Also by JJ Spain

Last Night in Sturgis

It Started in Laughlin

THREE DAYS IN DAYTONA

A MIKE SALAS NOVEL

THREE DAYS IN
DAYTONA

A Mike Salas Novel

J J SPAIN

HMS PRESS

Copyright © 2023 by JJ Spain.

All rights reserved. No part of this book may be reproduced in any form or by any electronic or mechanical means, including information storage and retrieval systems, without permission in writing from the publisher, except by reviewers, who may quote brief passages in a review.

This publication contains the opinions and ideas of its author. It is intended to provide helpful and informative material on the subjects addressed in the publication. The author and publisher specifically disclaim all responsibility for any liability, loss, or risk, personal or otherwise, which is incurred as a consequence, directly or indirectly, of the use and application of any of the contents of this book.

HMS Press
PO Box 2
Valentine, NE 69201

MikeSalasNovels.com
1-402-322-9197
jeffreyaspain@gmail.com

Printed in the USA

Ordering Information:
Quantity sales. Special discounts are available on quantity purchases by corporations, associations, and others. For details, contact the publisher at the address above.

Library of Congress Control Number: 2022923362
ISBN-13:   979-8-9872733-1-9   [Paperback Edition]
                979-8-9872733-4-0   [Digital Edition]

SALAS

S omeone once said, "Never make permanent decisions based on temporary feelings." Unfortunately, Salas didn't hear it, ignored it or maybe he didn't understand it. Instead, what was on his mind as he walked to the double glass doors of the Harley Davidson dealership was a sudden, powerful almost overwhelming desire for something you know is bad for you, known as lust. Salas opened the door, but an Indiana December wind beat him inside. A chill filled the entryway while his steel-toed-leather-lace-ups marked the wooden floor. Once again Salas completed his Deb check-list. Deb, bearing the title of "the ex-wife." Every girl he dated since the divorce, he compared to Deb; their smile, (hopefully with dimples), their eyes, the curve of their neck, their earlobes, even their laugh. No one compared to Deb.

"Hi, Michael. Great to see you again. Still thinking about it?" Candy yelled from across the showroom floor.

"Hey Candy, yeah I'm still thinking about you er… it. But now I'm kind of confused." Salas replied, putting his stocking hat in his coat pocket and rubbing circulation into his bald head. He stopped at his dream Harley, the 2016 black and white Road King Police Bike. Salas used the end of his t-shirt to buff out a fingerprint left on the black gas tank of the motorcycle. He thought Candy had Deb's smile.

"Confused about what Michael?" Candy was now face-to-face with Salas, her chin tilted up, she was looking into Salas's eyes. He liked her eyes. Candy's purple-black hair was falling between her shoulder blades; Deb never dyed her hair. She was close enough Salas could smell her perfume. Poison was the name of it. He had gone to department store after department store and smelled hundreds of samples until he found it. And she was poison. Poison to him. He took a deep breath, inhaled her, numbing the memories of what once was.

"I don't know if I am coming here to look at the bike or just to look at you, Candy," Salas said with a grin. This was his ninth or tenth visit to the Harley store since September. Salas had a burning desire to buy a Harley with an even more urgent desire to get his hands-on Candy. With each visit, she flirted with him more and more. Salas hadn't been in a relationship for years, he was looking for love and was receptive to her advances. He kept telling himself "Deb's remarried. Get over her."

"I hope it's me," Candy said softly, as Salas placed his hand lightly on the lower part of her back, gently pulling her into him. Their hips touched.

Candy looked right and left. The store was empty on a Tuesday night. The dealership closed in twenty minutes. The parts man was in the back; he would soon leave by the rear entrance. All the mechanics had already left, leaving Candy and Salas alone on the sales floor.

"Be honest Michael, are you going to buy that bike or just keep kicking the tires?" Candy asked, but not pulling away. She squared her hips to his and pushed in ever so slightly. Then she pressed in with her belly button touching his crotch, her back curving away.

"I think so; I just need to be sure. It is my first bike. I want my first bike to be the right bike." Salas now had both hands on her low back and was pushing a little harder than she did. Candy responded with an upward tilt of her pelvis. Salas responded inside his jeans.

"Oh Michael. Once you feel the 1690 cc's of power rumbling between your legs you will know you made the right decision." Candy grabbed his belt buckle and was prying it open. "And you can always come back in when you are ready for another one."

"I'm sure I want it. Are you?" Salas pulled the t-shirt out of her jeans. He placed one hand on her bare back, the other down the back side of her Lucky's, on a firm flexed butt. Her ass fit in the palm of his hand. That overwhelming desire something you know is bad for you was kicking in.

Candy didn't say a word, she just took Salas by the front of his pants and led him into the dressing room. She shut the door as Salas finished the unbuckling and lost the winter coat. Deb was still in the back of his mind. They made love standing. Salas picked her up, she wrapped her legs around his waist, crossing ankles behind his back. She was light, and Salas was strong. Her 110 pounds were nothing to Salas. He bobbed up and down as she wrestled her thighs and leaned back, arms around Salas's neck, her back in a u-shaped arch. She let out a low groan, Salas soon followed.

They were dressed and back on the storeroom floor at 6:05. The store was now officially closed. Hearing the door open and the wind rush in caused both Salas and Candy to turn, they looked at the front exit. A large man in blue bib overalls walked in. The man waved at Candy.

"Who's that?" Salas asked.

Candy's cheeks were red as if it was her that had just come in from the cold. Salas used his shirt sleeve to wipe beads of sweat off is head.

"That. That is my husband," Candy softly whispered. "Hi, Warren!" Candy called out.

"You have got to be shitting me. You are married?" Salas said, his back to Warren, they continued walking to the glass check-out counter.

"I have a wedding ring on." Candy proclaimed, showing him her left hand.

"You have a ring in your ears, your lip, your eyebrow, your nose, your nipples, your labia, and one on every finger, even your thumbs!" Salas said, now standing by a small Christmas tree. Ornaments hung lazily on the plastic branches of the phony evergreen and scattered haphazardly on the countertop. Red and white peppermint candy canes, each individually wrapped in plastic sat in a wicker basket next to the cash register.

Warren came forward in his farmer style overalls; he too was sweating. He wore a black long sleeve "Harley Davidson of Fort Wayne, Indiana" shirt underneath the bibs. The left chest buckle was left undone, the cloth and brass button bouncing on his belly as he walked. He had thick gray hair parted in the middle with a plug of chew in his bottom lip and right cheek; tobacco juice was running down the side of his face. He held a near-empty plastic 16-ounce Pepsi bottle in his right hand. He spit into it using the edge of the bottle to wipe his lip.

The man coming to Salas and Candy waddled more than walked. His cheeks bounced with each step, in synch with his belly as his arms stuck out to the side like wooden branches in a snowman. Candy's husband was, well fat, very fat. He hadn't seen what he was peeing with for years.

"What are you having this chilly evening sir?" The husband asked extending his hand to Salas. "Warren Jennings, owner of this fine establishment."

"I just had a piece of candy Warren." Salas held up a candy cane.

Candy had to turn away; she wanted to laugh. Salas shook Warren's hand. The handshake was soft. Warren grimaced from Sala's grip. Salas was a big guy, an ex-college light heavy-weight wrestler but Warren made Salas look small. When done with the greeting Salas looked at his own hand, it was now sticky. Salas caught a whiff of reefer emanating under the stench of the man's *Brut* style cologne. Salas looked in Warren's eyes; his pupils were dilated. Mr. Jennings was stoned. Salas questioned himself; obese and a pothead, how did he land Candy? Evidently, owning a Harley Davidson dealership had its rewards.

"Take what you need." Warren put a peppermint stick in his mouth, as did Salas, Warren tossed the plastic wrapper on the floor. "What bike you like my good man? It's Christmas; I'll give you a special present, a great discount. Don't you think we can give him a special gift this Christmas Candy?

"Absolutely Warren, I would love to." Candy winked at Salas as she picked up the disposed wrapper, placing it in the trash can behind the counter.

"How can I resist. I'll take that Road King," was Salas's answer, as he was pointing at the police bike.

"You a cop?" Warren asked.

"Yes, a detective, right here at the Fort Wayne Police Department."

"Tell you what, for our boys that serve, we will put a badge on the front fender. Your name and badge number on it. No charge," Warren declared.

Salas pulled a checkbook out of the back pocket of his blue jeans. Candy went to the sales desk and returned with a thin stack of paperwork. Warren punched the keys of a hand-held calculator then showed Salas the small green screen with black numbers.

"Her you go Mr. Salas." Warren put the calculator in front of Salas's face and showed him the numbers. He asked, "Will this do? A hell of a deal if I must say so myself."

"Geez for that price Candy should come with it," Salas said.

"No can do. I already came!" was Candy's response.

This time Salas had to hide his face to keep from laughing. He choked on the candy cane. He wrote the check out to Harley Davidson, signed it and handed the thin piece of paper to the both of them. Warren grabbed it first. He hand quick hands for his size.

Salas was now the proud owner of a 2016 Harley Davidson Road King. The exchange took less than ten minutes. Salas signed more papers as he kept an eye on Candy. He could feel himself getting erect again.

"We can deliver to your home or do you want to come back and pick it up?" Candy asked.

"Oh, I would love to come back, I need a leather jacket and a helmet. Get me in that dressing room and take care of me." Salas said with a grin. Inside his head he was wondering how he gets himself into relationships like this, married relationships and why would he do it, again.

"That I can do!" Candy replied.

Warren put another peppermint candy cane in his mouth, "I'm out of town Wednesday and Thursday of next week, got to pick up a few bikes in Indy." Candy's husband just gave them the days for their next date.

Candy was smiling as she placed a bright red "Sold" sign on the Police bike. Her husband Warren was smiling; he had just sold another Harley.

Salas was smiling as he said, "Wednesday works best for me. See you then." He put his jacket on and pulled his stocking hat over his ears. Salas zipped up his coat and walked out, hands in his pockets. His first thought was that Deb wouldn't be happy he bought a motorcycle. Then his mind raced to Candy. "Why do I do shit like this?" He said to no one. Not even he was listening.

RJ

RJ stepped out on to the front porch of his home, careful to not let the screen door bang against the door frame. He didn't want to wake Sheila; last night was the first night they had a sleepover. Usually, she would leave before midnight to go to her own home with her two kids and her mother. Since he was leaving for a week, she decided to stay. They, well Sheila, had "the talk." The talk about their future together. The talk RJ wasn't interested in. He nodded in acceptance, said nothing and committed to nothing. He wanted nothing. He hoped she took the hint and wasn't there when he got back.

Looking into the hazy morning sun rising off the Kansas border, RJ sat down on the top step and laced up his riding boots. He locked the door to his house. He had been living there for years, well minus the last fi e when he was in prison but before that, this was his home. When Deuce passed away, he got the key to the house, the club business, and the responsibility. He didn't want any of them. Over the past twenty years, Deuce was RJ's mentor, father fi ure, and best friend. Serving as Deuce's protector taught RJ more than the skills of being a bodyguard or bulwark. RJ was taught a code. The code of the club; loyalty, honor and you always paid back more than you received. Paybacks could be beneficial if you were loyal or very bad if you crossed the wrong person. He could handle the code. Handling the home, the business and the responsibility was different. And he especially didn't want to handle Sheila. He was glad to be leaving.

RJ hadn't completed more than a day ride since he and Deuce returned from the west coast. When Deuce was diagnosed with cancer in Rapid City, South Dakota, he found out during the Sturgis Motorcycle Rally; his response was "let's ride." Deuce longed to cruise the west and east coastlines of the United States. RJ took the challenge and led the way. From the Sturgis Rally in August they took I90 from Rapid City to Seattle, Washington. Stops in Missoula, Montana, and Spokane were quick hits of dinner, Jack Daniels, and sleep. As the pain in Deuce's back and hips grew more intense, so did his alcohol consumption. The pain pills doc had given Deuce didn't seem to help. Deuce rode well hungover but was thankful when they finally got off the interstate at Olympia, Washington and rode highway 101, the Pacific Coast Highway.

Today, RJ lifted his right leg over the backrest of his Harley Davidson Fatboy, sat on the seat, put the bike in neutral, pushed forward with both heels and coasted down the driveway, taking the grass to get past Sheila's Subaru. When the Harley's front tire touched the concrete RJ turned left to glide down the street. He was going over twenty-fi e miles an hour when he turned on the bike, gassed the engine and shot forward. Far enough away he hoped he didn't wake the lady in his bed. Riding through Boulder, searching for the interstate, he thought of Deuce.

After years in prison, to ride the open road as a free man, with your best friend was an answer to prayer. Deuce and RJ rode over 600 miles a day for the first three days leaving Sturgis, but once they hit 101, they slowed down, saw more of the sites, made more stops, ate more and drank more. RJ knew the pain had to be intense and played to whatever hand Deuce wanted to deal. At Tillamook, they rented a v-hull fishing boat with a local guide but didn't catch any fish. At Newport Beach, they checked into the Agate Motel, toured a lighthouse and got drunk on lady's night at the Asiatic Restaurant. The ladies loved the bad boy Son's vests and colors. RJ took a lady for a ride on his Harley and on another ride back at his hotel room, while Deuce closed down the bar. At Fort Bragg, California Deuce got reservations in the nicest hotel RJ had ever stayed in, the Ocean View Lodge. RJ knew Deuce was in a great deal of pain as he didn't talk much, took most of his pain pills then drank a bottle of Jack. Deuce spent the next three days in bed, where he could hear the waves breaking off the rocky shore and an occasional sea lion barking. Deuce wanted to tour the California Coastal National Monument, see the whitewater, the birds, and the sunset but lacked the energy and the will to fi ht the pain. RJ checked on him every few hours, with the bulk of his time at the Taphouse Lounge sitting alone listening to jazz. On the fourth day at the Lodge Deuce walked to the restaurant, it was his first meal since they arrived. When they got back to the room, Deuce told RJ he wanted to go home, back to Denver. It had been eighteen days since they left turgis.

That night sitting in Deuce's room, Deuce further changed RJ's life. He replayed the conversation in his head as he sat at a stop light. Clouds covered the sun; it looked like a snow day for Denver, Colorado.

Deuce laid out his plan, his vision for the club. The organization was started for those that needed help, a friend, a group of the same kind of people to hang with. It was about fellowship. The club had developed into a business. It was now employing people; they had an accountant, they were paying taxes and even had investments that were turning a profit. But like any volunteer organization, they lost their way. There were diffe ent people in diffe ent states doing some good things and some bad things. As a group, they lost their vision, their purpose. Deuce needed to re-organize the club. But Deuce knew his days were numbered. It was up to RJ now.

Deuce left instructions for RJ to finish his work. Clean up the club, make it and keep it legit. RJ didn't want the responsibility; he even told Deuce he wasn't qualified. Deuce told RJ there was a leader within him, that RJ just needed to let him out and the club would follow. RJ was raised on the streets where you lead by force and intimidation. Now he had to lead by influence, relationships, and knowledge. The change would be difficult.

The light changed to green, a honking horn urged him forward. He pulled into a BP station for fuel, coffee and to put on his rain suit. RJ looked over his bike, he washed the headlight, checked the tire pressure. He remembered the day he and Deuce rolled their bikes onto the driveway of Deuce's house, finally at home from their west coast journey. It was on a Thursday the eighth day of September. Deuce dropped his kick-stand and stood by his bike. He patted the gas tank as if it were a puppy. As he struggled to walk the steps to his home, he turned and took one last long look at his Harley. A tear ran down the side of his face. It was the last time Deuce rode his bike. He died in his home, RJ by his side on December 1st.

He finished his coffee, standing inside the BP watching a procession of cars make their daily commute to work. The line of cars with lights on, going so slow it reminded him of Deuce's funeral, the first funeral RJ had been to in over thirty years. He wasn't much for death. Deuce's two daughters, two ex-wives, three former senators, the mayor of Boulder, a colonel and a four-star general attended the ceremony. RJ, accompanied by over 100 bikers rode in pairs following the Herse and black sedans to the grave site. It was one of the warmest December days on record as a bright Colorado sun shined down on the procession. The four-star handed Deuce's girls the flag of the United States of America, thanking them for their father's service to his country. A tombstone was erected, it read "Beloved Father, Friend, and Soldier." A casket was placed in the ground. Tears were wept, hugs were given. The crowd parted, most likely never to come together again.

Unbeknownst to all, RJ had the cremated remains of Harold P. Wozniak, aka Deuce, in an urn, packed away in the saddlebag of his Harley. Deuce wanted his ashes laid to rest on Daytona Beach, the one rally he never attended. For RJ, after the funeral, it seemed Christmas and New Year's dragged on. He wanted to hit the highway to Daytona, one last ride with his friend. Daytona Beach was far away from the cold and snow of Colorado. The promise was that March would come. And it did, with more cold and snow.

RJ was back on the Harley, riding with Deuce.

RICHARD LOPEZ

e was sprinting, running in full gear, his head down, both hands on his weapon. The temperature was over 100 degrees, a cool day in Fallujah, Baghdad. This was his third tour in Iraq, his thirteenth year in the armed services, all as a Ranger and the first time his team had been split up by the enemy. Richard Lopez and six of his men were on a dead run. He led them down a side street, an alley in the U.S. The white stone buildings were abandoned, long since forgotten for business or habitation. Richard knew behind each broken window, each open door or fallen wall could be a hostile. His job, the duty of his team was to rid the block of such men and women, and now they were using children. As he was running he didn't care about the windows, the doors or the walls; he wanted his team back together.

Richard was running towards the firefi ht. They were getting closer. Engagement with the enemy didn't last long, mere seconds, minutes were an eternity. Richard knew this city better than he knew his hometown in Deland Florida. At the next block, they took a right, then up a flight of stairs to a rooftop. Richard and his six men huddled below the three-foot concrete and stone wall, Richard peered over. He saw his fi e men. They were trapped, laying behind what was left of a building. The roof was gone, the back and side walls crumbled to the ground. His men were laying on a bed of rocks and cinders; he could see blood on the white stone, a soldier helping another with a bandage, there was shouting, shooting, explosions, crying. It was chaos.

Richard could see his men pinned down by enemy snipers. Courageously they rose, returning fire with great skill and marksmanship. His men were outnumbered but perhaps, he thought, they were winning the battle. Even with the intense heat, the muzzle flash of their weapons brightened their faces. He cringed as Dylan Jacobs, a man he had known, lived with and fought with since basic training, his friend, was hit. The man falling to his back. Richard knew Dylan was dead. The enemy was advancing building by building. Richard could see their strategy as they broke into three groups, with ten men staying directly in front, firing heavily, as two groups of fi e ran to each flank. On the opposite rooftop, he saw more hostiles and a bearded man holding an RPG, a rocket-propelled grenade launcher. The enemy was going to blow up the barrier protecting his fi e men.

Richard pointed his fingers, he sent three men to each side wall, they had the flanks, Richard had the front. He waited as the enemy with the RPG stood. The hostile pointed the grenade launcher down, toward his men. Richard fired, an easy shot of less than 200 yards. The man holding the RPG was hit in the chest, his weapon now pointing straight down to the front of his own building. The RPG fired hurling a grenade toward his fellow al-Qaeda insurgents. The ten men in front, well they were nullified by the explosion of their own RPG. Blood and body parts hit the wall protecting the American Rangers like hailstones on the hood of a car. Richard's men unleashed hell on the right and left flanks as Richard eliminated the remaining men on the rooftop. The battle was over. Acrid smoke with screams in Arabic and English filled the air. Two of his men on the ground looked up at Richard on the roof top and smiled. Richard held his hand out to them with an extended arm, his fingers spread. In the corner of his eye, he saw it floating in the air. A black canvas satchel or backpack raising above the wall of the building, it hung in the air suspended in time. He read "OGIO" on the emblem. Then a blinding white light, the air being sucked out of his lungs, the impact of the explosion throwing him across the roof of the building. The searing hot pain in his head and shoulder.

Richard woke from the dream, his body sweating, his head throbbing. The room was dark. Where was Corrine? Where were his children? He stood from the bed, the floor cool to his feet, so cold compared to the hot roof in Baghdad. He went to the window drawing the curtain open with his right hand, the left arm still of little value to him. His head burned, as if it was still on fire from the metal ball bearings of the backpack that were once lodged in his helmet and skull from the explosion.

A fluorescent yard light illuminated the sign on the building across the driveway; it said: "We Found U Repo." Richard Lopez was home. Back in Deland, Florida.

He walked to the kitchen, the clock on the microwave said 3:35 pm. Richard grabbed the orange plastic container with the white top, "Tramadol" was on the label above a local pharmacy address and a doctor's name from the VA. He poured five tablets into his mouth and chewed them. Richard washed down the chalky powder with a long pull from a bottle of Johnny Walker Red.

Corrine had left him; she took the kids to her parents in South Carolina. His father had left him, dying of a stroke just weeks after his return from Iraq. Richard had his medical discharge papers; his father medical discharge was more permanent.

With his father passing, Richard was now the proud owner of "We Found U Repo." At We Found U, they confiscated cars, trucks, motorcycles, boats, trailers, recreational vehicles, furniture, even cattle, and horses. The repo crew worked the east coast, from Florida to North Carolina repossessing for banks, auto dealerships, credit unions and credit card companies. At "We found U" Richard was the team leader, Richard was in charge.

Richard Lopez ran his right hand over his hair, the standard military buzz cut. The thick black hair played the role well. Richard was wired for being a Ranger. Now sitting in the dark, he also knew he was wired for repossession. He loved the excitement, the hunt for the property and people, and he would admit, he enjoyed the occasional confrontation. Richard had a concealed carry permit, and even with a bad arm, he was way overtrained for hand to hand combat versus the normal civilian population. He enjoyed the battle with any red neck that wanted to fi ht for their banked owned property. The problem was the headaches. Bright lights, loud noises. The problem was the dream, the explosion, his dead men. The problem was the pills. The problem was his friends; Jim Beam, Johnny Walker, and Jack Daniels. The problem was Richard. Since his father passed and his wife left him, the business was failing fast. The business was dying. He was dying.

Then, entered brother Vincent.

VINCENT

“How’s your view?” A smoker’s voice asked. It was rough and raspy. A white wall of cement blocks separated the voice from Vincent. The front door to each box was metal bars, jail cells.

“Same as you asshole but mine changes today. You. Well, you got what, fi e more years?” Vincent asked back, as he paced inside the eight-by-eight-foot cell.

“Yeah, fi e more years. But I’m halfway there man. Then bitches and booze on the beach,” Raspy answered back.

“Look me up when you get out. I’ll be in Florida taking care of business. Maybe give your ugly ass a job,” Vince said.

“Lopez. You packed?” A man with a square jaw, shoulders the width of a mountain and thighs like tree trunks stepped in front of the bars. He was a large Black man in a brown uniform. He was carrying a nightstick in his hand. The stick looked like a toothpick compared to his chest and arms.

“Nothing to pack. You can keep all of this shit,” Vincent said, spreading his arms showing the pitiful collection of books and magazines.

“No books you want to keep? No letters or pictures?” The guard asked.

“Nobody wrote me a fucking thing in three years, man.”

“Well, you got a package from your brother. We had to check it. You will be happy to know it is an envelope full of cash. You are supposed to head home Vincent, back to Florida,” The behemoth guard said, as he escorted Vincent down the hall. A plethora of “see ya’s,” “fuck you’s,” "later bro," "send money," and "eat shit," came from the cells and echoed through the hallway.

"I'm so fucking glad to get the fuck out of Texas. This state sucks," Vincent said, as the guard pushed the security code and the metal door opened.

Another brown uniformed man stepped up. This one an opposite shell of his partner; skinny, short hair, sunken cheeks, he was carrying a sidearm and pepper spray in opposing holsters. He gave Vincent civilian clothes; new blue jeans, a white collared shirt, boxers, sweat socks and red converse tennis shoes. The clothes he wore when he entered prison three years prior no longer fit. Vince had gained a little weight in his years of captivity and no activity. He undressed and redressed in front of the guard, throwing the orange jumpsuit and white slip-on loafers into the black plastic garbage can.

Vincent opened the envelope. One thousand dollars in cash. He smiled. His brother Richard had called him the month before, his one and only phone call in prison. Richard asked if Vincent would come home and help run the family business. A thousand dollars, Vincent thought, Richard must really want him back.

Like his brother, Vince was also ex-military. Unlike his brother, in basic training, he was convicted of possession of a controlled substance. Like his brother, he received a discharge although Vince's was dishonorable. Basic training was outside of San Diego, California. His discharge made him homeless on the streets of a perfect climate. Streetlife wasn't too bad on Vincent. He soon hooked up with a local dealer and ran low-grade heroin from the Mexican border to Dallas. It was in Texas where he made the delivery, got the cash and got busted. Three years in lock-up and they told him that he was rehabilitated. Then, one phone call from his debilitated brother and he was game-fully employed at "We Found U Repossession."

He walked out of the state prison with a handful of cash, and with women, drugs, and whiskey on his mind. Two days later he called Richard for more money. He told him he got mugged. Richard wired another $1,000.

Four days later, Vince drove through the open gate of We Found U; he was back home. A home he couldn't wait to leave when he got out of high school, a home he couldn't wait to leave as he drove into the yard.

Richard was in the work area connecting the brake lights of a newly repo'd bumper hitch *Work and Play* enclosed trailer to a Chevy Silverado pickup. Richard looked up, smiled, and walked towards the brown rusted-out 1979 Monte Carlo. The car was Vince's graduation gift from their father. Vincent Lopez slammed the car into park, sprang out, and embraced Richard with a bear hug.

"Vinnie!" Richard returned the hug. "So good to have you home."

"So good to be here bro! Time for me to get to work. To help my brother." Vincent sounded excited. He towered over Richard, several inches taller and heavier than his older sibling. But where Richard was fit and firm, Vincent was sloppier, with long unkempt hair, a belly that sagged, bags under his eyes, and one long chin that drooped.

The two brothers worked well together, but over the course of the next few months Richard's headaches intensified and were more frequent. Vincent got Richard out of the Vets Hospital and into a private doctor who immediately doubled Richard's medication. Richard felt no better and was more out-of-it. He stayed in the house, avoided people and the sun. Thus, Vincent took over the business, more by necessity than force of will. Vincent called on his brother two or three times a day to be sure Richard was taking his medication. Richard spent his days inside his house. The bright sunshine gave him severe headaches. Richard was no longer driving any of the rigs. He wasn't collecting; he wasn't meeting with bankers. He wasn't contributing. Vincent was now in full control.

Vincent fired all of Richard's team and brought in his own crew. They were busy bringing in a few cars and lots of motorcycles. Richard could see new things, new people, new equipment and changes that he wanted to ask Vincent about. But before he could ask, Richard would fall sleep, pass out or stare into drug-induced emptiness. Richard was thankful he had Vincent with him. He loved his brother for helping him. Richard trusted Vincent.

SALAS

He had to admit…. Candy was growing on him. The past three months he had developed a sweet tooth with Candy satisfying the cravings. Salas found himself wanting more than meeting up with her in hotel rooms, dressing rooms and the back of her Suburban. He wanted, for the first time in years, and he hadn't admitted this to anyone, to be in a relationship. Salas looked forward to seeing her, he enjoyed their talks and thought less and less of Deb. Aside from Candy's beauty, gymnastic body, and athleticism in bed; she was smart, an intellectual, and she could carry a conversation. Candy was funny, and they shared the same views on religion, politics and climate change. For Salas it was becoming more than just the sex, his lust was developing into deeper feelings. He wanted her to be the first person he saw each morning. He wanted her to be the last person he saw each night. He wanted to introduce her to his friends, his parents, perhaps even his daughter. The problem, Candy was married.

The Indiana winter months drug on. Snow, cold weather, and freezing winds prevented Salas from playing with his new Harley. Salas was ready to use the Christmas gift he gave to himself, the Road King, and ride it on the highway. He had been dreaming of he and Candy cruising south to the Daytona rally. Just the two of them, sun in their face, wind blowing through Candy's hair. Salas had seen other guys ride with their ladies, it looked fun, a special bond. He wanted that.

After their regularly scheduled Wednesday afternoon workout at the Fairfield Inn, where Candy had been paying the hotel bills, Salas breached the conversation.

They were laying sideways on the king-sized bed; their legs were wrapped around each other, her head on his chest. Their clothes were on the floor, on the desk, on the couch and over the TV where Cameron from *Modern Family* was running, his arms flapping.

"Candy," Salas said. "Ride with me to Daytona. Just me and you, a week on the road."

"Michael," Candy responded. "I can't leave for a week; rally weeks are some of the best sales days at the store. Bike traffic is at a premium. Sturgis is better than Daytona, but we will be busy. You just go with your friends."

"You are my friends Candy. I want us to come out of the closet, tell Warren to move out and move me in." Salas was gently outlining her jaw with his index finger.

"Michael, please sweetheart don't do this. Let's not ruin what we have; this is fun, it is exciting. Let's keep what we have." She sat up and then on top of Salas. Her knees now on both sides of him, the heat off her bottom was warming his belly. She had her hands on his chest, rubbing in circular motions. Her butt doing the same on his abdomen.

She felt good, she looked great, and she smelled even better. Salas outlined the dragon tattoo on her chest and belly with his index finger. The dark tail of the dragon wrapped around the low part of her neck like a necklace, the triangle point of the appendage settling above her sternum. The body of the reptilian creature slid between her breasts, the wings cupping the bottom of each bosom. The neck of the dragon was gliding down her abdomen. Her six-pack abs highlighted the muscularity of the beast. The mouth of the serpent was open wide as the head reached down between her legs. Flames roared out of the dragon's mouth engulfing her vagina.

Salas closed his eyes. "I want more Candy; I think I'm falling for you. I haven't been in love for ten years, but I think this is it. I think that you, I know that we, are it. We can be one."

Candy leaned to the right, swung her leg off Salas and stood, her rear end to the TV; she was naked, she had the body of an athlete; muscular, lean, agile, and balanced.

"Michael that is so sweet." Candy was gathering her clothes as Salas lay flat on the bed looking at the ceiling, his arms under his head. She dressed quickly in black yoga pants, no panties, no bra, and a button-up striped Harley shirt that had her name embroidered over the left breast.

She tied the ends of the shirt in a knot over her belly button, walked back to the bed and kissed Salas on the lips. A long kiss. She ran her hand down his chest to his abdomen and beyond. "You go to Daytona. You will want me, even more, when you get back. You know you will." She removed her hand and walked to the door of the hotel room.

"Are you shitting me? You can't do that and leave me." Salas smiled as he lay still on the bed, his hands still under his head, elbows flat. He wanted her again, now.

Candy left the hotel. Salas knew this wasn't going to end the way he wanted. She wasn't going to leave her husband. He was hopeful but not optimistic.

Salas showered, dressed and drove back to work. He was seated in his cubicle at the Fort Wayne Police Department using his two index fingers to type on a keyboard. He had his cheaters on, a $2.00 pair of black-framed reading glasses from Walgreens. Salas accessed the county treasurer's office database, yes, he was using government equipment for personal use, and it wasn't his first time. Warren Jennings was the subject of interest. He found nothing in Warren's name but several pieces of property in the Jennings Family Trust, a local law firm was the executor, Warren the primary beneficiary. A $1.5 million home on 10 acres as the residence, with the Harley Davidson property assessed at over $3 million. The largest asset was 2000 acres of Indiana farm ground along with several rental properties ranging from residential dwellings, storage units to a small strip mall. Millions of dollars in property alone. All in a trust. Candy wouldn't get a dime in a divorce. She was waiting for Warren to kick the bucket. He was on the fast track given his weight and personal habits but death not imminent.

Salas's hope dwindled, his optimism turned to pessimism.

Captain Green knocked on the side panel of the cubicle.

"Salas. I need fi e minutes. Heard you are going on a weeks' vacation. Meet me in my office in ten." Captain Tom Green gave his order and stared at Salas for a response. The two had a rocky relationship for twenty years. A few months prior, Green took too much enjoyment in suspending Salas for beating up a guy and bragged to the division he was getting Salas fired. But as fate would have it, the assault charges were dropped, Salas arrested a serial killer in Sturgis, South Dakota and was an Indiana police hero with a new accommodation on the wall of his portable office. Green watched as Salas stood without objection.

Green's office was a shrine to his bromance with Larry Bird. Green and Bird arm-in-arm at golf events, Pacers and Indiana State basketball games. Again, arms around each other at charity events, social gatherings, and political fundraisers. Salas had seen most of the pictures of the two men hugging before. Green hugged Larry Bird more than he hugged his wife. A new picture caught Salas's eye: Bird, Green, and Vice President Pence standing in front of the DuPont Hospital, Bird in the middle, arms around each other.

Green walked in carrying a stack of papers. "Salas, where are you headed for your week off?"

"Daytona Beach. Hey is this a new picture?" Salas asked holding the frame of VP Pence.

"Yes, that is the opening of the new cancer wing at Dupont," Green said. He was looking at himself in a mirror that was hanging behind the door into his office. He was fixing his hair with his fingers. The hair never moved even after he ran his fingers through it. Thick hair that the wind couldn't mess with. Salas mimicked Green by tossing his head back and running his fingers through imaginary hair. Salas hated Green's hair.

"Wasn't that event Tuesday?" Salas asked. Today was Wednesday.

"Yes, a great addition to the hospital and for Fort Wayne," Green said.

Salas thought the guy must have extra matching picture frames hidden in his desk and direct access to Target's print shop.

"Update me on the Aztec bust you did last week. I have a press conference and need something positive," Green said returning to his desk. He sat down in a large office chair with a high back, he straightened his tie, checked his Rolex then interlocked his fingers while resting them on a flat stomach.

Salas detailed his interaction with the Aztecs, a regional motorcycle gang busted by Salas for running cocaine through Fort Wayne and the State of Indiana. A routine speeding ticket off Interstate 69 by the State Patrol, two men on motorcycles were pulled over doing 75 in a 55 mile per hour zone. Construction was in progress, so the fine doubled.

When the State Patrol officer ran their backgrounds for the speeding violation, the computer screen filled with prior convictions and current warrants for their arrest. Both men wanted for outstanding drug charges in Georgia.

State patrol called for back-up. The two men were arrested, and their bikes hauled to impound. It was there, after the crime lab technicians searched the motorcycles, that Salas was asked to participate.

Both men rode Harleys, one a Road King similar to what Salas had just purchased. Salas stood in a large metal building lined with confiscated cars and pickup trucks. Several of the vehicles had the interior carpet and upholstery not removed but torn out. Salas found the confiscated bikes and admired both Harleys. Every part of the bike that could have chrome on it did. The saddlebags shimmered under leather polish. Salas opened both bags just as the technicians had earlier in the day. Inside the right compartment, he found a quart of oil and a toolkit, the left had a black rain suit of bibs, and a jacket rolled into what resembled a log. Salas looked at the gear and looked at the saddlebags. Both bags were full. Salas knew he could get far more in his saddlebags than a quart of oil and a toolkit. He took his pocket knife, extended the four-inch blade and drove it into the bottom half of the leather saddle bag then he ripped the blade sideways. The bag split open as a white powder spilled over the floor of the garage. Salas found what the techs could not, a fake bottom filled with coke. Both Harleys carrying over three pounds of the white stuff.

Salas related to Green how he and Ronnie Higgenbotham, another detective, negotiated with the Aztecs. They offered reduced time for names and locations. By the end of the day, they had arrested the supplier and the buyers. Another five pounds of cocaine were confiscated, nearly $1,000,000 of product off the streets of Indiana. Six men were arrested. Salas related how Ronnie was the lead negotiator and did a great job. Salas didn't want to wait around for a presser and offered Ronnie as the lead. Let the young detective get the accolades to build his reputation in the field and highlight the Mayor's initiative; getting millennials into police and detective work. Green agreed, Ronnie would be with Green for the press interview and receive an accommodation.

Free to go, Salas was now officially on vacation.

The next morning, at his house, the alarm on the cell phone rang, it was 7:00 AM. Salas shaved his head and face, brushed his teeth. He did his morning ritual, one hundred push-ups and fifty sit-ups then stretched his hamstrings, quads, and shoulders while in a steaming hot shower.

He loaded his Road King for his first motorcycle rally. Well, his second rally but first with his own bike and first while not working. Salas packed a couple of pairs of jeans, five t-shirts, rain gear, extra socks and a daily change of underwear. He stuffed the clothes into a backpack which was then stuffed into the saddle bag of the motorcycle.

Using his index finger, Salas punched the keys on the Harley's GPS system, the destination: Daytona Beach Holiday Inn on Atlantic Avenue. The hotel had more than doubled their normal rate, but it was rally week. Supply and demand, capitalism at its finest. Per the GPS his hotel was sixteen hours away. The plan was a two-day ride there, three days in Daytona, and two days to get back. A one-week vacation. Day one was a nine-hour ride to Marietta, GA. Another Holiday Inn. Another inflated rate.

Salas went back into the split-level home; he slid a wooden dowel into the floor assembly of the sliding glass door facing the wooden deck. He checked the security of the windows, turned down the heat, and locked the front door on his way out. He put on his new leather jacket. The one Candy gave him. Her first gift to Salas. She gave him lots of gifts; this one happened to be a jacket. He zipped up the front zipper of the heavy roughened bomber style coat as well as the zippers on each arm sleeve. He tried to snap and close the top button, but his neck was too big.

Salas saddled on the Harley at 8:05. He wore the black leather coat, blue Cinch jeans, a black Bell helmet with white DOT letters and his dirty black lace-up boots; it was the standard rider attire. Plus, he carried a 9 mm Glock in the inner side pocket of the leathers. The only thing Salas felt he was missing was Candy.

VINCE

"Vincent Lopez, you have a shipment due in one week to Vancouver Canada. Are you going to make the order?" The man asking the question was face to face with Vincent, the top of his head barely to Vince's chin. He wore a blue silk suit; he was sweating through the fabric. His shoulders were broad; his waist was small, his back shaped in a V. The short man had thick black hair that fell below his ears, long bangs that covered his eyes. He swooped his head right, his hand catching the ringlets of hair pushing it behind his ear. He did this a lot.

"German, you know I will." Vincent replied, pronouncing the "G" in German as an "H." They were standing in front of the garage on the grounds of "We Found U Repo." Richard wasn't present, well he was, but he was in a medicated sleep. It was three o'clock in the afternoon. Richard had missed all the meetings with German and didn't even know of the man, much less this shipment. And Vincent didn't want Richard to know.

German again placed his bangs behind his ear. "Vincent, you are wrong. I do not know you, and thus far I do not trust you. Trust is earned not given. I don't care how you do it, but it must be done. Let us say. Your life depends on it." With his right hand, German handed Vince an envelope. German's hand was missing the tips of three fingers. The man's forearm was tattooed, skulls with red snakes coming out of the mouth and eyes of the skull. The muscles in his forearms were thick and defined like ropes that tie a boat to a pier. When Vince took the envelope, German grabbed Vince's wrist, squeezing it for effect. Vincent's hand went white; Vincent winced in pain. "I've given you too much already Vincent, and I have nothing. Stolen motorcycles? That is what you have for me? Stolen toys?" The accent was mixed; Hispanic, maybe Russian, English, Cuban.

Struggling to get his arm released, Vince pulled back to no avail. He was a foot taller than German, and 50 pounds heavier, but the short man had the grip of a gorilla. "Please German; you know my plan. The bikes are just a ruse, a ruse that will in itself make us money. Trust me, my friend."

"I am not your friend Vincent; I am your business partner. I am your banker; I am your future. If you do not make the delivery, you will no longer have a need for a friend, a partner, a banker, or have a future. You have three days…. Friend." German held up three fingers, each missing the last knuckle. He didn't say "friend" with love in his voice.

The short man turned his back to Vincent and returned to his car, a solid black Audi A7 with tinted windows. The driver of the car was leaning against the front grill. He opened the rear door for German, who was again flipping the hair behind his ears. Vince saw a handgun in a shoulder holster under the driver's black blazer. German sat in the back; he was looking at Vince through dark wrap-around sunglasses. The door slammed shut. The driver grinned at Vincent as he got behind the steering wheel. A sinister grin. A grin that made Vincent's blood pressure rise.

Vincent shouted at the car "No worries German, I have it all under control. The delivery will be made." The black windows showed only Vince's reflection. The driver pushed the accelerator speeding off, spitting dust, rock, and gravel at Vincent.

Vincent was sweating profusely. His blood pressure still elevated, and it wasn't because of the Florida sun.

"Terry, Jake, Rod I need you all in here. Now." Vince yelled as he watched the A7 exit the metal gate and cross the bridge.

The six acres of "We Found U Repo" were surrounded by a fi e-foot-tall chain link fence. Razor wire added an additional foot to the height of the barrier. Each fence post was cemented in. Vince had added the wire with the "down payment" from German. No one was going to sneak in and "steal" back their car or motorcycle back. The front gate sealing the compound was at the end of a 20-foot metal bridge spanning a 12-foot-wide pond. The pond nearly circumnavigated the grounds of We Found U. Richard referred to it as "the mote."

With Vince's arrival, the gate was now locked each night. "Security reasons" was Vince's response, even though Richard had never had any property stolen. His father had put the fence up years ago to keep the decreasing number of deer, the ever-increasing number of alligators, and the occasional random crocodile and kids off he property.

The three men walked over to Vince, in no hurry to the command. Terry was the leader of the three; he had a baseball hat on backward, greasy brown hair pulled back under a Marlins baseball cap. He was smoking a cigarette. He always smoked cigarettes. Terry wore a white t-shirt with the number 93 in big numbers on the front and back. The name SUH over the back number. His pants were down low on his hips, plaid red and green boxers sticking out. If he had to run with anything in his hands, he was screwed. He needed both hands to keep his pants up. Terry's skin was a ghostly pale white. For living in Florida, he needed sun.

Jake rarely if ever spoke. A black man from Louisiana, Jake dropped out of college when he blew out his knee. He was a running back for the LSU Tigers. From an NFL first rounder to driving a truck in two steps. Jake was still built like a pro; six pack abs, no body fat, dreads that hung to his shoulders, a lean muscular face, you could see the muscles move when or if he spoke. Jake never wore a shirt, never drank alcohol, never ate sugar, and didn't like Vincent.

Rod had crazy eyes that darted from side to side. His thick brown hair was also pulled back under a dirty baseball cap, which was missing a logo. Rod was nervous, excited, and jittery. He was on something Vincent just couldn't fi ure out what it was. For so much energy you think he would be thinner, but he carried a roll on his belly, an extra chin and rosy cheeks. Rod was the opposite of Jake. He ate junk food all day; donuts, candy, chips, Pepsi, Bud Light, and of course, cigarettes. There was always something in his mouth. It was Rod that spoke first. "What's up V?"

"We got 42 bikes guys; I need at least 50. Fifty-fi e would be perfect. Good bikes. Harleys, 2005 and up." Vince was pacing back and forth in front of the three men. "Your cut is 10%. About twenty grand each.

Eight more Harley's boys. Spread the risk, work Daytona, especially the hotels. Go out about thirty miles." Vincent was wringing his hands, beads of sweat formed on his upper lip. He looked tired; he had bags under his eyes. Vincent had slept in his Wranglers and was wearing the same shirt for the past few days. He smelled of sour body order, coffee breath and nervousness.

"Well go!" He yelled waving them away.

Vincent turned and went into the garage. He had forty-two Harleys loaded in a semi-tractor trailer attached to a Freightliner truck. The bikes were alternately parked one to the right then one to the left. There was room for at least eight more. His three-man crew had stolen each bike. Each bike was documented with a new, phony titled issued by his connection at the county treasurer's office. For $10,000 he got 55 titles.

Vince watched as the three men left the grounds in the enclosed truck. The straight truck had a diesel engine with the Tommy Lift under the rear door. It was mid-afternoon. They would be back by sun-up with six bikes. The Daytona bike rally was scheduled to start Saturday; it would be easy pickings. The first 42 bikes had been taken nearly every week for the past year. All for this one big score.

As the truck left the grounds, two more men came out of the modular home where Vince was housed. The men looked like twins. Big, brown, and bald. Tattoos were on their necks and arms. Each in blue jeans and white tank tops. Black rubber flip-flops for shoes. They looked juiced up, muscles on muscles. You don't get that way from just lifting weights. They were medicinally enhanced.

"Vincent. German wants us to keep a close eye on you." Bald guy #1 yelled at Vincent from across the driveway. He didn't have a neck, just a jaw sitting on top of pectoral muscles.

"I am standing right here Raphy. See me?" Vincent yelled back standing at the entrance of the garage where the truck storing the bikes was housed. He waved at them with a large circular motion from his shoulder.

"I'm Marco. He is Raphael." Marco said tilting his head right towards his partner. Marco had a Springfield XD Model 2 handgun tucked inside the front of his pants. Aimed at his manhood.

"Yeah. We are watching." Raphael grunted as he spun brass knuckles around his right index finger.

The two men turned and went back into the modular. Vincent thought all they did was play video games. The only time they left the compound was for two hours, every day, always announcing they were going to the gym. German had dropped them off nd left hem.

RJ

The ride from Denver to St. Louis was, in motorcycle terms, a bitch. Getting through Denver was always a pain, the traffic seemed to get worse each year. He rode alone, no members of his club alongside him and he rarely had a passenger. No one cared to notice the lone man on the Harley. He was cut off in traffic by a Range Rover, a Tahoe and a Porsche Cayenne. Everyone in Denver drove an SUV whether they claimed to be a tree hugger or not. The liberals in Boulder had to get to work safely regardless of climate change. RJ laid on his throttle with the clutch engaged, the roar of the engine got the female driver in the Porsche 's attention but no apology, she was too busy looking at her phone. It is said that loud pipes save lives, but not in Denver. At least she was cute.

RJ was bored as hell through Kansas, thinking why does anyone live in this state? It was flat, no trees, no curves and lots of cold. Cold even without the wind. Riding a Harley is twenty to thirty degrees cooler than standing outside. RJ was layered up with extra socks, long underwear, and heat pads in his gloves and boots, yet he was still shivering.

The sky was spitting snow as he left Colorado and spitting rain through Colby to Hays, Kansas. RJ didn't have a windshield on his Fatboy, preferring the wind in his face but not the rain and snow. He cursed himself for not snapping on the detachable windshield. His broad shoulders caught a great deal of wind pushing him into the backrest of the Harley. RJ wore Gore-Tex rainwear he purchased at a Bass Pro Shop in Denver. He always carried the gear in the saddlebags on his bike; he thought this was the first time he had worn them. The bibs of the rain suit were snug against his chest, warming the layers.

From Kansas City to St. Louis, what should have been four lanes of traffic, was on a two-lane interstate. The traffic was intense, and it was still cold. He was the only motorcycle on the road. His bike had a whip on the clutch side, the left if you were riding the bike. If a car got to close, RJ would flip the whip, striking the passing car door or side panel. The end of the whip was equipped with metal lug nuts hanging off the leather. It made a great loud cracking noise when it made contact with the side of a car.

RJ stopped every two hours for fuel, coffee, and to stretch his legs. At six-feet-two and 220 pounds, he needed to stand and get the blood to his extremities. Turning fifty-years-old while in prison wasn't celebrated, but the time in the house allowed for lots of weightlifting. The extra muscle mass and low body fat made him look leaner and younger than the half-century he was.

RJ rode through the evening and setting sun into the night hours, something he rarely did. He wanted to get through the traffic and past the damn state of Missouri. He zipped by Wentzville at over 80 miles per hour. Thirty minutes later, after passing miles and miles of strip malls and car dealerships, he saw the Gateway Arch to his right. To his left, the lights of Busch Stadium were on even though there was no baseball in March.

In his hotel room, a Motel 6 near Interstate 64 and Fairview Heights, Illinois, RJ replied to several business emails and personal texts. Emails and texts were new to him, as cell phones were not allowed in prison. He hated emails, seems people never stopped sending them, you never had a moment without the damn phone vibrating or ringing. RJ refused Facebook, calling it "Spacebook." He wanted nothing to do with Snapchat or Instagram and thought Tweeting was the most dumbass thing he had ever heard.

He had several text messages from his semi-girlfriend in Denver. She was more into him than he was into her. RJ didn't ask her to ride with him to Daytona; he even doubted he would contact her the rest of the trip and most likely not when he got back to Denver. After spending several years in a state penitentiary, he didn't want to be tied down to anything or anyone for too long. Taking over the club gave him enough headaches without the responsibilities of having to care for someone else.

RJ was up and down several times during the night, looking out the window to check his bike and the cargo he was carrying. He had left the ashes, the remains of Deuce, in his leather saddlebags. The bags were locked and secure, yet he felt uneasy about Deuce sitting out there by himself. He should have just gotten dressed and brought Deuce to his room but put it off thinking he would fall asleep. RJ swore the next night he would have Deuce, his ashes, in his room.

After a long shower, coffee, a few more emails and a free continental breakfast of bagels, cream cheese, fruit and orange juice, RJ was ready to ride. He pulled his hair back in a pony-tail, put on cheap wrap-around Bolle sunglasses, dabbed his nose with sunscreen and was back on the road. No rain gear was needed, just his leather jacket.

Next stop would be somewhere near Atlanta for the night.

As he was riding, RJ was thinking and planning the rest of the trip. At Daytona Beach, he was meeting up with other members of the Son's motorcycle club. Deuce's request to spread his ashes on the beach would be a private affair between RJ and Deuce. But while in Daytona he had club business to attend to.

RJ had asked to meet privately with Big John Ballard, the club president for Florida. RJ didn't care for the operations and management of the club, but it was a duty Deuce left to him and something he promised Deuce he would do. He also didn't care for Big John Ballard.

RJ had met Big John, who truly was big, at 6' 5" and 480 pounds, at a club meeting near New Orleans. RJ was guarding Deuce. Big John was guarding Tanker Jones, who was then the Florida, club president. Unlike the name, Tanker was a skinny little shit who could out eat Big John. No one knew where he could put all that food. Thus he had a big tank and became Tanker. That's how biker's get their names; it's not rocket science.

Big John Ballard, behind Tanker's back, was lobbying for the Florida club president position. Big John thought he could manage the club better than Tanker. He was trying to get votes from other presidents, and club members. He wanted Deuce's vote. Deuce told him to fuck off. Big John got in Deuce's face, and RJ put Big John Ballard in the hospital.

Tanker got re-elected only to die of stomach cancer within the same year. It seems his big tank was cancer-related. Big John was voted in.

The ride to Atlanta went quick, very little traffic, good weather, no bugs and no need for the car whip. After he checked into his room, RJ had a couple of beers at the hotel bar and was sound asleep at 10:00. His friend Deuce was sitting by the TV.

The next morning, up before the sun, RJ skipped the hotel breakfast and went to the nearby Waffle House. It was packed with couples waiting in line to be seated. A ten-minute lull and he was given a table for two. He sat facing the parking lot, an easy eye on his bike. RJ carried a book in with him, Lee Child, the Persuader. A Jack Reacher novel. He ordered coffee, two pancakes, bacon, OJ and wheat toast. RJ opened the book and began to read.

SALAS

Leaving Fort Wayne, Salas rode Highway 27 'til he merged to Interstate 75 at Wapakoneta. At a BP gas station, he was sipping hot coffee while sitting in a two-seater booth. He was studying a map he had downloaded on his cell phone. Salas looked up as three loud-talking young men entered the store. Not that Salas never dropped the f-bomb, but these three kids managed to say it every other word. F this F that, F you, F me, F them all. Each grabbed a Mountain Dew from a stand-up cooler. Salas knew this because he was still watching them.

At the front counter, the young man attending the cash register asked them, "Is this-this-this all?" The kid stuttered.

The largest of the three boys, all of them in their upper-teens, stuttered back "Yes-yes-yes that's-that's-that's all. You dumb f-f-f-fuck." The three boys laughed.

"That will b-b-b-b be $5.07," The clerk responded.

"N-n-no t-t-today it is f-f-fre-ee," The leader said. The three boys laughed, then all turned around to leave. The largest grabbed a bag of potato chips off the counter, looked at the store clerk and said, "T-t-tanks."

Salas stood and was waiting for them at the door. Salas gave the leader a short jab of a flat palm to the chest. It knocked the wind out of the kid who then coughed and gasped.

Salas held out his badge. "Pay the clerk. Apologize, or you are going to jail for robbery, assault and being assholes."

The two followers each had dollar bills out of their pockets and handed them to Salas before he could finish the sentence. The leader gave Salas a fi e-dollar bill.

"Now tell the cashier you are sorry for teasing him," Salas said as he pointed in the direction of the young boy behind the counter.

The three boys each apologized by saying, "I'm sorry."

"Did it sound sincere to you?" Salas said as he was looking at the young man behind the counter.

The cashier nodded.

"Well, it didn't to me. It sounded to me like they may come back when I'm gone and be assholes again. Is that going to happen assholes?" Salas had his hand on the neck of their leader. He was squeezing hard, his knuckles turning white.

Two boys said "no" in unison. The one with Sala's hand around his throat shook his head right to the left. Salas let go of the kid's neck.

"This young man will have my cell phone number. If you come back and are assholes, he will call me, and I will call on you. Understand?"

This time they said "yes" in unison. Salas grabbed the arm of their leader as the other two exited the building.

Salas said softly to the young man, whispering in his ear, "I have found that boys who bully other boys are being bullied at home. If your dad is being an ass to you, call me. I will help." Salas gave the kid his business card. "Now get the hell out of here. And quit cussing so much. It makes you sound stupid."

"T-t-t-tanks" is what Salas heard from behind the counter. He followed the delinquent boys outside turning to wave at the cashier. Salas started his Harley and left he parking lot.

Salas rode past Dayton, stopping outside of Cincinnati for fuel. The ride through the Daniel Boone National Forest was springtime at its finest. The trees were gaining leaves, flowers blooming, lots of birds in the air. He saw many side roads that looked fun to explore but stayed true to his course and his plan.

Studying the map in Knoxville, Salas was tempted to head south and ride the hills through the Great Smoky Mountains near Ashville, North Carolina. He had been to the Biltmore on vacation with his ex-wife Deb years ago. It was beautiful country, probably even more so on a bike. The Vanderbilt boys knew how to spend money, make a forest, and build a castle. Their daddy was one hell of a businessman, their offspring, like Anderson Cooper, maybe not so much. Salas skipped the excursion, staying true to the course. It was the first time he had thought of Deb without Candy in days.

Riding on, he was in Chattanooga with less than two hours to his hotel. The nine-plus hour trip was winding down, and so was Salas. Cruising between 75 and 80 miles per hour the last hundred miles got him to his hotel on schedule.

Salas had a couple of beers at the hotel bar engaging in conversation with an attractive woman who worked for a life insurance company out of Lincoln, Nebraska. She said her name was Joyce. The beer and the conversation went smoothly; she was easy on the eye, intelligent and funny. A woman, Salas thought, he would like to get to know. A picture of Candy, not Deb, came to his mind, he liked that and felt guilty talking to Joyce. He felt he was in a relationship and committed to someone…. who was committed to someone else. A vision of Warren flashed through his head. Salas knew he needed to break his "relationship" with Candy but was drawn to her like a magnet. The insurance lady, dressed in a woman's business suit, her brunette hair pulled back behind her ears, small diamond studs in her earlobes, took his hand while he was thinking.

She asked, "This will sound corny but a penny for your thoughts?" She had no ring on her finger, neither did Salas. She was tattoo-less from what he could see; absent were nose rings, no studs in her tongue, only one set of earrings, she hadn't uttered a swear word. She was the opposite of Candy, in several ways she was more like Deb. She turned Salas's hand over, took a writing pen from her purse and wrote 327 on his palm. She stood and walked away.

From his seat in the hotel bar, Salas could see her standing at the elevator. Joyce turned back and smiled at him. Salas ordered another beer. He texted Candy and finished the beer without a return message. Salas took the stairs, he paused on the second-floor landing and looked at his hand. 327. He walked to room 214, his room.

His phone vibrated on the nightstand, an annoying sound. Salas woke, wondering where he was. Oh yeah, he realized, a hotel in Georgia. Salas looked at the alarm clock sitting by his phone. It was 5:44 AM. He cussed out-loud. The screen on the phone read "Deb." This couldn't be good. Deb never called him. Their divorce was amicable, both sides wanting the best for their daughter, Sami. There was no fi hting, no squabbling over property or bank accounts. No arguing over custody of Sami or who got the dog. Salas had nothing but good memories of his ex-wife, too many memories of his ex-wife. Deb hadn't called him in over two years, not since Sami picked Notre Dame for a college and she called to tell Salas he had tuition to pay. His heart raced. It had to be about Deb or Sami.

"Deb. Are you ok? Is Sam ok?" Salas asked. You could sense the fear in his voice.

"Yes, Mike I am fine. Sami is fine too. Sorry to bother you so early but I got a call from Sam last night. She lost her wallet and credit cards; she needs cash."

Salas sighed a huge sigh of relief. "Ok, give her some cash. You are an hour away Deb."

"No Mike. She is at Panama City Beach. On spring break."

"Are you shitting me? Panama? What the hell Deb, you let her go to Panama? Why didn't you tell me about this? What were you thinking? She needs more than cash. She needs an ID to get back on the freaking plane." Salas was standing now. He opened the curtains and was looking out the hotel window. The sun was trying to peak over the horizon.

"Panama City Beach in Florida, Mike. Not Panama, Panama."

"Oh. Well, you scared the crap out of me Deb. Damn it." He rarely cussed in front of Deb.

"Sorry, I thought she told you she was going there. Can you swing by her on the way to Daytona? Give her some money? Please." Deb said it softly.

Salas remembered that voice. She owned him with that voice. For a second he saw Deb when she was pregnant with Sami, beautiful hazel eyes that could look right through you. Olive skin that never sunburned or wrinkled. The most gorgeous pregnant woman he had ever seen. She glowed. She was perfect. How did he mess that up?

He asked, "How do you know that I am going to Daytona?"

"Sami told me. That's why I called so early. I wanted to get you before you were on the motorcycle. I know you can't check your phone while you ride. At least you hadn't better be."

"No, I don't use my phone while I ride. And yeah, I can go over there. I'll find it on the map. Florida isn't that big of a state."

"Mike, how do you like your bike?" Deb was still in the soft speaking mode.

"I love it Deb. Very relaxing. Gets your mind off, off of stuff." Salas was remembering Deb in a good way. He was smiling.

"Yeah, we like ours too. Jack bought one last year. We just ride around Springfield. No rallies like you." Her tone was sharper.

"I never figured an actuary would ride a motorcycle. A bicycle maybe. And never fi ured you for the biker type. What kind of bike do you have?" Mike asked, no longer smiling. It had been several years since their divorce, but she was still his first love, and now they were visiting about his replacement.

"A Goldwing."

"That I guessed right. I will call Sami later and meet her in Panama Beach."

They said their goodbyes. He had been thinking of Deb nearly every day for several years. He finally finds someone new, and then he hears Deb's voice. Salas took a cold shower. He laid down again with no hope of sleeping. Too early to call a college kid on spring break. Breakfast sounded better.

Salas re-packed the Road King, swung his right leg over the saddle and rode down the street to a Waffle House. In a crowded parking lot, he parked his bike next to another Harley. He thought maybe there were a lot of guys who got early morning calls from their ex-wives, and afterward they all went to the Waffle House for breakfast.

Inside the restaurant, he couldn't find an open table. He scanned the booths, the bar stools at the counter, all lacking empty chairs. He walked back to the entry door, one guy sitting alone at a table for two was reading a book. Salas approached.

Salas said to the man sitting at the table, "Hey. You like Lee Child? I love Jack Reacher. Mind if I sit? Place is packed." He was pointing at the book.

"Sure. That was you that parked by my bike. May as well join me." The man responded.

"Salas. Mike." Salas extended his hand to shake as he sat.

"RJ, please to meet you." RJ closed the book, sat up straight and shook hands.

"You could pass as Reacher. Not like that little shit Tom Cruise, they cast in the movie. Which, by the way, I refuse to watch," Salas said.

"Ha. Agreed. Can't fi ure out what the hell they were thinking when they cast Cruise. Reacher is six-foot-five, two-hundred and fifty. Cruise is five-foot-five and one-fifty. He can't do what Reacher does," RJ replied.

They sat in silence as Salas scanned the menu. RJ went to the front counter and squeezed by a waitress. He grabbed a white ceramic coffee cup from behind the counter. He sat back down and poured coffee for each of them.

"Hey, thanks," Salas said then he looked up, over RJ's shoulder. He sat quietly for a few seconds. Still staring past RJ.

Salas frowned. "You have got to be shitting me."

"What is it?" RJ asked without turning to look.

"Two rednecks. Meth-head white boys. They just walked in. One has a handgun in the front of his pants. They are going to the front counter. You carrying?" Salas asked.

"Yeah. And, you will like this. Their buddy just came in the door behind you. Trench coat. Double barrel shot-gun. Barrel sticking out the bottom of the coat. I agree on the meth, or maybe they are British."

Salas laughed and said, "I'll go to the counter. Can you take the double barrel?"

"Yeah. I got him," RJ said.

Salas walked toward the two boys standing in front of the cash register. The guy with the gun was wearing a Confederate flag t-shirt, Salas thought he could smell the kid over the eggs and bacon. He paused by a young lady on her cell phone. Salas bent down and whispered in her ear, "You may want to video this for me please."

As Salas neared the counter, the redneck pulled the handgun from his pants. Salas beat him to the draw. In his right hand, Salas held his Glock 9 mm; he was pressing the barrel against the boy's cheek.

"Morning Kid Rock. I don't think you want to do what you want to do," Salas said quietly. No one in the restaurant was aware of what was happening. People were talking as usual, cooks yelling orders were ready, waitresses filling coffee. "You lay the gun on the counter. Or I will remove what teeth you have left."

The other redneck stepped forward. He had greasy red hair that was haphazard, bed-head. The kid looked like he just woke up. He had a face full of red freckles or red acne, Salas wasn't going to study it. He wore a white tank top featuring sweat stains under his chin and armpits. With his left-hand, Salas grabbed him by the throat and lifted. Salas liked to do that. Redneck's toes were barely on the floor. Redneck gurgled something about kicking ass. Salas squeezed harder, and the noise stopped.

Across the room, RJ walked towards the door when the third redneck started to raise the double barrel shotgun. As the kid lifted the gun to his shoulder, RJ grabbed the barrel of the long gun and drove the shotgun upward, smashing the top of the gun's barrel into the kid's forehead. A huge red imprint emerged from his nose to his hairline as the young Georgia man crumpled to the floor. RJ was now holding the shotgun. The morning breakfast patrons still unaware.

The redneck with the handgun slowly laid the gun on the counter. Salas scrunched his nose to his eyebrows and looked toward the floor. A clear, yet stinking liquid was running out the bottom of the redneck's pants over the top of a red and white Puma logo.

Salas looked back up at the boy saying, "Why didn't you tell me you had to go poddy?"

Salas cleared his voice and said loudly, "Listen up everyone. I am a police officer, and we are arresting these three young men. Please remain calm. We have the situation under control." Salas looked at the waitress who looked bored, as if this happened every morning at the Waffle House. She was chomping gum and scratching her left breast. Salas said, "Dial 911."

One of the cooks, a Mexican in a hairnet and white latex gloves came from behind the counter. He was carrying black plastic zip ties. Salas said, "Thanks, please zip him up." The cook took the ties and secured both men as if he had done this before. The third guy, by RJ, was still unconscious, the cook zip-tied him too.

The restaurant was back to normal. People talking, cooks yelling that orders were ready, and waitresses filling coffee.

Salas turned to RJ, "You a cop?"

RJ looked Salas in the eyes and said, "No. To tell you the truth, I'm fresh out of prison. Still on probation. I don't need any of this."

"Are you shitting me? I fi ured you as a cop. Well, give me your gun." Salas stuck out his hand. He was sure no one was watching the exchange as people were looking at their phones, those that recorded the incident were posting it on Facebook. Salas looked at RJ's weapon, a Glock 9 mm like his own and put the handgun in the small of his back, under his shirt next to his own weapon. His leather jacket concealed both.

The police arrived minutes later. Two black and white squad cars, with two officers in each front seat. Questions were asked. RJ's background was run. He had permission to leave the state of Colorado and had reported to his probation officer already that morning. Salas's badge, handgun, and permit were confirmed. Salas left RJ's handgun in the back of his pants. The officer in charge didn't search Salas but did pat down RJ. It was decided Salas was just an Indiana cop on vacation.

Witnesses were documented, and paperwork completed. An ambulance arrived and took redneck number three to the hospital. Rednecks number one and two were each in the back seat of different squad cars. RJ and Salas were free to go. The three rednecks would probably be out of jail soon, after all, they never committed a crime.

RJ and Salas got a free breakfast courtesy of the Waffle House management.

In the parking lot, Salas reached behind his back under his leathers and pulled out a Glock. He handed it to RJ, his large hand masking the exchange. RJ took the weapon and placed it in the small of his low back. RJ opened his saddlebag, careful to not upset Deuce, and took out his vest. He put on his colors, the vest further covering the handgun.

"Where you headed?" Salas asked.

"Daytona Beach. Hitting the rally. I made it to Sturgis so thought I would get another rally in." RJ responded.

"Hey, I was in Sturgis too. Can't believe we didn't meet. There were only a million people there. Want to ride together? I have to spin off to Panama City Beach and see my daughter though. Taking the long route."

"Sounds like a plan. I rode out of Denver. It will be nice to ride with someone. I have some friends near PCB I need to see, so yeah, I can follow you there," RJ said.

The two men fired up their Harleys and rode east. Salas leading the way.

RICHARD

As his headaches intensified, Richard withdrew from the business and from life. His wife leaving him and no contact with his children made matters worse. He had no reason to get out of the bed, much less get out of the house.

Richard was staring out the front window. The sun was well over the horizon, he thought maybe it was 10 or 11 in the morning. It looked like it was raining on the coast. Every day it rained somewhere in Florida. Vincent was in the work yard talking to the men.

Richard didn't know any of his new employees. He had heard Vincent calling out the names of Jake, Rod, Terry and an occasional Raphael. Richard didn't like the looks of any of them. And didn't know why the two muscle heads were even there. All they did was walk around. He never saw them load, unload, drive a truck, or clean the shop.

For being in the house so much, and in bed, Richard couldn't sleep. He would lay there in pain, his head ready to burst. Richard had been to the VA, Veterans Administration Hospital several times, with the same results. More pain medications. He had been to orthopedists, neurologists, internal medicine docs, chiropractors, massage therapists, naturopathic physicians, psychiatrists, and had been acupunctured, neuro-stimulated, adjusted, heated, cooled, ultra-sounded, hung upside down, suffered through colonic irrigation, and was shaked and baked. All with no improvement.

At his physical peak as a Ranger, he would run five to six miles a day. Richard had spent three days a week in the weight room and countless hours in the field, target practicing, mountaineering, parachutes, hand-to-hand combat training, and studying battlefield tactics. Now he spent hours looking out this window. The lights always off, just Richard sitting in the dark, staring at nothing. He had so many questions to ask Vincent. Who were all these guys? Who was the short guy in the Audi? How did we get so deep into the motorcycle repo business? How many bikes are in that truck? Did Vincent get a contract with Harley Davidson? When did we buy a Freightliner and an enclosed trailer? When did he put a garage door on the back of the shop and why? Where did he get the money? The questions made Richard's brain hurt.

Richard was still staring when he saw the muscle head with the handgun in his pants. Richard thought that they didn't need guns in the work yard. More questions clogged his head. Yes, Richard carried a weapon when collecting but why carry at the office? Why all the security? The razor wire, the cameras, and now guns? He had to visit with Vincent. He needed to see what was going on. Richard needed his questions answered.

Opening the front door to go outside brought in bright rays of sunshine. Richard had forgotten to put on his sunglasses. He grabbed his temples with both hands and closed his eyes. Richard dropped to his knees, then fell back on the hardwood floor of the house. He kicked the door shut with his foot and crawled back to his recliner. Richard dry swallowed two Meperidine tablets. He would talk to Vincent tonight or tomorrow when the sun wasn't shining.

BIG JOHN BALLARD

Big John wore gray sweatpants that were held up above his waist by red suspenders. His white socks were dusty gray with the hem of the sweatpants at the high-water mark. John's shirt could be a tent, housing four or fi e boy scouts. On his feet were Converse tennis shoes. The laces tied, the heels of the shoes were flat. He used the shoes like slippers, easy on and easy off.

He rode up to his store, a Jiffy-Lube, one of two franchises he owned on the Atlantic Coast of Florida. Both stores were slowly getting more profitable and cash flowing extra income. Work was steady though he was always turning over new staff. Constant training and re-training. No one worked for Big John very long. John thought it was the wages. If you asked the employees or former employees, it was because of Big John.

John parked the Harley Davidson trike near the rear garage door. He struggled to get off the bike. His body, in its enormity, didn't want to lift and bend the way it needed. John Ballard was better built for a Walmart scooter than a Harley trike. He wasn't always this big. In his early twenties he worked the oil fields of Wyoming, was lean and cat-quick but he didn't like the work. Manual labor was too much effort and not enough pay. Ballard jumped from job to job, from Wyoming to Louisiana. It was in Baton Rouge where he got his first taste of "easy money."

John was asked by a friend to deliver a package from the Bat to New Orleans. A cardboard box, each seam taped shut. There was no address, no names, and no post office box listed on the carton. Ballard knew the box didn't weigh over two pounds.

He drove to New Orleans to the address he was given. John stood in front of a law office with the sign on the door stating, "Davenport and Davenport Attorneys At Law." He went through the door and stopped at the front receptionist and told her he had a package for Mr. David Davenport. John was told by his friend to give the package to David and watch him open it.

The receptionist tried to take the package, but Ballard insisted on a personal face-to-face delivery. After a ten minute wait, Mr. Davenport appeared and thanked John for the carton. Davenport asked where to sign, and Ballard said: "No need to sign, just open the box."

Davenport hesitated, John Ballard said, "Open the damn box."

The attorney gave John an odd look but opened the carton. He used a letter opener from the receptionist's desk to break the seal. Mixing through papers inside the box David Davenport extracted what he thought was a hotdog. He held it up to the light. The receptionist screamed. Davenport dropped the object to the countertop. A look of horror on his face. Ballard stared at the object sitting oblong on the counter. It was a thumb. Ballard smiled.

At least the thumb was minus a hand, which was minus an arm, which was minus a body. Davenport gasped, grabbed the thumb, threw it in the box, and gave the package back to Ballard. To which John did as he was told to do and said: "Kingston wins in court, or your thumb is delivered next." Ballard added free of charge, "And I will shove it up your ass."

The friend of John's gave him ten-grand for the delivery and the message. It was easy money. Ballard ran more errands for his Baton Rouge friend. The errands were easy, but no manual labor made him gain weight. When his friend suddenly disappeared, John took his stash of cash and invested in a franchise. The body weight kept adding on.

Today Big John shuffled through the open garage door, his inner thighs rubbed together, the rubbing continued well below the knees. The sweatpants had holes in the crotch from the friction. The waist of the pants dragged down by the suspenders and was hopelessly hanging on by the metal clips.

"Hector, you Mexican piece of shit, clean up this crap on the floor," Ballard yelled at an employee. "Kevin, get your ass off that phone and

get in the bay. I don't fucking pay you to be on your phone you pissant."
You get the idea why Big John Ballard goes through help.

Ballard went to his office on the other side of the garage, away from
the waiting room that was designed for people getting their oil changed.
The office was small. No computer, as John didn't know how to run one.
He took out his cell phone and punched in some numbers as he was
looking down his nose, his arm extended as he was looking at the phone.

"What was last night's run?" Ballard yelled and asked into the phone.

"Down. Net was a couple of grand. I need more feet on the street,"
was the response. The voice was weak, whiny; it lacked conviction.

"Quit bellyaching, you pussy. All you do is bitch and moan. Don't
you think I know that already? I'm your brother James, not your fucking
mother."

"When is your boss coming in?" was the response.

"I told you, he ain't my fucking boss, you shit for brains. I'm
expecting him today or tomorrow," John replied.

"You think he will go along with your plan?"

"No. You dumbass. I know he won't go for it, him and Deuce got self-
righteous. When Deuce got cancer, he saw Jesus or something. Wants
us to be boy scouts, not bikers. I'll give him a chance and ask him. If he
don't like it, then we will have to go on without him. Everybody wanted
me as club president, not some half-assed bodyguard that wasn't smart
enough to keep himself out of prison." Big John snorted as he spoke.

"Let me know. I'll be ready for ya'all. Tell Momma hi." The voice on
the other end jumped into a Southern accent.

"Fuck you and Momma, neither one of you are worth a shit." Big
John Ballard hung up the phone.

SALAS

The two bikers started out on I85 to Atlanta, they drove fast and hard through the rest of Georgia and into Alabama. Spring had sprung, early tree blossoms, the smell of pine and moisture in the air, it looked as if it must have rained during the night. Salas took the lead with the GPS screen on his Road King guiding the way. RJ followed off Salas's right shoulder less than fifteen feet behind. They rode with the cruise control set at 75 mph. No helmets. Salas's bald head glistened in the morning sun. RJ's hair was blowing back like the mane of a horse running in the derby. Dennis Hopper, Jack Nicholson, and Peter Fonda would have been proud.

Off of highway 431, they pulled their Harley's into Eufaula, Alabama. Lunch was burgers and fries at a mom and pop diner. Salas checked Google maps, they had another 150 miles to Panama City Beach. Salas asked how and why RJ was on probation. RJ told him about the Denver strip club, and Deuce getting his ass kicked, and RJ kicking the ass of the guy who attacked Deuce. How he became a member of the club. RJ told him about the arrest in Denver after, of all things, a Toys for Tots bike run. Again, RJ defending Deuce, with RJ serving time for assault. Salas and RJ connected. Salas asked, and RJ answered, a first for RJ.

When lunch was over, with both men sitting in the booth of the restaurant, Salas dialed Sami's cell phone number. She answered on the third ring.

"Daddy!" Came through the phone. Her voice and the word "daddy" made Salas smile.

"Sweetie!" Salas said. This made RJ smile.

"Mom said you would call. I am at PCB!" Sami was yelling into the phone. Salas could hear music in the background. Well, it was rap, if you like that as music.

"Yeah. I am on my way to see you, Sam. Be there in a few hours. Where is a good place to meet up?"

"We are staying at the "Beach Tower by the Sea" off Front Beach Road. I will text you the address."

"Ok, and I will text you when I get there! Can't wait to see you."

"Thanks, Daddy. Love you." The phone went dead.

Salas sat for a minute as if thinking. He went back to his phone. He looked at Deb's number then called Candy in Fort Wayne. The phone rang four times and went to voicemail. He didn't leave a message.

Within seconds he got a text. It was Candy. "Michael, you know I can't take your calls while I am working."

Salas responded, "I miss you. I wanted to hear your voice."

"Have fun on vacation," was the response.

"Candy, I wish you were here with me."

"NOT going to happen. Don't call. I will text you when and if I can."

Salas looked at his phone, he didn't like this. He felt dismissed. He placed the phone in the inner compartment of his leather jacket, same pocket as his Glock. He zipped the pocket shut.

Salas turned to RJ "I'm not a spring break fan for women, especially for my girl. I went to Padre Island when I was in college. It was crazy. I imagine it is worse today with this group of kids." He said it more to himself than to RJ.

"I've got some guys near Panama City Beach. If you want I can have them keep an eye on her for you," RJ said.

"Really? Some guys? What are you into?" Salas asked. He went from thoughts of Sami to what and who was RJ?

"Told you. I help run a motorcycle club," RJ's replied.

"A club. Not a gang? You a Hell's Angel type?"

"Nope, not at all. Just a bunch of guys looking for a family. That is how I got in."

"Your world. I'm good with that." Salas recalled the teams of guys riding at the Sturgis Rally. They had each other's backs, a bond. Salas understood this. As a wrestler, he knew the value of a team, the meaning of brotherhood, friendship, and commitment to each other. "And yes. I would like the extra eyes on her. Thanks."

"I'll meet with my crew when you see your daughter." RJ slipped out of the booth, sending a text on his phone. "So, let me ask you. Who was the girl you were texting?

"How you know it was a girl?" Salas asked.

"Cuz you don't seem to be into guys."

"Yeah. Ha, you are right. It was my girlfriend. My very married girlfriend. I have a tendency to make mistakes, especially with women."

"Got you there, brother. Been there done that. If it don't feel right then walk the other way," RJ said.

"Just walk?" Salas asked.

"Just get on your bike and ride the other way. That's what I would do," RJ replied.

Salas paid the check.

Two hours later, the two bikers took a left on highway 231, riding the highway 98 bridge over the Grand Lagoon. Another left on Front Beach Road had them parallel to the Gulf of Mexico. They could see the water, the waves and the thousands of college students lined up on the beach. Passing Pineapple Willy's, Walmart and a Holiday Inn, they rode into the Beach Tower parking lot and the weekend home away from home of Sami.

They parked their bikes in the shade under the portico entering the hotel. There was no valet parking. Salas texted Sami. "I'm here! At the lobby."

RJ said, "Just so you know. I'm not supposed to wear this because of my probation." He turned his back, so Salas could see his colors on the vest. "Don't tell. I'll go meet my boys." RJ smirked and walked off, leaving Salas alone waiting for his daughter.

Within ten minutes Sami responded to the text: "On my way." A happy face accompanied the text.

Standing in the Florida sun, Salas was soon drenched in sweat. His leather jacket was draped on the handlebars of his bike. His Sturgis t-shirt was dark under the arms and under each pectoral. Sweat dripped off his forehead.

It was early afternoon, and kids were asleep or passed out on the balconies, even on the couches in the lobby. Music was pulsating everywhere. You could hear loudspeakers announcing contests and drink specials. DJ's were barking songs and nobody, boys or girls, had enough clothes on.

Sami saw her dad and came running up. She gave him a big hug. The three girls following her, standing in the background, were all on their phones, the white glare of the screen highlighting their faces. Each girl was sunburned to various degrees. All four of them had little red noses and burn lines from yesterday's swimsuit, which obviously was a diffe ent style than today's.

"Daddy, this is Cindy, Tamara, and Steph. Friends from school. We all drove here together and are sharing a room."

"Hi ladies." Salas smiled at them. They looked up briefly and went back to their cell phones. "This place is cool Sam. How much longer you staying?" Salas hoped they were leaving tomorrow. Tonight would be even better.

"Another three days. I lost my wallet. Well actually I left it in a bar when a fi ht broke out, and we all ran outside. When I went back to get it, someone must have taken it."

"Did you have Mom cancel your credit card and tell the bank about your debit card?"

"Yes, Dad!" was Sami's response as she rolled her eyes.

"What about your ID? How do you get into the bars without it?" Salas, again hoping she was spending the evenings in her room watching TV.

Sami reached into her swimsuit top and removed a driver's license. "I keep the driver's license here. Along with my phone. Lost my credit card, debit card, and my cash. And some make-up."

"Ok, sweetie. Here is some cash. And just so you know you are very spoiled. I would keep the cash with your ID. And could you put some more clothes on, please? At least leave something to the imagination." Salas handed her a roll of crisp twenty-dollar bills courtesy of the hotel's ATM.

"Oh, Daddy. We are at the beach! You wear swimsuits at the beach," was Sami's response.

Father and daughter talked for the next 15 minutes. School, classes, her mother. Salas could tell Sami was getting restless. Spring break at PCB was not the time for a father and daughter catch-up talk.

"You go with your friends. I will run up to South Bend soon, and we can have coffee. Maybe you could have a beer with your old man."

Sami kissed her dad on the cheek. "Thanks again, Daddy. Love your motorcycle. Have fun in Daytona." She turned and was lost in the wave of half-clad college bodies.

Across the street, RJ was sitting under an umbrella that was advertising *Mike's Hard Lemonade*. There were four chairs and three men. They were behind a small temporary metal barrier. The kind used for crowd control. In this case, it was being used to designate where the outside seating for the bar and grill started and stopped.

The two guys were members of the Son's. All three had their vests/colors on. The two men with RJ were both young, early twenties. Salas saw the three men talking while he was with Sami. Sami didn't see the three men. When Sami left with her entourage of friends, RJ stood as did the two younger members of the Son's. He shook their hands. Both were shorter than RJ. One way heavier, chubby pink cheeks with a buzz cut. The other lean and muscular in jeans and no shirt, just the leather vest. His hair was pulled back in a pony-tail like RJ's.

RJ crossed the street as the two men walked the opposite way. They too were soon lost in the mass of people. He approached Salas. "Those are my boys. They will keep an eye out on your Sami."

"How? They just left. They will never find her in all of this." Salas was pointing his hands out to the crowd.

"She is here at this hotel. Room 433. Her balcony is right up there." RJ was pointing up. "Nothing bad happens at the beach during the day. They will keep an eye on her tonight. There is one way in and out of the lobby. They will take care of her."

"How you know her room number?"

"Simple phone call Mike. The hotel gave it to me." RJ held his Samsung up for RJ to see. "Relax, you are acting like a dad, not a cop, especially a detective."

"Who are they? You trust them?" Salas said. Looking for the two men.

"The bigger kid. His dad and grandpa are in the club. Over in Tallahassee. They own a couple of *Subway* franchises. That's how he got a little hefty. The other, we call him Tripp. His parents died in a car crash when he was a small boy. His uncle Deuce, the friend of mine I told you about, raised him in Denver. He came out to Florida State for college. Really a smart young man. Going to law school next year."

Salas was rubbing his bald head. "Ok. I trust you RJ. Let's get out of here, we got another three-hundred-and-sixty miles to go. And I just want to ride."

RJ smiled. He had heard that line before.

VINCE'S CREW

Terry, Jake, and Rod were crowded inside the straight truck, their shoulders touching, the diesel motor humming, black exhaust streaming from the tailpipes. Jake was driving. Terry had the passenger side window. Rod was asleep, his head on Terry's shoulder. Drool from Rod's mouth was soaking into Terry's t-shirt. The air-conditioning was on high. They had driven from Deland to Crescent Beach Florida and were working their way back down the coast.

The three-man crew had their bike stealing system down to a matter of seconds, not minutes. Spot a bike, parking lots were the best. Ideally, find a guy while he is parking his motorcycle, then watch the owner walk away being sure he didn't come back. Next, drop Terry and Rod off by the bike. Their job is to get the bike loaded. Jake was better at the lifting since he was stronger but something about a black man hanging around bikes drew unneeded attention. Terry would test the handlebars of the Harley, always a Harley, to see if it was locked at an angle. If it was, then not a good candidate. Most riders forgot to lock their handlebars.

Terry would signal Jake, who had lifted the back door of the truck open and set the Tommy Lift down near the ground while Terry checked the bike. Jake would then back the truck to the motorcycle. Terry and Rod push the bike on to the Tommy Lift. As Jake drives away, Rod would jump into the back of the truck while Terry raised the lift and closed the door. Their best time was 27 seconds. Once enclosed, Terry and Rod secured the bike to the hooks drilled into the floor with ratchet straps using a front wheel chook to prevent the bike rolling forward. A couple of miles down the road, Jake pulls the truck over, Terry and Rod change the magnetic decal on the doors and get in the front seat.

The magnetic decals were Terry's idea. He got them in Deland. No one pays much attention to a repo truck loading a motorcycle, but they do notice the name. The decals on the doors read "We Found U Repo." Terry got similar decals that read "Gotcha Repo." They used the "Gotcha" decals when they stole the bike then removed it down the road when they were away. So far, the system worked as they were 42 bikes for 42 bikes. No one was caught, and no one was turned in. A perfect plan.

Four bikes were in the back of the truck. They got lucky with the first one, a 6:00 pm pick-up along the beach. A biker left his Harley unlocked, dropped his clothes, jumped the sand dune in his boxers and went into the water for a swim. The barrel key was left in the front pocket of the pants that he had just taken off, so they even had the key. The next three Harleys were taken near Ormond Beach between 10:00 and 11:00 at night when the bikers were in a bar. All three bikes were on the same block. Three bikes in under fi e minutes. Terry said it was a world record.

The truck carrying the repo men entered the city of Daytona Beach. The doors of the truck read "We Found You Repo." They would change it before the next lift.

Jake pulled the truck into a rest area; the asphalt of the parking lot was covered with a thin layer of sand. He put the truck in park with the windshield facing the beach and the waves and the beach walkers. There were dozens of people strolling the beach enjoying the same view as the men in the truck. Terry left the other two men in the truck to get their evening meal. He walked back up the road they came in on towards several fast food restaurants they had passed on the way in.

The waiting game began. After the bar scene, the next best time to steal a bike was four to fi e in the morning. Hotel parking lots were the easiest. The three men sat in the cab of the truck, Terry, and Rod with an Arby's sandwich, Cokes and curly fries. Jake had an apple. Steely Dan was playing on the radio.

They had five hours until time to go back to work.

VINCENT

Vincent was sitting alone in his mobile home. In Florida, they are known as ETDUs, Early Tornado Detection Units. He stood and walked to the far wall of the bedroom. He was looking at a gun safe he ordered online from an outdoor sporting goods store from Nebraska called *Cabela's*. The white and yellow *Cabela's* logo stared back at him. The keypunch security card on the door of the safe was waiting to be triggered. The Outfitter 86 gun safe could hold 64 shotguns or rifles, 16 handguns and several rounds of ammunition. *Cabela's* guaranteed the safe would be good to 1,200 degrees Fahrenheit and stated that the safe weighed over 700 pounds. They used a forklift to get it off the delivery truck and a reinforced dolly to get it inside the mobile home. When they sat the safe down, the home shook, Vincent thought the safe would drop through the floor. Vincent purchased the Outfitter 86 to protect his cargo from fire and wind, obviously a perfect fit.

He entered the code and opened the safe. Twenty pounds of heroin sat inside, looking tiny in the large metal box. Last week the safe was full, as German had delivered 100 pounds of the powder and stacked it inside the gun safe. That was the only time he saw Marco and Raphael work. The street value of the entire load was over $10,000,000. Vincent's job was to get the 100 pounds to Vancouver within two weeks. He had less than 5 days left, and it was a 3,200-mile drive. At least 48 hours on the road in the Freightliner.

Vincent hatched the plan the year before he went to prison when crossing the border from Mexico to San Diego. He was carrying a pound of cocaine. Vincent couldn't fi ure out the metric system, so he went by pounds not kilos. Vincent was sitting in a stall at a men's room truck stop, a mile from the United States border. He poured the white powder into a ziplock bag and rolled it like a cigar. Vincent added a half dozen more ziplocks, each encasing the prior bag. In the parking lot, he pushed the now banana-looking package into the gas tank of his Vespa scooter.

At the border, waiting in line, he remembered sweating profusely and not because of the sweltering heat. Two border crossing guards approached him as he sat on the scooter, motor idling. One of the guards had a dog, a yellow lab. The dog was sniffing every person, tire, and door and the dog was not looking for a place to piss.

The lab sniffed Vincent then sniffed the bike. The guard made him shut off the scooter and push it out of the way of the traffic. A Mexican border patrol officer checked Vincent's ID and said something in Spanish into a hand-held radio. The other officer had him stand away from the scooter. They patted him down. The dog was still sniffing.

The two police officers huddled together. They looked at Vincent. He was frisked again. The dog laid down, his tongue hanging to the side of its mouth, he was panting. The officer holding the dog leash told Vincent he was free to go. They turned away and went to the next vehicle.

Vincent started the Vespa. As he was riding away, he was smiling. The dog couldn't smell the coke because he was smelling gasoline. Vincent pulled into a McDonald's. He took the package out of the gas tank as he sat in the parking lot. The fuel had eaten its way through a couple of layers of the ziplock. Another few hours and the package may have been contaminated and ruined. But it worked.

From one pound to one hundred. That was the project. Once out of prison, Vincent wanted to work the plan. He needed capital, he needed a truck. He needed better packaging than ziplock bags. Oh, and he needed a hundred pounds of drugs. That is when he thought of his brother Richard. Richard could be the answer he was looking for. The perfect fall guy. Who would have thought Richard would enlist Vincent before Vincent even made it out of prison?

Arriving at the acreage where he grew up reminded Vincent more of what he didn't want out of life than what he was there for. As a kid, helping his father clean the shop, servicing the trucks and vehicles was beneath him. Vincent wanted more than scrubbing cars and driving a truck.

When Vincent returned home, he was surprised how sick Richard was. The headaches Richard experienced crippled him. The migraine type pains made life terrible for his brother. But it worked great for Vincent. As the mayor of Chicago says, never let a good crisis go to waste. Vincent secured an operating line of credit from the bank, further leveraging the business, buildings, and land. Richard signed the papers without looking at them.

With the money, Vincent was able to put in the security system. He made a down payment on a truck and trailer, both of which he would leave in Canada. And he solved his biggest problem, the packaging he needed.

A simple google search and Vincent discovered the material *Viton*. Their military grade fluoroelastomer, whatever the hell that was, was the solution he was looking for. A powdered product could be poured into a flexible container that could be sealed and sitting in gasoline for over a week, a month or a year. His special order of fifty-fi e bags was completed, shipped and received within thirty days. It was expensive.

Now out of money, he needed more cash and 100 pounds of product. Through a friend he met in prison, (are there really friends in prison?) Vincent was connected to a mid-level supplier and told him what he needed but not the plan. Vincent was then connected to German.

German had a distribution problem. German was getting over a hundred pounds of product a quarter thanks to the never-ending war in Afghanistan. He had saturated the Florida market with more distributors than *Amway*. German needed to contract or expand, there was no middle ground. Vincent's plan intrigued him. He had the product to spare if Vincent screwed him, so he could take a chance. German didn't like Vincent, so if Vincent failed, German would have Vincent, a win-win.

Product was delivered. Raphael and Marco were put in place to stand guard. The clock was ticking.

Vincent rolled a cellophane-wrapped block of compressed white powder in his hands. It was packed tight, secure, it took a knife to break through the packaging. Millions of dollars sitting right there in front of him. Millions of dollars of a fine yellow-white powder.

He smiled. He was going to be rich. His brother, Jake, Terry, and Rod would probably end up dead. Too bad he thought, but they are big boys. They should know better. He locked the door to the safe.

GERMAN

German was sitting in a high-backed leather chair, he could scoot from side to side on the wheels. He was perched behind a mahogany desk; no drawers were attached making it look more like a dining room table than office furniture. On the flat table top were a Microsoft Surface Pro, his cell phone and a coaster made of marble. The coaster supporting a plastic cup containing iced coffee. German took a slow sip of the dark liquid. He flipped his hair behind his ear.

"Diego, This Vincent situation. I am thinking this was perhaps a bad move on my part. I do not trust him. I fear this will end badly for our repossession man. Let's go there tomorrow night. I wish to repossess our supply and get my cash back. Does this work for you as well Diego?" German asked.

"Of course, German. Do I get to eliminate the risk?" Diego asked back.

"I think we should Diego. He knows more than he should."

"I will enjoy tomorrow night," Diego responded as he brewed himself a cup of coffee, the Keurig machine hissing at him.

"Which reminds me," German said. "Things I enjoy and things I do not enjoy. Thursday night at my wife's charming cocktail party, I hate those events, Diego. Politicians trying to kiss my ass while their hands are in my pockets. Were you able to obtain DayVonte's cell phone?" German asked as he was typing on the Microsoft evice.

Diego was sitting across from the flattop desk in a straight back Victorian chair. His legs were crossed in a twisting fashion, he had skinny legs. Diego was drinking his coffee out of a small white ceramic teacup. A matching white saucer was on the magazine stand in front of him. He glanced out the 5th story window, seeing the white sand beaches of St. Augustine.

"Yes, German. Your invitation for him to join you in the pool worked. He left his clothes, and cell in the cabana area. I was able to place the device on his phone. We now know where his phone is located at all times." Diego continued to slowly drink his coffee.

"So, Diego. Has our All-pro DayVonte's cell phone and Michelle's cell, have they connected since Thursday?" Another question from German, he pronounced Michelle as Meeechelle.

"Yesterday, German at the Park Place Plaza Hotel. The two phones connected." Diego answered.

"This has been confirmed?"

"Yes, Danny has photos of their cars. A photo of them getting into the elevator. They ordered room service German; champagne, strawberries and Banana's Foster."

"My wife Michelle does love Banana's Foster," German said. "And where is our favorite Jacksonville Jaguar enjoying his day off today Diego?"

"Danny related he watched DayVonte board his yacht at the marina this morning. One other passenger also got on the boat. The phone app says he is fi e miles in the Atlantic. Not moving at this current time." Diego was looking at his phone.

"Get Danny and arrange for my boat, the 38 Top Gun, to be available at our dock. Thank you, Diego. Let's make a yacht visit," German said.

Less than an hour later German had the twin Mercury's cruising well below the capabilities of the 850 horsepower engines. The boat planed out on the silky-smooth waters. The three men; German, Diego and Danny were five miles out in the Atlantic on the cigarette boat gliding in the water. None of the men were dressed for a fishing excursion. German in his favorite blue silk Brioni with straight legs, the jacket stretched tightly at the shoulders. Diego wearing khaki pants with a blue Ralph Lauren blazer, and Danny in a Stafford JC Penney off-the-rack outfit. The men were riding towards the electronic pinging released by the cell phone on the boat of DayVonte Robinson, the All-Pro defensive back for the Jags.

They spotted the 44-foot Viking Billfish and slowed the Top Gun to approach without a wake. DayVonte was on the starboard side watching the boat coming towards him. He recognized German and waved. He was shirtless in bright yellow to the knee swim trunks, the baggy kind. He sported six-pack abs, traps and deltoids cut like diamonds, and his biceps and triceps were larger than most people's thighs. DayVonte was smiling, his hair was pulled back in thick cords of black rope.

German gently slid the 38 against the 44 Valhalla. Danny and Diego tied the two boats together. There were no waves, a perfectly calm ocean. No noise, no birds, no bugs, no music, no other people for miles.

"German," DayVonte said. "What are you doing so far out? You are not dressed for fishing."

"Just out for a mid-day cruise. Thought I recognized your boat. I love this Billfish. May we come aboard? What are you fishing for?" German asked.

"Barracuda are hitting, aggressive as hell," DayVonte responded.

German and Diego stepped from the cockpit of the 38 to the back deck of the Billfish. Diego took a position behind DayVonte's friend, who was not introduced.

"D-Rob," German said extending his hand.

"It is actually Day-Rob." The friend of DayVonte's spoke. His tone was sharp as German and Day-Rob shook hands.

"Pardon my error," German said. "Day-Rob, I have some questions to ask of you. It would be to your advantage if you spoke the truth."

"Just who you think you are bro?" The friend spoke again as he stood with chest out. His voice aggressive.

German looked the man over. DayVonte's friend was shorter than the six-foot-two-inch Robinson. Darker skin dreads like DayVonte, held back with a red bandana that covered his forehead. He was muscular but not at Robinson's level. Perhaps an ex-jock. A college friend out for a ride with his millionaire former college teammate.

"And you are?" German asked.

"None of your damn business," the friend replied.

"Tray, relax man. It's cool," DayVonte said.

German looked the man over, seemingly bored with the conversation. He repeated the scan head to toe and back again. Then said "You have worn out your welcome. I have no use for you." German nodded at Diego.

Diego took a six-inch blade out of the inner pocket of the Ralph Lauren. In a single sweeping movement, Diego slit the throat of DayVonte's friend. He tossed the man over the side of the boat as the man gasped for one last breath. Blood was spurting in a pulsating motion creating a fine arc from the cut, over the railing, and into the ocean. DayVonte screamed in surprise, agony, and disbelief, as did Danny who was still sitting in the 38. Diego was so quick only a few drops of blood were able to hit the deck of the Billfish.

"German, what, why did you do that? Tray! Tray!" DayVonte screamed as he tried to step forward, to look for his friend over the side of his vessel. Diego pulled out a handgun and told Day-Rob to back off.

"DayVonte, please place your hands behind your back. We are going to handcuff you. We know we cannot wrestle you to the floor. So, you have two options. One. Allow yourself to be handcuffed or option two, we will shoot you in the kneecap. It is your decision. I don't believe anyone will hear the shot. Do you DayVonte?" German looked out into the ocean. Scanning the empty horizon. "Are you in need of your kneecap Day-Rob? It may be hard to repeat as All-Pro with only one kneecap. What do you say Day-Rob," German said, he too pulled a handgun from his suit coat, like his boat, it was a .38 Special.

"Danny, grab the bolt cutters and the rope from the side panel. Please give them to Diego."

Danny did as he was told, as did DayVonte who placed his hands behind his back. He was looking into the water for his friend.

Diego cuffed Day-Rob's hands behind his back, then pushed the man hard against the boat's railing, pressing DayVonte's head firmly to the metal.

"I pray you to stay still," Diego said as he tied the football player to the metal bar, DayVonte's face was compressed against the chrome. Diego wrapped the poly-manila rope around the chest and arms of DayVonte, pulling the rope tight. The cords ripped into the skin of the athlete with his blood soaking the fibers. DayVonte winced in pain.

German and Diego heard the sound of a stomach emptying its contents, that roaring sound of an elementary dinosaur. Both men turned towards the 38 Top Gun boat. Danny was throwing up over the side.

"The Barracudas. They are eating that guy," Danny said as he whipped spittle from his lips and chin with his right hand and pointed to the water with his left.

German looked annoyed and turned back to Diego's work. "DayVonte," German said the name softly as he leaned into the All-Pro. "Have you been sleeping with my wife?"

"What? No, No. German. I would never do that," DayVonte screamed into the rail. His spit running down the metal tube.

"I am going to ask you again. If you lie again, Diego will snip off the end of your finger," German said as Diego put one of DayVonte's fingers between the two blades of the bolt cutter. Blood forming from a small cut on the side of the Robinson's finger.

"Did you have sex with my wife?" German asked.

"No German!" DayVonte yelled.

German nodded again to Diego. Diego used the bolt cutters. DayVonte screamed. Danny repeated his vomiting protocol; lean over, throw-up and wipe.

"Let's see. He only took maybe a quarter inch off your finger Mr. All-Pro. Again, I ask, have you been sleeping with my wife?"

"No, German. Please. I told you. No," DayVonte yelled as he looked at German, his eyes wide with fear.

German now heard crying and weeping coming from his boat, the 38. He turned to Danny. "If you continue to cry, I swear I will kill you myself."

He nodded to Diego. DayVonte screamed.

"Maybe a third of the end of your middle finger. You will play football again Day-Rob, but you will have difficulty catching the ball. But then if you were good at catching the football, you would be playing offense and making far, far more money. Isn't that so Day-Rob?" German said as DayVonte was now crying.

Danny turned his back to the boat, to Diego and German. He stared into the vast emptiness of the Atlantic. Tears ran down his cheeks, but no sound came from his mouth.

"Diego. I hate to request this of you. But before I again ask this lying piece of shit if he has been fucking my wife, please unzip this man's shorts, take out his manhood. Then let me ask him. If he lies, take the end of his penis off," German said.

DayVonte yelled out, "Yes, Yes I have been sleeping with your wife, German. I love her. I love her, and she loves me. Yes, German. I am sorry, so sorry." DayVonte had tears streaming down his cheeks. He could feel his own warm blood running down his back and the hamstrings and calves of his legs. He could see a small pool of his blood collecting at his feet.

No one spoke for over a minute. DayVonte got his breath back. Danny was pale, gasping for breath and looking at German to show mercy. Diego had his blade at the ready, the bolt cutters still in his grasp.

"See my hand DayVonte?" German held his hand in front of DayVonte's face. "I was 16 years old when a man held my hands in front of me while another cut off my fingers. Cut them off at the knuckle. Not the fingertips like you. At the first knuckle. They asked me four times DayVonte, and I lied four times. You are weak Day-Rob. You broke. You are a coward. You are not fit to fuck my wife," German yelled.

German left Diego and went back to his boat. He started the engines. DayVonte was still tied to the rail. Diego went below deck, inside the Billfish. Within minutes he came back out of the hull and was on board the 38 with German. Danny was ordered to untie the lines. The two boats disconnected, the 38 drifting away. German lowered the accelerator, pushing it towards the console. The boat responded, all three men braced and leaned forward against the acceleration. They were less than 200 hundred yards away when the Billfish exploded.

RJ

RJ followed Salas off highway 98 down the Florida coast. Interstate 10 would have been faster but not as scenic. The sand beaches to their right were pristine, the water crystal blue, the waves with white flashes pounding the beach. The sailboats floating in the Gulf were a painting of a life neither rider would ever know.

They stopped in Perry Florida for fuel and bottles of water, then took Highway 27 across Florida to Gainesville where they jumped on Interstate 75 to Daytona. This ride not as memorable, the scenery, RJ thought, was better than Kansas but only because he wasn't shivering.

The two approached Daytona Beach on the back side, away from the Atlantic Ocean. Turning left they passed the Daytona Motor Speedway. Highway 92 took them to the beach. Before them the ocean was dark, the moon defining a small section of the horizon with no waves to be seen. Their first day in Florida, tomorrow they would catch the sunrise.

Salas pulled into the Holiday Inn Resort off A1A. RJ behind him. The parking lot was lined with motorcycles. Mainly Harleys, a Victory, and an occasional customized look-at-me, look-at-me, chopper that was trailered in. Salas backed his bike into an open slot, looking over his right shoulder as his feet fought for traction. He hit the kill switch shutting off the engine. Salas locked the handlebars with his barrel key and got off his bike. He put his thumbs together, reached up with both arms above his head and arched his back, the DDP diamond cutter. Salas let out a loud grown.

RJ stayed saddled on his bike, he checked his phone while Salas stretched. Putting the phone back in his vest pocket as Salas approached. The two men shook hands.

"Thanks for the help at the Waffle House and for having your crew watch over my girl," Salas said.

"Any time Mike. Thanks for the ride," was RJ's response.

Salas pulled a business card from his wallet and gave it to RJ. "Here, call me next time you are in Fort Wayne Indiana." Salas smiled.

RJ took the card and stuffed it in the right front pocket of his jeans. "I can honestly say that is one place I have never been." RJ did a two-finger salute with his clutch hand and rode out of the parking lot. Salas watched as RJ checked traffic to his left and right, then he turned east up the coastline.

Riding on Highway A1A RJ stopped at the *Starlite Diner* for a hamburger, fries and two Coors Lights. The diner was packed with bikers, most of them smelled of beer, were talking loudly and flirting with the waitresses. He relaxed with the beer and read a few more chapters about Jack Reacher. RJ tipped the waitress an extra fi e dollars. He felt bad for her for having to deal with drunk bikers.

RJ arrived at the Super 8 at 11:45. He found a parking spot at the end of a row of bikes. He parked his Harley under a bright light, the light pole serving as a barrier to the bike next to him. Like Salas, he backed the bike in, shut down the motor with the kill switch and dismounted. He grabbed a duffel bag from the right saddlebag, entered the hotel and checked in.

His room was on the 7th floor. From his window, he could see the hotel canopy over the entryway, the endless expanse of a black ocean and the light illuminating his Harley. He pulled the curtains wide open, preparing for the morning sun. RJ turned the AC on high. He sat in the desk chair and unlaced his boots before kicking them off with his opposite foot. He removed his vest and placed the Glock by the flat screen TV. He looked again at his handgun. He picked it up and turned it over in his hands. This was not his gun. Salas gave him the wrong weapon. RJ made a mental note to call Salas in the morning at the Holiday Inn. He took a hot shower, using the entire bottle of shampoo and conditioner. He toweled off then crawled under the sheets. He was asleep within minutes.

RJ suddenly sat upright in his king-sized bed. Rubbing his eyes, he looked at the digital alarm clock sitting on the nightstand. The red lights told him it was 5:15 in the morning, he had slept about fi e hours. He realized in his sleep that he left Deuce in the saddle bag on his bike. RJ went to the window to check on his friend.

Looking over the parking lot, RJ spotted his bike still sitting quietly under the light. He also saw a straight truck, like a UPS truck, parked to the side of his Harley. RJ grunted in jest at the wording on the side of the driver's door: "Gotcha Repo." The message was tilted at an odd angle. You had to turn your head nearly parallel to get it straight.

RJ watched as two men went to his bike. His mouth dropped open as they straightened the handlebars on his Harley. He watched in disbelief as a guy bent down and flipped the gear obviously putting the bike in neutral. The men then pushed his Harley Fatboy forward towards the truck. RJ screamed at the window, "Stop!"

He ran to the door of his room, opened it and sprinted down the hall. Wearing only his boxers. RJ pushed the down button on the elevator. The light read 1. The elevator was on the first floor and had to come up. He took the stairs. Running down the steps, his left hand on the railing then turning at sharp left angles to the next series of steps, RJ took fi e and six steps at a time. He busted through the exit door and ran into the parking lot.

The truck was taking off, gaining speed. RJ saw the rear door of the truck closing. He ran at an angle cutting across the parking lot, zig-zagging between cars, bikes, and pick-ups. RJ was level with the truck, perhaps thirty yards away. The truck now on A1A. His eyes met the driver's as he looked out the cab window toward him. The driver smiled and waved. RJ reached behind his back for his Glock. No pants, no gun. He looked at the driver side door, the sign read "Gotcha Repo." This sign was level not pointed down. RJ tried to give chase on foot down Highway A1A but gave up as the distance widened between himself and the straight truck. He inhaled diesel fumes as he ran. Under the lift of the truck was a Florida license plate but he couldn't get the details as dirt, mud, and grime obstructed the numbers.

RJ walked back to the hotel and re-entered thru the front doors which opened automatically as he approached. He went to the front desk and asked for a room key. He had no ID. He had no pants, no shoes or shirt for that matter. RJ stood before the night clerk in his boxers and told her what had just happened.

The woman assigned to the night and early morning front desk duty wore a silver name tag that read, "Marge, Portland Oregon." She looked RJ over, the good morning smile turned to concern as she examined the nearly naked man before her. Without thinking, Marge reached across the counter, running a finger along a scar on RJ's chest, an eleven-inch raised colloid, void of hair, that stretched deep from his right pectoral muscle to a light wisp of a scar on the left pec. A present from his days in lock-up. Marge touched another round, raised, and roughed scar on his right shoulder, a bullet wound from years ago. She followed his abdominal muscles to a missing piece of his body on his lower left. Where most men in their forties and fifties had a roll of love handles, RJ was lean but missing a chunk of his side. Another wound with a story of its own. She met his eyes, a small scar on his cheek barely noticeable unless looking for it, another scar on his left eyebrow, she could tell his nose had been broken in the past.

Marge advised RJ to call the police, she then ignored Super 8 policy and made him a new key to his room without identification. She watched the man in his boxers walk to the elevator, his back with more scars. She thought perhaps he had been whipped or dragged. Marge couldn't imagine what the man in white boxers standing in front of her had been through in his life.

In his room, RJ sat on the end of the bed. The bottoms of his feet were black and dirty. "That was a phony logo on that truck," He said aloud. "Those bastards, those dirty fucking bastards." Then, as realization struck, he said even louder, "They got Deuce."

RJ grabbed his jeans off the desk and found Salas's card in the front pocket. He punched in the numbers. It was 5:30 in the morning.

SAMI AND TRIPP

The four girlfriends from the University of Notre Dame were dressed to the nines. None of their parents would be happy with their chosen attire. Sami was perhaps the most conservative of the four which didn't say a lot. Shoulder-less dresses, sprayed on tight, length at mid-thigh or higher, open backed with tanned lines exposed, and high heels that could draw blood. They would, however, blend in with the rest of the female crowd.

They exited the hotel after pre-gaming in their room. The girls each had a slight buzz due to shots of cinnamon flavored Fireball and Busch Light beer chasers. The Fireball was warm, the beer chilled inside a large red Igloo cooler stacked with more beer and ice. They had to carry it in with a luggage cart.

None of the four ladies noticed the two guys shadowing them. Both men were dressed in baggy shorts that hung past their knees and wore flip-flops with a cord between their big toes and the rest of their foot, at one time the flip-flops were called thongs. Names change.

The guy with his hair pulled back wore a black t-shirt with the face of Bill Murray on the front. The other bigger fella wore a yellow tank top with a happy face on the belly. They too blended in. The girls were dressed for a sleazy prom and the guys dressed for the pool.

The men to women ratio was even. Men are just louder, stupider and more prone to arrest. It must be a testosterone thing. As the girls walked the lane in front of the hotel, they were met with an onslaught of catcalls. From the balconies, two to ten stories up a variety of comments rained down. Most were innocent, the guys who were yelling vulgarities would be the ones passed out within the next hour. It was Mardi Gras without the smell of urine.

Several bars were within walking distance, but it was too late to get a table, much less a chair. All the establishments were packed with college-aged students. Occasionally you saw a thirty to forty-year-old man thinking that he still looked 20, that he was thinner and that he still had more hair. These guys tried the hardest to mix in with the crowd, usually by purchasing drinks.

Their first bar stop was the *Swallow.* The girls quickly found out why there were more men than women in the establishment. The guy's first line was … "Do you swallow?"

Unfortunately, they had a beer coming, paid for by two men at the bar who immediately let them know they were students at Harvard. They said Harvard without the R. The girls said thanks for the drink and turned away only to have the boys round the corner to get face time. The taller of the two placed his hand on Sami's rear. She swatted it away. He did it again; she slapped the hand this time. The Harvard preppy smiled at his buddy and placed his hand once again firmly on Sami's butt. Sami turned and faced him. She looked the man in the eyes, smiled then doubled her fist and punched him in the face.

Preppy was none too happy, blood was running from his nose, down his upper lip, and into his mouth. The four girls left the beer on the table top and walked out, Sami leading the way. Harvard's finest didn't care for the outcome and went after the ladies.

"That bitch" was heard coming out of the mouth of the bloodied Ivy Leaguer.

The two bodyguards assigned by RJ met the two preppies at the entrance of the bar.

"You don't want to do what I think you are going to do." The guardian with the ponytail and Bill Murray shirt said.

Harvard looked his newfound opponent up and down, while his friend did the same.

Harvard said, "Fuck off illbilly," and pushed him back.

The man with the ponytail responded with a fast right and tagged him on the chin. Harvard wanted to drop to the floor, but his friend caught him and was holding him up.

"Don't mess with those ladies. You understand." The guy that delivered the punch said. It wasn't a question. He pointed his finger into the chest of the Harvard man he had just hit. He said it again, this time with each word he poked Harvard hard in the chest with his finger. Don't. Mess. With. The. Ladies. You. Understand. The two body guards walked out of the bar while the two Harvard boys held on to each other.

The girls walked to the next bar and squeezed into the *Lemon Drop*. This bar was only open during the spring break season. The rest of the year the *Lemon Drop* was a flower shop. There was no way they could get to the counter to order a cocktail, too many people, too small of a bar. The two guys shadowing them were close behind. The girls didn't notice.

A man walked up to the guy with the ponytail and the Bill Murray shirt and said, "Bill fucking Murray." The two men exchanged a fist bump.

A young girl in an outfit she had grown out of the year before, was offering shots of Jesse James Bourbon for $5.00. Given the circumstances, the four girls on spring break stopped her. A thirtyish-year-old man with a comb-over hairline offered to buy the shots. Thank you very much. Tamara and Steph took doubles. The four girls, as well as the out of place older guy, raised their shot glasses for a toast. The two bodyguard guys were keeping an eye on the four girls, well one of the four girls. The guard with the ponytail smiled when he saw Sami dump her alcohol shot on the floor of the bar while the others drank.

Another shot was purchased, this time by the older guy's friend. Another round of tapping shot glasses and throwing them back. Another shot dumped on the floor by Sami.

Comb-over excused himself for the restroom. They were yelling to communicate over the thumping base of the rap music; it was Fifty Cent or Nelly, maybe Tupac, no one over 35 years old really knew. Comb-over's friend stayed with the girls, acting as if he was protecting their territory. The taller of the two guys watching the girls, the guy in the Bill Murray shirt followed comb-over to the men's room.

Inside the bathroom, both comb-over and the Bill Murray guy stood at the urinal. There was another patron washing his hands.

"Man, this water is cold," Comb-over stated loudly.

"You ain't supposed to drink the water old man." The guy washing his hands said as he left the room. Just Bill Murray guy and comb-over were left.

Comb-over ignored the comment and pulled a bag of pills out of his front pocket. As he was dangling the plastic bag of pills from his hand, he turned to the guy next to him and said, "Chive on bro," then returned to peeing.

"Hey!" Comb-over yelled. "You want to buy some Rohypnol? A little roofie to help close the deal?" Comb-over asked Bill Murray. Then comb-over said, "Slip one in her drink, and she is all yours. I got my gal picked out for tonight."

The man comb-over was talking to, the guy with the Bill Murray shirt, zipped his pants and said, "No thanks." Then he smashed comb-over's forehead into the ceramic tiled wall. Comb-over dropped to the floor, still peeing as he fell. The man then pulled comb-over by the shirt into the bathroom stall. He placed comb-over's knees on the floor and his head into the toilet bowl. The guy with the Bill Murray shirt, the bodyguard, washed his hands and left he men's room.

Back in the main bar, more people seemed to have entered; the place was even more packed with kids. The man who just knocked-out comb-over guy nudged and pushed his way to his friend who was drinking a Miller Lite in a large aluminum can and watching the four girls. The crowd was so dense it took several minutes to get near them.

As he approached his friend, a girl was suddenly in his face. She kissed him hard on the mouth and said: "That was a random act of kindness." She stood there smiling, expecting a return kiss. He gently pushed her to the side and said, "Thank you, but no thank you."

Bill Murray man finally reached the people he was after. He leaned forward and shouted/yelled into Sami's ear, "Hi! I'm Tripp."

Sami looked up; her brown eye's staring into Tripp's blue. She didn't say anything, she just smiled. A perfect white smile.

"I said my name is Tripp."

"I heard. Hey. I'm Sam." She held out her hand.

The entire crowd moved at once pushing Tripp into Sami. He couldn't shake her hand; he was pushed into her. He held her with his hands on her hips. Protecting her from the mass of bodies being pushed to the side.

"Nice to meet you Sam," Tripp whispered into her ear. His lips touching her earlobe as he spoke. "Let's get some fresh air," he said as he grabbed her hand and led her out the front entrance. Tripp's friend with the smiling face shirt was several people behind. Sami left her friends with a quick wave as she followed Tripp.

At the door they squeezed past a security guard who was holding people back, his arms spread wide.

"Nobody in, only out. Let the paramedics do their job people." The large man wore a black shirt that read "Security" on the front left chest and also across the entire back of the polo.

Tripp and Sami watched as two paramedics brought a man out of the Lemon Drop Bar on an ambulance cart. The man was tied down, secured on the gurney with yellow bands, a thick white neck-brace in place. The man's forehead had a white bandage covering his receding hairline.

Sami said, "I think that guy bought us a drink."

Tripp laughed to himself, thinking, "Yes he did."

The legs of the cart folded automatically as the paramedic pushed the gurney into the back of the ambulance. He lifted as he kept pushing. Through the open back door of the ambulance, Sami and Tripp could see the paramedic was going to put an IV into the arm of their new patient. The couple heard the police officer say to the large man with security on his shirt, "This guy had a large bag of different kinds of pills. He could be an O.D. Looked like he fell and hit his head on the toilet."

The red and white ambulance with PCB Community Hospital detailed on the driver side door drove away as it's lights were flashing and with the siren crying to warn people to get out of the way.

Tripp still had Sami by the hand as they walked to the beach, their shoulders touching with each step. Neither looked back for their friends. They were only looking at each other.

They passed a boy laying on the sidewalk; he was passed out. They walked by a young lady throwing up on the street while her girlfriend held her hair back behind her head. There was a male and female couple making out on the grass, the young lady's dress was hiked up showing off a fluorescent glow-in-the dark thong. There was a circle of boys watching two guys wrestle and fi ht in the street. Tripp and Sami noticed none of this.

Sami spoke first. "So, Tripp. Are you like the third generation to be named the same name? How do we get to a name like Tripp?" Sami asked as they went from the asphalt to the sandy beach. She stopped and took off her heels never releasing her grip from Tripp's fingers. She held the shoes in her other hand.

"Well, my initials are A.A.A. You know, so they called me Triple A. Like the batteries. Then it was just easier to just call me Tripp."

"And your real name?" Sami asked.

"Anthony Aaron Anderson. The first." Tripp - Anthony smiled.

"I like the name Anthony. Can I call you Anthony?"

"Sure, that's what my Mom called me."

"Called you?"

"Ugghh. Yes. My parents were killed in a car accident when I was a kid."

"I'm so sorry."

"Do I call you Samantha?"

"No. Only Mom and Dad call me Samantha. And only when they are really mad at me." Sami smiled as she said this.

The two walked the beach. They had yet to break hand contact. They found a quiet spot away from the people, the noise, the cops, the ambulances, the fi hts and the make-out sessions. They sat on the beach, knees folded to their chests and talked, and talked.

The sun was rising in the east; the couple sat silently as the yellow glow broke the water. They finally stood.

"I can't believe the sun is up already. It seems like we just sat down. We need to get some sleep tonight. I mean today," Sami said.

"Can I see you tomorrow? I mean later?" Tripp asked Sami.

Sami replied, "Yes. At least I hope so."

Tripp escorted her back to her hotel. Sami pushed the up button on the elevator. They were the only ones in the lobby. As the door was closing, Tripp leaned forward and kissed Sami on the cheek, then smiled at her as the elevator door closed. Sami waved to him, a four-finger wave. They were both flushed, excited and exhausted.

SALAS

The cell phone was ringing. Salas groaned. "You have got to be shitting me." He said aloud. Two days in a row with an early morning call. He was supposed to be on vacation. He grabbed the phone hoping it wasn't Deb or Sami but kind of wishing it maybe was Deb. He knew it wouldn't be Candy. Salas didn't recognize the number. He answered on the 4th ring just before it went to voice mail.

Salas cleared his throat.

"Yeah," was the greeting.

"Salas, it's me. RJ."

"Hey RJ. What's up? You always awake this early?" Salas asked as he leaned on his left elbow, still under the covers. He turned on the lamp next to the bed.

"Not always, no. Say. I got your gun. You got mine," RJ stated.

"Shit. Glad you noticed. That could be bad." Salas got out of bed and looked at his weapon.

"Yeah, I'm sure mine is stolen."

"And mine is registered with the State of Indiana. But this couldn't have waited at least until six in the morning?" Salas said with sarcasm.

"Well yeah but, get this. I just watched my Harley get stolen. They hauled it off n a straight truck."

"You got to be shitting me? Stole it while you at your hotel?" Salas asked as he stood and looked out his hotel window.

"Yeah. Stole it while I was watching them, from my room on the 7th floor. Some bullshit name on the truck. "Gotcha Repo" was the name on the driver door but the passenger's side door was way off-kilter. So, I think they were using those magnetic logos you can take on and off."

"You think it was local thieves? Not another club getting back at you?" Salas asked.

"No way was it a club. This was local. Pros. A three-man team. The truck had Florida plates, but I couldn't get the numbers. Truck had one of those lifts on the back; you know those kind that can lift heavy stuff, like a motorcycle." RJ paused as Salas listened. "They knew to hit the hotel early in the morning. Like a smash and grab. They had done this before; they had a routine," RJ said. "And Salas. In the saddlebags, there is an urn with the ashes of my best friend. I got to get him back."

"I have a guy that can help. He is in Fort Wayne. A computer guru." Salas said.

"I have to have those ashes back Mike." RJ said softly.

"On it. Once I get some Intel, I will talk to local PD. I got your number. We will get him back. Call you later." Salas swiped the screen left, and the call was over.

Looking at his phone, Salas went to his contacts. He found Ronnie Higgenbotham's name. He had known Ronnie for less than a year. Salas started to call him Higgens after the guy in "Magnum PI," but it just didn't fit. Ronnie was best called Ronnie. He was the skinniest man Salas had ever seen that was still in good health. A 22-year-old computer genius who was assigned to Salas from the Mayor of Fort Wayne's millennial police recruiting program. It was the mayor's way to get young people into the field of police work. Salas had no idea how Ronnie passed the physical requirements to be on the force, other than Ronnie was related to his boss, Captain Green.

Ronnie had proven his worth in August when Salas was tracking a serial killer into the state of South Dakota. Ronnie could break into any computer database whether it be the government, DMV, or a credit card company, Ronnie Higgenbotham could get in and out without being noticed.

Salas found the number and pressed call. A squeaky voice answered.

"Hello." It was a female.

Salas looked at his phone. He had the right number.

"Ronnie. I'm looking for Ronnie Higgenbotham."

"Just a sec. Honey, Ronnie. Wake up; it is for you." The sleepy female voice said. Salas could hear the rustle of a phone being handed off.

A man's voice got on the line. He too sounded tired; the voice creaked out "Ron Higgenbotham."

"Ronnie. Salas. Who was that on the phone?"

"Hey, Mike." A long pause. Ronnie yawned. "That was Doris. Aren't you on vacation in Florida? At a bike rally? Doris wants to make that rally someday too. And just so you know. She is not a morning person."

Salas recalled Doris from Sturgis. He had been the one to get the two together. A matchmaker by happenstance. Ronnie had never had a girlfriend before; now she was spending the night.

"Oh, yeah. Sorry about the time," Salas said. "I need some computer help, Ronnie. A friend of mine just got his bike lifted in Daytona. He saw the truck that took it. It was a straight truck, with a lift on the tailgate. Magnetic logos on the doors read "Gotcha Repo." Need you to find them, Ronnie. It has got to be a local crew, near Daytona. And Ronnie, I need your help. like now."

"You fi ure another repo company. Like maybe they repossessed the wrong bike? Gang-related? Maybe a random bike grab?" Ronnie asked.

"No gang, not random. Three-man team, organized, not their first time. Maybe it was a repo of the wrong bike, never thought of that."

"Mike, let me get online. I'll go to the office. I have better access there. I'll text you what I may need," Ronnie said. The line went dead.

Salas shaved his face and his head, showered then went for the free breakfast downstairs in the Holiday Inn lobby. Sweet rolls, a banana, coffee, and OJ. As he ate, he got online on the hotel's business center computer. He googled for local repossession businesses in Daytona. There were too many to count. Most were one and two truck units. Salas decided the team that did this would have to be a bigger business with multiple units. He texted Ronnie what he thought; the bigger repo guys, not the mom and pops, repo units with lift kits, repo with large garages and buildings, repo with more than four employees, repo that specialized in motorcycles, repo business that posted bonded and insured, repo guys busted for stealing, people stealing multiple bikes and their locations. The more ideas he thought of, the more he text to Ronnie.

Salas could imagine Ronnie at his desk in Fort Wayne. His fingers sliding over the keys, three monitors at work, dressed in biker boots, jeans that were too short, his skin a pale, pasty white, and a Sturgis t-shirt that flapped on what little biceps and triceps he had. That reminded him, he had to get Ronnie a Daytona Bike Week shirt.

Salas knew it would be a few hours before he heard back, so he got on his Harley and went for a ride.

VINCENT

Vincent's crew was back at the compound at 7:00 am, they had six bikes. The three men unloaded the motorcycles in the garage near the Freightliner, parking the bikes in a straight row. Terry then parked the straight truck, and the three men left the compound. Vincent sent them home to get much-needed sleep.

Once Vincent knew he was alone, as none of the crew members knew of the drugs they were smuggling, he went to work putting the heroin in place. The three man team was under the assumption they were stealing motorcycles for a shipment to Canada. Jake, Terry, and Rod were anxious for their year-long efforts to be rewarded.

Vincent placed two tubes of heroin in each of the bike's gas tanks. He had four pounds left. He took the remaining tubes and stuffed them into the gas tanks of four of the newly stolen bikes. He hated to double up, fi uring the more in a tank, the greater the chance a drug-sniffing dog would catch the scent. Vincent grabbed the red plastic fi e-gallon gas can and topped off the tanks, fuel spilling over the side and onto the engine, on the exhaust pipes and the floor of the garage. Vincent jammed the gas caps into their receptacles closing their fate, hoping he didn't tear a tube. They would load the last six bikes later in the day.

Vincent was planning on driving the truck to Canada by himself, getting his money wired to an offshore account, and then flying out of the country. The stolen bikes would fetch over $250,000; he had the buyer lined up and ready to receive the shipment. The heroin buy was guaranteed, netting Vincent $5 million and he still had a duffle bag full of cash from German. The amount in the bag, $200,000. Vincent felt, screw his crew, and screw German. He was taking the entire $5.45 million.

The bikes were parked at the rear of the Freightliner's trailer, on the concrete floor, waiting patiently to be loaded. Vincent would have Terry and Jake load them later in the day. The duffle bag of cash was sitting on the rear seat of one of the Harleys. A small suitcase containing Vincent's clothes was in the cab of the truck.

Vincent checked the security cameras, the gate was locked, and all was clear. He had to get into Daytona to clean out his personal bank account and the accounts from "We Found You Repo." Yes, he was going to take all of Richard's money too. Vincent thought he may as well take all he can get, with Richard's health, he would lose everything to the bank anyway. And Richard always has his disability check from the military, not like he would be broke.

As he drove out the back entrance of the compound, the exit Richard didn't even know of; Vincent was smiling. He was about to become a multi-millionaire. Nearly $6 million tax-free. Vincent was going to be living large in Costa Rica. He could see himself on the beach, drink in his hand, two beautiful women by his side. Twelve more hours and he would be on the road, sixty more hours and the bikes and the heroin would be in Canada, and he would be swimming in cash.

Vincent thought…. Life is good.

SALAS

Salas rode, what the motorcycle enthusiasts referred to as "The Loop." Thirty-eight miles starting and ending at the Holiday Inn. Taking off on Highway A1A to Granada Blvd and Ormond Beach Salas shifted into fourth gear at 55 mph. At High Bridge Road he slowed slightly as several bikers formed a long line, all on the same route. A left on Walter Boardman Blvd had them on Old Dixie Highway then hugging the Intracoastal Waterway. The bikers rode in a staggered formation, the line a mile long.

The procession came to a stop. Two bikers were standing on the shoulder of the highway looking at their motorcycles which were laying on their sides blocking the lane. Both riders appeared to be fine, no blood no foul. Each passing rider slowed to stare at the accident, their heads turned to the side, their bikes weaving, a new accident ready to happen. The two wrecked bikes had mirrors broken, glass on the road, a piece of the faring of one bike lay on the surface of the highway. Police sirens were in the background. No ambulance was needed.

The pace slowly resumed but held under 45 mph. Old Dixie Highway turned into North Beach then back to Granada and AIA. With traffic and the wreck, it was an hour ride.

Salas pulled his Harley into a large parking lot; a Wal-Mart sat in the background. Bikes were crammed in, parked side by side, he joined them. He was in the 8th row back, ten bikes in. He parked between a purple Harley Trike and a silver 75th-anniversary Ultra. Salas checked his phone: no calls or texts. He put the phone on vibrate and followed the crowd. Hundreds of men and women clad in black leather, Harley T-shirts, black boots, and bandanas faced the ocean, craning to look over the person in front of them. Salas could see two large ramps, a take-off ramp and a landing ramp. Both of the metal structures were painted black with plastic banners tied to the support beams promoting Budweiser, Monster Energy, Harley Davidson and Papa John's. He took to the edge of the crowd and walked on the grass to find an open spot to at the end of the rows of people. Like a football game everyone wanted 50-yard line viewing, Salas went for the end-zone.

The draw was three young men straddling dirt bikes. Long tangled hair sat on each rider's shoulders. They wore bright yellow jerseys with Monster Energy Drink logos over shoulder pads. They each wore black leather pants with knee and hip pads. Another long-haired young man with a ZZ Top beard and the same logo shirt was holding a microphone. He was walking between the bikes into the crowd, announcing the young men's names and advising the gathered group of motorcycle riders of the daredevil feats they were about to see. "Please," he said, "do not try these stunts at home."

The three stunt bikers strapped on their full-face helmets and fired up their 125 CC engines; the bikes whined as black dust shot out of the exhaust. Knobby tires, not much use on asphalt, were the tread of choice as the three bikes did wheelies and road the one-hundred-yard length of the crowd on one wheel. The bikes gathered at the opposite end of the runway, away from Salas. Bike number one wheelied again and took off. With both tires on the asphalt, he rode onto a ramp which had a sharp incline. The bike and biker shot into the air, thirty feet or higher into a cloudless sky. With both hands, he let go of the bike's handlebars. He glided through the air as the crowd was looking up then grabbed the handlebars as he touched down softly on the landing ramp. He came to a stop near Salas, skidding sideways like a snow skier coming to a stop.

Biker number two sprang forward, same pattern; wheelie, then the ramp, then in the air. This biker held on to the handlebars but let his rear and legs come off the seat; he was doing a handstand on his bike - in the air. He too landed on the down ramp coming to a stop in front of Salas, high-fi ing his friend.

Biker number three was already in the air before his partner stopped. On his bike, he performed a perfect backward somersault landing gently and pulling to a stop beside his two partners. They all exchanged high fi es then roared their engines, slowly releasing their clutches, so they did burn-outs, then wheelied the length of the driveway. The crowd cheered and applauded.

Round two was more intense; double somersaults, somersaults with no hands on the handlebars, then with no feet on the bikes. Round three was two bikes at one time in perfect synchronization in backward somersaults and then all three at one time in perfect unison, synchronized freestyle motocross. The crowd was still cheering as Salas drifted away, leaving the show.

Salas left his bike parked in the parking lot and walked the ocean side of the strip. His goal was the IHOP a couple hundred yards away. He entered the restaurant, found a booth in the corner and ordered coffee.

Salas considered calling Candy. He had his phone out ready to dial and decided to wait.

Ronnie called after his third cup.

"Talk to me," Salas said.

"Mike, I actually have two items I need to discuss with you. First per your request. I went several directions with this search. I thought of the trucks, the lift, and thanks by the way for your ideas. Did you know there are over 30 repossession businesses just in the Daytona Beach area alone? And then when you take in the surrounding population and repossession companies that have a regional and national influence the search was quite daunting."

"Ronnie. Results. Now," Salas interrupted.

"Yes, my findings. Well per your directions. I eliminated the mom and pops as you called them. Then went after the trucks. I found through the DMV that they list trucks with those lift gates. I searched for Tommy Lifts, again as you called them and other forms of lifting devices that could handle a 1200-pound motorcycle. Did you know, the Tommy Gate was invented by Bus Brown in a little town called Woodbine, Iowa in 1965? Bus named it Tommy after his son, wouldn't you know, named Tommy. It is the original hydraulic lift with sales in the millions of dollars."

"Ronnie. Please. I am on vacation," Salas pleaded.

"Yes. So, I created a list; trucks with Tommy Lifts, businesses with more than five trucks registered with the DMV, and business advertising bonded, insured, and workers comp. I fi ured we would start at the top, the largest businesses first. Well, this gave me less than 15 operations in Daytona and another 20 within 50 miles. Thus 35 prospects. Still, a massive undertaking to find any concrete information. Don't you think so Mike?" Ronnie asked.

Salas did not respond. He thought it was a rhetorical question. Seconds ticked away.

"Yes. Yes, Ronnie, I agree. Do have you anything at all for me?" Salas asked rather loudly.

"Of course, I do Mike. Do you think I would be calling if I didn't have a solid lead for you?" Ronnie asked, then was waiting for an answer. More seconds ticking away.

"Ronnie, give me the name of the damn guy you found," Salas yelled into the phone. IHOP patrons were staring at the bald guy screaming at his phone.

"Then I went with the logo, the magnetized decal. This intrigued me. My cousin does magnetized decals in Indianapolis. I called him. He related that you can order them online from several places around the world. Probably a dead end, right? But wait. I thought this business owner perhaps would not be the most tech-savvy. Pardon me, but I am assuming repo guys are, how would you say it? A little on the redneck side. I know not a fair assumption but bear with me. I thought this guy would most likely use a local service. I thought this guy would call a signage store within two miles of his place of business. A signage shop he probably drove by every day on his way to work. And guess what? I found three repo companies within the two miles of a customized sign shop that advertised magnetic decals for vehicles." Ronnie stopped for breath.

Salas was silent. "Mike are you still there?" Ronnie asked.

"Yes, Ronnie but my cell is ready to die." Salas was still talking rather loudly.

"Recall Mike I requested you obtain a new battery for your cell. Every time we talk it seems you are always running low on battery power." Ronnie was off topic again. "I carry a *Morphie Powerstation.* Mike I would encourage you to look at this product. It works very well with Smartphones and tablets."

"The person of interest Ronnie. Do you have someone for me to go find?" Salas said loudly. Everyone at IHOP was looking at Salas. The manager came over to his table and told him to shush by putting a finger ton his mouth and saying "shush."

"I had three sign shops identified. So my plan was to call all three and to comment on a particular decal I fancied. I told them that I liked a specific decal called "Gotcha Repo." And asked if they did the work. I realize it is not telling the truth, but it was easier than going through the entire story of a stolen motorcycle. And don't ya know, call number two was it. So, I asked who "Gotcha Repo" was so I could call them and ask about the service and pricing. And guess what Mike? They gave it to me." Ronnie took another deep breath, then said: "There I found him."

"And his name Ronnie. His name and address would be great," Salas said slowly.

"The name of our buyer is Terry Johnson. He lives in Deland Florida in Volusia County. Mr. Johnson works for "We Found You Repo" also in Deland. And Mike, just so you know, Terry has a long rap sheet. Grand theft auto which he did some time for. Drug possession. Armed robbery. Assault. Resisting arrest. Selling stolen goods. I will email you his arrest record as well as a picture."

Salas asked, "Ronnie, who owns "We Found You Repo?"

"Yes, I anticipated you would ask that. And the owner is, Richard Lopez. Richard is a very heavily decorated military veteran, a Ranger in fact. He served tours in Afghanistan and Iraq. Honorable Discharge. He was wounded in combat a couple of times. Mr. Lopez is now on full disability. He inherited the repossession business from his father who recently passed away. Oh, and he is going through a divorce."

"Anything else Ronnie? This is great stuff."

"Yes. Richard Lopez's brother, Vincent Lopez. Seems Vincent was also in the military, following the steps of his older brother. But Vincent was dishonorably discharged for possession of drugs. He spent time in a Texas prison for distribution of a controlled substance. Per DMV and licensing, Vincent's name is on the truck in question as well as a Freightliner; I suppose a Freightliner is an 18-wheeler." Salas could hear Ronnie gulping water over the phone connection.

"Thanks, Ronnie, once again good work." Salas hung up before Ronnie could say goodbye.

Salas's cell phone vibrated, the email was in. Salas opened the attachment and stared at the picture of Terry Johnson.

He kept the phone out to follow up on his previous idea. He couldn't get her off his mind, at least this time it was Candy and not Deb. Salas dialed Candy. This time the call was answered.

"Hi Candy," Salas said.

"This ain't Candy. Who is this?" It was a man's voice.

"Oh, is this Warren? I had a question on the jacket I purchased." Salas was lying.

"No, this ain't Warren." The man said, his voice added a laugh. Salas could hear a woman talking in the background.

"Who are you talking to? Wait that's my phone." It was Candy's voice. The line went dead.

Salas got online and found the Fairfield Inn of Fort Wayne's direct phone number. He dialed it.

The phone rang three times then was answered. "Hope you are having a wonderful Marriott morning! This is Becky how may I help you today?" The voice was chipper.

"Morning, can you connect me to Candy Jennings room please?" Salas asked.

"One second please." Salas heard typing on a keyboard. "Ah yes, I sure can. Please hold while I connect you."

Salas shut off his phone. "You have got to be shitting me," he said loudly. Again people stared.

He paid his bill at the cash register. Several dirty looks continued to come upon him from the staff and some patrons. Salas skipped leaving a tip and went outside. He walked the distance back to the Walmart lot. The daredevil show was over. The lot was empty; a crew was disassembling the ramps and taking down the advertising banners. His bike was sitting alone on the black asphalt.

Standing to the side of his machine, Salas turned on the accessory key. He found the Volusia County Sheriff Department on the GPS. He tapped on "find directions" then "start." The screen said he was 30 miles away. He got on his Harley to ride to Deland. Salas was not in a good mood.

RONNIE

"Mike. Mike," Ronnie yelled into the phone. "I didn't get to my second request." Ronnie was yelling with no one listening. Beside Ronnie, the only other person on the floor was the night janitor and not even he was paying attention.

Ronnie rechecked the voice mail on his office phone. He punched in his four digit security code, his mom's birthday 0415. The response was a female computer voice, "You have one new message dated Thursday at eight o'clock pm. Press one for your new message." Ronnie pressed one. The next voice wasn't female, it was soft but authoritative, "Mr. Higgenbotham. I saw you on TV and the arrest of those drug guys. I have information that may be of use to you. Can you meet me downtown by the Firefi hters museum at 9:00 tomorrow?" That was it. No name was given, and the number was blocked, most likely a burner phone.

Ronnie had never been out of the office without Salas and wanted Mike's advice as to the best option to address the voice mail. Yes, Ronnie had arrested a few people and almost drew his weapon once when a drugged-out man was resisting Salas and coming towards him. Ronnie had forgotten about the holster clip used to keep the weapon in place and fumbled trying to get his gun out. Before the crazy guy could touch Ronnie, Salas punched the drugged man in the side of the head and knocked him out.

He knew this day would come, the day he would have to be out by himself, but he didn't think it would be so soon. Ronnie looked at the other desks on the detective floor, he could ask Fisher to go with him, or Phelps. Osborn was not very friendly. He could ask Captain Green; maybe Green would enjoy being back in the field for a few hours?

Downtown Fort Wayne consisted of hundreds of businesses, hotels, restaurants, bars, artsy stuff. Ronnie fi ured it would be safe, lots of people going to work at nine in the morning. And the meeting would be by the fireman's museum; it would be safe, he told himself again.

At 8:30 Ronnie drove to downtown Fort Wayne. He parked on the first floor of a fi e-story parking garage. His Ford sedan faced a four-foot tall concrete wall that open to the eight-foot ceiling. Large concrete pillars were placed every twenty parking stalls, which were marked off by yellow lines. Ronnie locked his car as he walked out of the structure, the car beeping it was secure. Ronnie read the sign as he left, "First Two Hours Free Parking."

Ronnie purchased a large coffee from a Starbucks across from where he was to be met. It was 9:05. He crossed the main street in a slow jog and went to the door of the museum. The sign stated it would open at 10:00. He held the cup with both hands to keep his hands warm as he sipped the coffee. At 9:30 Ronnie was tapping from toe to toe, it was cold in early March. At 10:03 a gray-haired man in a red and yellow one-piece jumpsuit opened the door to the museum.

"Come in young fella, great to see you."

Ronnie entered telling the greeter he was to meet someone, then he stayed by the front door. At 10:15 Ronnie went back outside, stood another ten minutes, tossed his empty coffee cup in the trash and walked back to the parking garage. He unlocked the car with his remote several feet from the Ford, placed the key back in his jeans as he opened the driver side door. It was then that he was punched in the back, over his right kidney. Ronnie crumpled to the side of the car; a man was holding Ronnie up with both hands under Ronnie's armpits.

"Mr. Ron, so nice of you to come," was whispered in Ronnie's ear, the same soft oice that was recorded on his office phone.

Ronnie was gasping for air, the muscles in his lower back were cramping. He felt nauseous and wanted to vomit.

"Mr. Ron, congratulations on your arrest of the Aztecs. I have a few questions for you Mr. Detective."

Ronnie tried to take deep breaths. His eyes were glossy. He tasted bile.

"Take your time Ronald. We are in no hurry," the man said as he slowly turned Ronnie's body to face him.

The man had brown skin, dead brown eyes that didn't move when he spoke. His mouth was surrounded by a salt and pepper goatee. He had dyed jet-black hair pulled back over his head. He was as tall as Ronnie, not as big as Salas. The man had both his arms on Ronnie's shoulders as Ronnie leaned back into the car. It would appear as if two men were just talking.

"Tell me Mr. Detective. How did you know about the drugs? Who tipped you on this? We were supposed to have a clear path through your shitty little town." The man spoke softly and with a slight grin. Again, two men having a visit.

"I don't know what you mean," Ronnie said in a burst. "The two men were speeding." Another burst of air. "It was a traffic stop."

"There was no speeding Ron. You told your men to pull them over. We pay you to not be pulled over." The man with the goatee said into Ronnie's ear, spittle from the man's words hitting his ear. Ronnie pulled his head back. "You tell me now, and there will be no more pain. Tell me now Ron for I am impatient with you and my time is nearly up, or I will have to pay to park."

"They were speeding in a construction zone." Ronnie gulped in more air. Both of Ronnie's hands were on his right kidney. "Your men turned on you." A gulp of air. "Go beat them up." Gulp. "They got fi e years instead of 25. For ratting out their suppliers."

"Not what I want to hear Ron." The man pushed his hand into Ronnie's right side. Ronnie cried out in pain, his knees buckled.

"Uggghhh." Ronnie groaned. "I just did the interview." A gulp of air. "I had no idea the State Police would arrest them." A groan. "How could I know that? They gave me the bust to make the mayor look good. Honest."

"You don't know anything, do you? I believe you are clueless. You do not even look like a cop. I am talking to the wrong person Ron. Who is your boss?"

"My boss?" Ronnie groaned in pain. "My boss is Captain Green." Another gulp of air and another groan in pain. "But he doesn't know anything either. He assigned the case to us."

The man with the goatee and dead brown eyes helped Ronnie sit down in the car. "Sorry, Ron." The man said as he shut the door to Ronnie's car. "Don't worry. I will leave you alone. You are of no importance to me."

Ronnie could see the man in his rearview mirror as he walked away, he had broad shoulders and walked with a swagger, shoulders rolling from side to side. Ronnie sat in his car for several minutes, his breath returning, his back, and abdomen cramping. The nauseous feeling was subsiding. He backed the car out then pulled forward to the kiosk, which was telling him to "Please insert your parking ticket. Please insert your parking ticket." Ronnie struggled to get the ticket into the machine. "Please insert the appropriate payment" was the next command. He owed two dollars. Ronnie's side and lower back went into spasm as he tried to get his wallet. The car behind him was honking. He pushed his credit card into the machine and was allowed to leave. He didn't get a receipt.

The car swerved left to right as he drove to the Dupont Hospital Emergency Room. He parked the car and limped towards the door, both of his hands were on his right side. Dragging his right leg, Ronnie went to the counter. "I'm having kidney pain," he said to a red-haired receptionist with a name badge that read, Glenda RN.

Glenda asked for an insurance card and Ronnie's driver's license. She photocopied both documents handing them back to Ronnie. She gave him a clipboard with several sheets of paper and a ballpoint pen telling Ronnie to please complete the forms. She was pointing to the chairs behind him. Ronnie sat down hard with a grunt of pain. Sweat was building on his forehead, dripping on the papers. The nauseous feeling was back. He looked at the TV, Neil Cavuto was talking. He looked at the coffee table, Julia Roberts was smiling at him from the cover of a *People Magazine*. Neil was then standing next to Julia, or Julia was running away from Neil, the room was spinning when Ronnie passed out and slid to the floor.

When Ronnie woke, it took time for his eyes to adjust to the bright sunshine coming through the large window in front of him. He was in a hospital bed; an IV was in a vein on the back of his left wrist, there were electrodes on his chest, a white clip on his right index finger and a blood pressure cuff on his arm. The monitor beside his bed said his pulse was 50 and his blood pressure was 123 over 78. He felt no pain. A white remote was on his lap. A button would turn on the TV, another button for volume, a third for volume and a 4th button to call a nurse. He pushed the 4th button. Within seconds three women entered his room, two wore blue hospital surgical scrubs, one donned a white lab coat.

The lab coat lady said, "Afternoon love. I am Dr. Harper. You gave us a scare. How are you feeling?"

"I was punched in the side. But it doesn't seem to hurt now," Ronnie replied.

"Yes, we found black and blue bruises on your side when we examined you. We have taken an X-Ray and an MRI. You have a severely bruised kidney. You most likely passed out due to pain. We have given you a little medication but not much. Do you know who hit you, Officer Higgenbotham?" The doctor asked.

"No, I do not."

"Hazard of the job I guess. We will keep you here a couple of hours. Monitor your vitals to be sure you will be able to urinate. You will most likely pass some blood, but that is expected. You will also get some abdominal and lower back muscle spasms, it is your body telling you that you are hurt. So, listen to it." Dr. Harper was taking his pulse.

"Please let the nurses know when you have to urinate. We need to measure volume. You will be fine Officer. I suggest a few days off to rest. No running or sharp movements, you shouldn't drive either. Your kidney needs to stay still. I will stop back in a bit." Dr. Harper left the room while the nurses placed a new bag of fluid in the IV and checked the wires on his chest.

Ronnie asked for his cell phone. He called Doris, told her what happened; she was on her way. He dialed Salas, no answer. He pictured the man with the goatee and dead brown eyes. *Who tipped you? Who was his boss?* Ronnie closed his eyes and went to sleep.

SHERIFF GROFF

A wooden sign sat on two fence posts dug into the grass, the sign read, "County Court House." Etched in stone at the top of the building read, "Volusia County." Salas parked his Harley across the street, locked his bike and entered the white brick structure's double doors. Inside the facility the temperature was cold, the air-conditioning on high, the room was painted light blue. Salas heard someone yell in the office, behind the laminated reception counter.

"Sum Bitch! You tell those spoiled little snowflakes if they knock over that statue their pansy asses will be in the county lockup." Salas heard the man say, "It's the Citrus Wizard for goodness sake. I don't care if they call Geraldo, Wolff Blinker, or that constipated pissed off lesbian, I will put them all in jail." The phone was slammed on the receiver with an additional outburst, "What a freaking fart festival."

The man yelling was short and stalky, built like a fire hydrant and just as solid. He walked out of the office wearing a brown colored baseball hat, VCPD above the brim. He had a crimson face; his shirt was white with short-sleeves. The top two buttons were undone, with light red hair bulging through the opening. There were brown stains on the chest and belly of the shirt. He was carrying a cup of coffee; his bicep flexed when he took a drink. The name embroidered on the front pocket read, "Sheriff Groff."

"Can I help you, sir?" The Sheriff named Groff said, his voice back to normal decibels.

"Yes, sir. I'm Detective Mike Salas. Fort Wayne Indiana." Salas flashed his badge. "I'm here on vacation actually, the Daytona Bike Rally." Salas stuck out his right hand.

"Oh, we love that rally. Drunk riders, fights, drugs, hookers and want to be badass bikers. Like we don't have those same problems without the rally doubling the population of dumbasses." Groff grumbled as he walked towards Salas.

Groff shook the extended hand causing him to spill the coffee in his left. "Sum bitch," were the words that followed the spill.

"You didn't get those cauliflower ears playing basketball Sheriff," Salas said, looking at the side of Groff's head.

"Hell, no I didn't. And neither did you," Groff replied as he gave the same inspection. "Where you do your time?"

"Nebraska. About 50 pounds ago," Salas responded.

"Sum bitch. Hell yeah, Salas, I remember you. Mike Salas. I was at Chadron State, out in western Nebraska," Groff ountered.

"I know it well. Shot some turkeys out that way," Salas said.

"Damn. You are taking me back. You remember the Cowboy Open? You wrestled our heavyweight Slick Willie Long. Willie was a tough sum bitch. A returning All-American. You weighed maybe 210 or 215. Willie was all of 285, hell you was half the size of Willie. Slick, he is a good buddy of mine. He said he was going to kick your Nebraska ass. You two were tied up head to head; you did a left shoulder shrug into a head lock. You had Willie so tight he was ready to tap out. Then boom!" Groff slapped the counter with the palm of his hand. Everyone in the room looked over.

"You turned your hips in and tossed old slick Willie. He got more flight time than a fucking United Airlines pilot. Willie hit the mat so hard the building shook. People thought Laramie, Wyoming was having an earthquake. Ah hell, that was funny." Groff got quiet then said, "Slick never wrestled worth a shit after that." Groff   as shaking his head.

"That was a few pounds ago sheriff. How did you end up in Florida from Nebraska?" Salas asked.

"Spring break. The ladies wore pants so tight I could see their religion. Thought what the Sam Hill was I doing freezing my ass off in Nebraska? Been here ever since." Said Groff. "Good to meet you, Salas. Now, what can I do for you, Detective?"

"You know a guy by the name of Terry Johnson?" Salas asked.

"Hell yeah, I do. Terry don't know whether to check his ass or scratch his watch. Hell, I've arrested that sum bitch half a dozen times. What he do now?"

"I'm missing a motorcycle. We fi ure he stole it or mistakenly acquired it. In a truck with a Tommy lift. "We Found You Repo" was the name on the side of the truck's door. You know of it, Sheriff?"

"Yeah, I know them too. Richard Lopez is the owner of the repo. Now Richard, he a good man, a war hero. His brother Vince, he is a sum bitch. Vincent could piss off the Pope. Has to be a misunderstanding. Richard wouldn't go for no stealing. Let's jump in the truck Salas. Sounds like a house call is in order. Let's see if they got your bike." Groff placed his coffee cup on the counter. He grabbed his holster with a handgun latched in and cinched it tight on his hips.

"Bob. Let's roll," Groff yelled out as he passed Salas and opened the door. "You coming Salas?" Groff sked.

"Yeah, but where is Bob? Salas was looking back behind the counter.

"Right there." Groff pointed down. Bob was a Jack Russell Terrier. A round brown eye patch over the right eye

Salas followed Groff and Bob out the front door to a white Ford F150 with "Volusia County Sheriff Department" painted on both the side panels. Under the name, it read, "To Protect and Serve." Salas rode shotgun while Groff drove, an actual shotgun sat between them, barrel pointed down. Bob was leaning against Groff's thigh. Salas reached over to pet Bob and was met with a snarl and a snip on the fingers.

"Bob. Be nice. He don't like most folks, Salas. He is a good judge of character." Groff l ughed.

Groff continued talking while driving, "I wrestled that Powell kid from Nebraska. He was one tough sum bitch. He got me in a cradle so tight my nose was three inches up my ass. He didn't stick me but after that match, I couldn't walk upright or take a shit for a week."

Ten minutes passed as they drove. The two ex-wrestlers exchanged stories, discovered people they both knew and decided they were both heavier and balder. Groff approached a small lake and stopped the Ford, so he and Salas could assess the grounds.

A one lane bridge spanned the water connecting where they were sitting to what looked like a small construction or business site. Groff drove on to the bridge, stopping the truck again. The gate was closed. The two men looked ahead. A chain-link fence with barbed wire at the top surrounded the large island. Two metal shops, a framed house, a small single wide mobile home and a double wide modular house were the out-buildings. You could see a semi-tractor and trailer in the larger of the two metal structures. There was a straight truck with a Tommy Lift, the truck in question parked near the mobile home. Two tow trucks were parked on the west side of the modular home with a white Ford F250 pickup parked in front of the framed house.

Groff honked the Ford's horn four times. Then honked again. Salas noticed each time he pressed on the horn an alligator jumped into the water. He couldn't see the gators on the grass, just when they entered the pond. The creatures blended in well.

"Lot of fucking alligators," Salas said.

Groff had a speaker system on the outside of the pickup. He picked up the handset of the loudspeaker and said, "Richard. Richard Lopez. This is Sheriff Groff of the Volusia County Police Department. Please let me in. Need a few words with you, sir."

Two large muscular men stepped out of the modular. They wore blue jeans and white wife beater tank tops. Both were wearing baseball hats on bald heads, the caps on backward. Their arms were the size of Groff's legs.

"Sum bitch. Look at the size of them two dipsticks. Even from this far away, those two look big and stupid," Groff aid to Salas.

Bob had his paws on the dash. He growled at the two men.

The gate slowly opened as it rolled to the right. More gators went into the water. Groff drove his truck through the opening, crossed the acre of driveway and parked in front of the two muscle men.

Groff said to Salas, "Them two boys so ugly they'd make a freight train take a dirt road."

Salas and Groff got out of the Ford. They slammed the doors shut in unison.

"Bob. Guard the truck," Groff said as Bob barked and placed his paws on the steering wheel. Both men were looking over the compound. Each wore dark sunglasses. Salas was a foot taller than Groff, both men with broad shoulders, small waists, and mangled ears.

"We are closed for business Sheriff. Organizational restructuring. You and your boy can leave," came from one of the two mouths.

"Well Mr. Warren Buffett, we don't give a shit about your restructuring. Is Richard Lopez around? How about Terry Johnson?" came from Salas.

"Buffett? What'd you call me asshole?" Salas couldn't tell if it was the same guy that spoke before or the other one.

"Those steroids shrink your brains and your balls you know," Salas said.

Both muscle guys stepped forward. Their fists were clenched. Salas could see brass knuckles in one of their hands. Salas stepped forward too.

"Back off you sum bitches. I'll arrest you faster than green grass through a goose." Groff pointed to the two men in t-shirts. He had his hand on the butt of his gun. "Where is Richard?"

On que, Richard Lopez came out of the house. He wore dark sunglasses with his baseball hat pulled low over his eyes. He looked sickly; a grayish tone was his body color.

"Hey, Sheriff Groff," was Richard's greeting. "Raphael, you two can go back in. I got this. No worries." He too was pointing at the two muscle men.

"What, Raphael, you a fucking Ninja Turtle?" Salas yelled at the two.

The twins stopped and glared at Salas. One of the men, Salas couldn't tell them apart, gave Salas the finger.

Richard introduced himself to Salas, then led the two men away from the house. They walked towards the large garage that housed the Freightliner, away from Raphael and his brother. As they walked, Salas thanked Richard for his service in the military listing the accommodations Richard had earned and received. Salas let Richard know he was aware of Richard's medical discharge from the military as well as his battle with headaches. Groff was impressed with the background information Salas had gathered on Lopez.

Salas asked Richard if he was married and if he had kids. Richard told Salas with his head held down, his chin on his chest, that his wife, Corine, had left him. Richard spoke slowly and deliberately; his speech was hesitant, even slightly slurred. Richard said Corine had taken the kids and went back to stay with her parents in South Carolina. Richard admitted to Salas he had been drinking too much and was popping pills. Richard said he was thankful she left before he did something worse. He said he had quit drinking and that his brother Vincent had gotten him new medication.

Salas then asked Richard the names of his kids; he got back that Grace was eleven, Ruth nine, and Little Richard was five. They all laughed at being called Little Richard.

Both Salas and Groff looked at each other at the same time. They could see from Richard's eyes and his speech patterns that Richard was under the influence. Drugs were in his system most likely painkillers.

Groff got them back on track and related what amounted to be an issue about a stolen motorcycle. He assured Richard that his team didn't steal it, but they could have repossessed the wrong bike. The Sheriff stated he wanted to look for the Harley and they were canvassing several repo businesses.

Richard said with his headaches; he had given the business over to his bother. He said he didn't know what his team was working on, but they had been busy. Busy with lots of motorcycles being repossessed. But yes, they were free to look around.

The three men stepped into the large building via the open garage door. A white Freightliner truck with no sleeping quarters and a trailer were parked inside. The truck was facing the rear wall of the metal building with the trailer doors open. The doors which swung to the sides of the trailer, were tethered down. Salas could see a lot of bikes inside the unit, had to be close to fifty motorcycles. All the bikes tied secure to the floor with ratchet straps, one strap on each handlebar, each front tire was secure inside a metal chock bolted to the floor of the trailer.

"That's a lot of motorcycles Richard," Salas stated.

"Yeah, I didn't realize they had repo'd that many," Richard said.

"Richard that would be a record number of motorcycle repo requests. From what I can see, all Harley Davidsons. That be odd to just repo Harleys," Sheriff Groff said as he stood at the rear of the trailer, his finger was counting bikes.

"Maybe my brother Vince got a contract with Harley Davidson. I don't know. You know they do their own financing now." Richard countered.

There were six bikes parked on the concrete floor. Salas was looking at those. Two Fatboys, a Dyna, a Street Bob, one Night Train and a 1200 Sportster. Salas was looking through the saddlebags of one of the Fatboys.

"Hey, leave those bikes alone sir." It was Vincent. "You have no authority to be here much less be examining our property." Vincent walked in to the garage and towards the men. He stopped and grabbed a duffle bag off ne of the parked bikes holding it in his hand.

"You must be Vincent. I am County Sheriff Groff." Groff extended his hand. Vincent ignored it, walking past Groff o Salas.

"You must leave the motorcycles alone mister. Leave it be now I said," Vincent said as he pushed Salas's hand away from the bike.

Salas didn't care for the swat on the hand. He doubled his fist and looked Vincent in the eyes. He had seen what he needed. The Fatboy's saddlebag was locked, but Salas knew the bike was RJ's.

Salas said "My apology sir. It seems you have repossessed the wrong motorcycle. This Fatboy here belongs to a friend of mine named RJ. I would like to take it now." Salas had his hand on the bike's handlebars.

"That isn't possible. My crew doesn't make mistakes. We have orders on all of these bikes. We confirm all vehicle identification numbers prior to the transaction. Your friend must be late on his payments. Take it as a lesson learned. Now if you will, I am asking you kindly to leave the premises." Vincent was pointing to the open garage door.

Richard was sitting on a stool at the workbench rubbing his temples. He was oblivious to the conversation.

"Vincent the easiest thing to do is to allow us to take the bike. This is Mike Salas; he is a detective in Indiana. Just here for the bike rally. He wouldn't be here if this wasn't a legit claim." Groff aid.

"Sheriff you know the law. Show me a warrant. Or even show me the title to the motorcycle in question and I have no problem helping Mr. Salas and his friend, RJ as he is called. Until then, the motorcycle is my property to be delivered to the location deemed by the bank on the note. That is my job Sheriff," Vincent said.

"Nobody rides to Daytona with the title to their bike. And this is RJ's bike," Salas shot back.

"Sum bitch. Vincent is right. We will go through the paperwork process." Sheriff Groff was walking out of the shade of the garage, into the Florida sun.

"Fuck this. I'll be back later," Salas said.

"You heard the man Sheriff. That was a threat," Vincent said standing by Richard. "I'll be right here when you are ready." He had his arm around his brother.

Groff and Salas walked to the Ford and got in. Groff started the engine and turned up the air conditioning. Hot air blew out of the vents. Bob jumped on Groff's lap and held his head out the window.

"That Vincent looks like ten miles of bad road. Hell, when his lips are moving you know he is lying." Groff aid backing out of the driveway.

The two muscle men were standing in front of the house. One of the men looked at Salas. He had his hand in a fist, the thumb extended and ran the thumb across his throat. This time Salas flipped him off.

Groff drove the pickup out the front gate, across the bridge, turned left and stopped the truck. Both men sat looking at the compound. The water in the pond took their attention. It was alive with thrashing as gators tore apart a white plastic bag. The water turned darker, what was in the bag was dragged underwater, the gators killing and drowning its prey. Salas and Groff atched the feeding frenzy.

"There is more to this than those repossessed motorcycles," Groff said, taking his eyes off the pond. "That Vincent is slicker than owl shit. No way in hell that many bikes get repo'd here in Deland. Stolen bikes are worth some serious cash. Fifty bikes is worth what, two or three hundred thousand dollars?" Groff sked Salas.

"Yeah. But the risk. Stealing bikes, paying a crew. Cost of a truck. And shipping somewhere means there must be some kind of a paper trail to cover their ass. Bill of lading, copies of titles, bank orders that kind of stuff." Salas added.

"I can get a warrant. Going to take time. It is a weekend. But those bikes and truck, they looked ready to ship. Could be going out tonight."

"Well then, I say we come back this evening. We will be better prepared." Salas looked at Groff. The meaning was apparent.

"Sum bitch Salas, you can't be going rogue over a motorcycle. And it's not even your motorcycle."

"In the saddlebag of that Fatboy are the ashes of a friend. Vincent isn't going to give up anything. There is something more to the bikes. Tonight, I can find out just what that is."

"Hell let's just go back in now," Groff aid.

"No, you heard him. We have no rights; he has the law on his side. We need that warrant. I can come back and check around later."

"Sum bitch Salas you are in my backyard. You work with me, or you don't work. Got it? I am serious Salas I'll tan your hide and throw your ass in my worst stinking jail cell. You will have to shit in your helmet."

Salas didn't answer. They drove in silence to the Sheriff's office.

"I'll work on a warrant. Let's grab some chow, Salas. I'm so hungry I'd crawl up a hog's ass just for a ham sandwich."

RJ

RJ took a ten-minute Uber ride to the Jiffy Lube Store owned by Big John Ballard. The Uber driver gave RJ his life story within the short time frame of the ride. A retired insurance executive bored out of his mind, with a wife that wants him out of the house. RJ wanted out of the Nissan Altima. The car pulled up to the business and RJ made a quick exit out the car door. The Uber bill automatically paid with his credit card on file.

The store was cream-colored with red strips on the top and bottom of the building. It had a flat roof with the air conditioning unit on the side of the building. One of those elongated inflatable balloons, a yellow one, danced on the three-foot section of green grass separating the store from the street. RJ saw Big John inside the office looking out the window at him. If possible, Big John had put on some weight; he was bigger.

"Mr. RJ. Good to see you, my friend." Big John greeted RJ with an arm halfway across RJ's back. The expanse of John's belly made it more awkward than normal to hug a person you didn't care for.

"Hey, John. How is business?" RJ asked.

"One thing about it, people always need their oil changed. Pay me now or pay me later. And they love fast and easy. In and out in less than twenty minutes is our standard. It is a fast food world out there RJ, and we have to fill that need." Big John was pitching RJ already. John took a white handkerchief out of the front pocket of his sweatpants. Blue suspenders were struggling to keep the pants above his privates. Big John whipped sweat off is forehead.

"John, is there a place for us to talk? In Private," Salas asked. He expected John Ballard to smell of oil and fuel, but he reeked of body odor.

The two men crossed the service bay, past three parking stalls with underground pits where the mechanics were housed. The cars drove over the top of the pits. A large metal cage separated the pit from the vehicle. The sound of air pressure tanks buzzing, hydraulics, oil compressors, vacuums, and a laser computer printer printing filled the air.

They entered a small room with two folding chairs and a portable table. The room got smaller when Big John sat down. The metal chair on the brink of collapse. He again took out his handkerchief and dabbed his forehead. Then Big John raised his chin and belched in the air. The smell made RJ want to gag.

"What can I do you for RJ?"

"John let's get right to it. Word is you are running dope under our club colors," RJ said.

"No way RJ. That is against the Son's policy."

"Thus, why I am here. You know the rules. You break them, and I pull your charter and your colors."

"Who told you this RJ? I need to know who is out to get me."

"Not your concern. I will take care of that."

"I wouldn't run an operation like that without your consent RJ," John said. "But I will tell you I have been approached by several. RJ you know, hypothetically with our network of members, our distribution, we could really make a financial impact for the club. You ever thought of being a distributor? You know low-level stuff. Nothing fancy. Just fulfilling the need. I know some key players RJ. Organized right and we could be on easy street in no time. Easy street for everyone in the club." Big John was trying to lean forward but you couldn't tell it.

"John unless you mean some multi-level marketing for vitamins, selling life insurance or if you have an exclusive distribution agreement for a new synthetic oil, the club will not go there. Period. Non-negotiable."

"RJ you need to look at the bigger picture. Think beyond you and me. We could help a ton of our boys get financially secure, set for life."

"We are not transporting or peddling dope. Let's expand the Jiffy Lube business, get some more franchises. We have guys with Subway stores, storage facilities, and those dollar stores. That is where we need to be. If it is get rich quick, then it is get dead quick."

"RJ, let's get the other chapter presidents involved. This is a democracy RJ. We believe in capitalism. And we also believe in the right to vote."

"I speak for the entire group John. You want to peddle dope to young kids, then do it on your own. You don't need us. And we don't want you. Deuce wanted us to be legit. He was working us that way. I am going to see it through. You want to deal drugs then join the Saints, the Aztecs, or some other startup. I guarantee that you will lock horns with them or others and someone will end up dead. And I won't let it be our boys. You want to branch out then do it but give me your vest."

"Ok. That's it then?" John asked.

"Yes, that is it." RJ stood to leave. "I can count on you right John?"

Big John didn't comment; he followed RJ out of the small room.

RJ was getting claustrophobic; the smell of body odor was getting to him. He was afraid the smell would permeate his clothes. He was glad to get out of there. RJ took out his phone, using his thumbs, he put a destination in the Uber app.

"Where is your bike?" John asked.

"Getting some minor repairs. It was a long ride here," was RJ's response. No way was he going to tell Big John his bike had been stolen.

"Where you staying during the rally?" Big John was curious today. "You could have stayed with me or one of the boys.

"I'm at the Super 8 on highway A1A. I'm leaving tomorrow. Need to get to back to Denver and take care of business, legit business."

Big John left RJ standing by the front entrance of his service store. He didn't say goodbye, good luck, or travel safe, and RJ didn't say any goodbyes either. RJ watched Big John waddle back into the service bay. John yelled at someone named Hector, telling him to get off the damn phone.

His Uber arrived, this time a Prius. RJ noticed the female driver. She was cute, a short, well-groomed afro, smooth, clear skin, bright brown eyes, and beautiful lips. RJ thought maybe he would text that girl in Denver after all. He sat in the passenger seat, the driver told him to buckle-up, sit still, that she didn't like fidgety passengers, no drinking, no smoking, no eating, no sunflower seeds, no gum and no small talk. What was he thinking? RJ decided against calling the lady back in Colorado.

Big John Ballard watched RJ get in the car and leave the area. He took out his cell phone. John scrolled through his contacts and hit send. Someone answered on the second ring.

"He just left. Told you he would be here," John spoke into the phone. "And? Is he in?"

"No. He has no interest in talking. I say fuck him. You know what to do. He is staying at the Super 8 on A1A. He is going there now."

The man on the other end of the phone asked: "When you want this completed?"

Ballard's answered, "Tonight. Hit him tonight. He is leaving town tomorrow. Has to be tonight. And don't fuck it up, James." The line went dead.

SAMI

nthony, aka Tripp, met Sami where he dropped her off earlier that morning, at the elevator door. It was midafternoon in Panama City Beach, they each managed six hours of sleep. Dozer, Tripp's friend followed the couple, staying back a few yards, a bodyguard for the bodyguard, but Dozer had nothing better to do. The trio headed to the beach, trying their best to find an isolated spot away from the crowds, the drunks, and the incessant noise.

They walked over a mile on spotless sandy beaches, the rhythmic pounding of the surf in time with their conversation.

Sami spread a beach towel on the sand. She saw Tripp's friend hanging back. "Is he with you? Sami asked Anthony.

"Yeah, he is a friend of mine. He is kind of shy," Anthony said.

"Tell him to join us. I will call my friend Steph. She loves the strong silent type. And she is easy," Sami said smiling.

Tripp called him over. "Sami, this is Dozer. Dozer, Sami." The two twenty-somethings shook hands. Dozer blushing slightly as Sami was in a low-cut bikini top. Dozer looked at her chest and thought he was busted, but Dozer's sunglasses concealed his stare.

"Just a sec Anthony, I'm calling Steph." Sami turned and walked away as she spoke, her toes in the salty water.

Dozer turned to his friend, "Anthony? Your name is Anthony, or you make that up?" Dozer asked Tripp.

"Yeah, it's Anthony. You didn't know that?" Tripp asked.

"No. Do you know my real name?" Dozer asked

"You know, I don't. That sucks. What is your real name Dozer?"

"Will, Will Dossier. I guess Dozer is easier to say than Dossier." Dozer responded to Tripp's question.

"She is on her way! You will love her, uugghhh, it was Dozer. Right?" Sami asked.

"Call me Will. Please." Dozer was blushing again.

Sami reached up and stroked his cheek. "You are blushing. That is so cute. Steph will love you," Sami said. She could see Steph jogging down the beach.

Dozier saw Steph running too. She looked good running, like something out of Baywatch. Will looked at Anthony, he was all grins.

The two couples sat on the beach. They put suntan lotion on each other's shoulders, went for a swim in the gulf, dried each other off and repeated the lotion application. Steph opened her beach bag bringing out a small bottle of Fireball. Steph took the first sip. Will, the second. Will passed the bottle to Sami, skipping Anthony.

Sami asked, "You don't want a drink?"

"No thank you. I don't drink," was Anthony's response.

"His parents died in a car accident. The guy that hit them was drunk." Will provided the info. Anthony gave Will a stern look.

"Go ahead Sami It's ok. I don't mind," Anthony said.

"No, I like that in you. Thanks for telling me, Will." Sami turned to Will and rubbed his shoulder.

"Well, give it back then. Will and I will drink it. And we ain't driving," Steph said loudly.

"Sorry about her. She didn't mean any offense. She doesn't have a filter," Sami said softly to Anthony.

The men turned their backs to each other and focused on their girl. Everything was quiet.

"So, is this your annual spring break fling?" Sami asked avoiding eye contact.

"I hope not Sam."

"But I'm just a junior and at Notre Dame. You have graduated and live in Florida. We will probably never see each other again."

"Do you want to see me after this week Sami?"

"Of course," Sami said as Anthony was now touching her cheek.

"Sam, I have been accepted to law school in Chicago. At Northwestern. I start in August. It is 90 miles from South Bend. I googled it already."

"Are you kidding? This is fantastic!" Sami shouted. Steph and Will looked over.

"But Sami there is something I have to tell you. And I hope you don't get mad at me." Anthony was now the one avoiding eye contact. He was digging his toes into the sand, burying his feet to the ankles.

"What? You are married, aren't you? No way you are gay? Are you? Are you an atheist? Tell me you are not a Democrat! You didn't vote for Hillary, did you?" Sami said, sitting up straight.

"No Sam, I'm not any of those and no I didn't vote for her silly." Anthony laughed out loud. "Sami, is your dad a bald guy with huge biceps, tattoos on his arm? Does he have mangled ears?"

"Yes, he wrestled in college. His ears are a mess. But what? Wait. How do you know all of that?"

"Don't be angry. A friend of mine is a friend of your dad's. When they heard you were here, they wanted us, me and Dozer, err Will, to keep an eye out for you," Anthony said; he was now holding her hand.

"Kind of like a bodyguard?" Sami asked.

"I like to think of it as like a guardian angel," Anthony said.

"Well, a bodyguard sounds pretty tough. But I like the guardian angel too." She kissed him on the cheek. "Wait, you're not getting paid to be with me, are you?"

"No, no money at all. Actually, I wasn't supposed to let you know I was watching you. But after seeing your smile, your brown eyes and watching you punch that Harvard asshole. Then when you dumped those shots on the barroom floor, the ones the old guy with the comb-over gave you, I had to meet you."

"You saw all that?"

"Yes, you dumped two shots on the floor."

"And you saw me punch that guy?"

"Yeah you got a mean right."

"Don't tell."

"Our secret."

Anthony leaned forward and cupped Sami's face in his hands.

Neither knew it, but they had their last first kiss.

VINCENT

Vincent was standing in the garage; he was on the phone. He called Rod, Terry, and Jake; he told them to haul their asses to the compound.

The three men were at his side within the hour; Jake arrived first. Vincent told them the time frame had been accelerated and they were not going to steal any more bikes He had Jake and Rod load the last six motorcycles in the trailer connected to the Freightliner. He gave Terry instructions to top off ll the gas tanks.

Vincent lied to his men and told them another crew, a motorcycle gang found out about the load of stolen bikes and were coming this evening. This gang was going to take over all their hard work. Tonight, was all or nothing. They had to protect their investment.

Vincent had a diagram of the compound spread out on the work table in the shop. This building was the smaller of the two metal structures. The table was sitting more outside than in. He needed a full view of the grounds to describe his plan and give instructions.

"Terry, I want you across from Richard's house. In that stack of empty oil barrels. You can't let anyone into the garage." Vincent went back to the diagram. "Take the AR15. Lock and load blow the hell out of them bikers."

Terry grinned. "I've always wanted to go batshit crazy on someone. This will be fun." He lit a cigarette as he spoke.

"Vincent where do you want me?" It was Rod speaking.

"Rod you stay between the garage and the modular. Opposite of Terry and a little farther away. You are line two of our defense."

"I got my shotgun. Will that do?" Rod said.

"Yeah, that will do. Be sure and take out the plug. You want more than three shots before you have to reload. Terry be careful when you fire as Rod is across from you." Vincent said pointing from the oil barrels to the cement barriers Rod would be standing behind.

"Jake, you got the Freightliner. That truck makes it out of here no matter what. You got a gun?" Vincent asked.

"Yeah, I got my Browning 9-millimeter, but I don't do any shooting Vince. You know that. No killing from me man." Jake replied.

"I know, that is why you got the truck," Vince replied. "If things go to shit you haul ass out the back exit."

"What about the two muscle heads?" Terry asked. "They going to help or be pussies and stay in the house?"

"I will talk to them. We have a plan for them as well. Don't worry about Marco and Raphael. We will finally get some work out of those two. And don't worry about my brother. I gave Richard some pills. He should be out 'til tomorrow. I expect them bikers to show up when it gets dark." Vincent was loading his own pistol as he spoke, a Smith and Wesson .357 magnum.

"What about the security system Vincent? Why don't we just keep the gate locked? Keep them out?" Terry asked. "Shoot them as they enter?"

"Cuz they will blow it open anyway. We let them in, and we have the advantage. I have a couple tricks up my sleeve." Vince said.

In a way, Vince wanted this. He wanted a showdown. Vincent's entire life was an ultimatum, it was always do or die, and to live and learn. Vincent enjoyed stress and living on the edge.

The three men went to their assigned locations. Terry set up a shooting stand built of plywood on top of four empty fifty-gallon barrels. Barrels were stacked two high in front of him for protection. He lit a cigarette, sucked it down to the filter in three long drags, stomped it out and lit another.

Terry had never before shot an AR 15 but didn't want to tell that to Vincent. He had never killed a man before either, though he had told all of them that he had. He practiced bringing the rifle to his shoulder. Terry popped out the magazine and put it back into place. He pulled at his pants. He lit another cigarette.

Rod set up behind a concrete barrier, the kind you see at road construction sites. The barriers had to be lifted by a tractor or a crane, they were so heavy. He wished he had more than one and that they were higher. The concrete barrier only went to his waist. Too high for him to shoot from his knees so he would have to stand which exposed more of his body. He was nervous and sweating. And scared.

Jake didn't want anything to do with this adventure. He wanted out. Jake was in this for the money but had yet to see anything but minimum wage and free lunches. Too late to bail out now, he swore if the money wasn't there he was going to deal with Vincent himself. Jake didn't like Vincent. He thought about beating the man with his own hands.

Richard sat in his house, staring out the front window. He saw Vincent talking with his arms. He was waving them back and forth, giving directions, pointing here and there. He saw Terry go right, Rod to the left. They each had weapons. Richard rubbed his temples. He wanted the medication Vincent gave him but threw the four pills to the floor. Richard knew he had to gut this one out. He had to overcome the headaches. He knew something big was going down tonight and he had to be prepared. Richard hoped it didn't involve the police and Sheriff Groff.

Richard watched Jake walk out of the shop and into the garage. He saw Jake carrying what looked like a weapon, had to be a pistol maybe another 9mm. The three men were locked and loaded. Whoever was coming to the property was in for a huge surprise, an ambush. Richard knew this wasn't right and that Vincent was doing something wrong, something illegal with his family business. His, their father's business.

He sat in the living room; the lights were off. The sun slowly going down past the horizon, the room getting darker by the minute. Richard could see Terry smoking and Rod sweating. The two muscle heads were still inside their modular. Jake was in the garage, and Vincent was walking the compound. Vincent also had a weapon, a large handgun. Richard recognized a .357. He never liked that gun. Too much power, not enough accuracy. He preferred the Glock 9mm. He thought, when did they buy so many guns?

Rubbing his temples, Richard walked the length of his house to his bedroom. He passed by his kid's rooms, mourning their absence. Their beds were made with the toys lined up against the wall. Richard had the room ready for their return, yet knowing it would be an event that he would never get to see. He walked past his den, pausing to look at his military citations for bravery, his Purple Heart framed and hanging on the wall. His Medal of Honor for saving his team in Falluja. He took a round to his chest that day and rubbed the scar under his shirt. Richard went to the walk-in closet, where his wife's clothes used to be. Hangers on a long white wooden pole lacked dresses, shirts, and slacks. Evidence someone once used them, now no need for so many. He opened the footlocker which was covered, hidden under old blankets. He bent over and dialed the three-number combination, right then left and back to the right, the lock opened. Richard lifted the lid looking for his own 9mm, his own weapons. The locker was empty. His guns were gone. Vincent must have taken them. Vincent had left him alone, with nothing to defend himself with but four sleeping pills.

JAMES BALLARD

James was in his mobile home, or as he referred to it, his one-bedroom POS. Piece of Shit. The unit was built in the 70's and thrown away in the 90's after a tropical storm submerged the mobile unit six feet under water. His brother, John Ballard brought it back to life when James got out of prison two years ago. John also owned the three acres of water-soaked Florida real estate where the POS sat.

James could smell and see black mold running up the side walls of the living room. He used Clorox on the walls in the bedroom, it seemed to help, but he never got around to cleaning the living area and kitchen combination room. He wasn't in the POS very often, he stayed at his mother's condo a couple days a week or at Sherri's place. Sherri was a coke head, she had no teeth, was anorexic skinny, but she had a nice house in suburbia and a trust fund courtesy of her parents. James treated her like crap, slapped her around and stole money from her. But she always let him back in her house.

Looking out the two-feet-by-two-feet picture window of his POS, he could see the latest improvement to his own home. James had stolen, off a Kenworth truck and trailer, two cargo straps, the one-hundred-foot yellow ones with ratchets that truckers use to tie down the load on their trailers. James had used the straps to tie down his mobile home. The ends of the straps were secured to long metal posts hammered into the ground. The straps were on each end of the mobile home. His improvement was a success as the house didn't move as much now when the wind blew.

John kept telling James he would get him a newer unit or move him out of this flea and mosquito-infested swamp. James wanted something near the beach, something like John had. So far James felt he did all of John's dirty work with no financial return for his effort.

This distribution idea was to change his life for the better, but this RJ fella was in the way. James was excited about being rid of RJ and even more so that he was the one to get to end RJ's existence. They two had met once, in Tallahassee the year before at the grand opening of a Subway store owned by one of the members. James had a little too much celebratory beer, wine, and recreational Ritalin. RJ took offense and slapped James around. RJ slapped him to sleep then slapped him for sleeping. When James woke, he was bruised, battered and embarrassed. RJ was due.

James had been thinking about this hit for over a month. He offered to John that he would walk up to RJ and shank him. He had done that in jail more than once, and it worked well. John thought RJ would be too tough, that RJ was too aware of everything around him. James didn't think RJ was that smart but perhaps RJ's eight years in Federal lock-up made him wiser than he looked. James promised he would do what John told him to do, for now.

James placed two weapons on the sofa, a .243 caliber Parker and Hale deer rifle with a scope and a Ruger .38. He would carry both and wait for opportunities, after all, he had all night.

James drove a later model Toyota Tundra pick-up, also a gift from his brother, to the Super 8 Hotel in Daytona. He sat in the cab of the truck staring at the front door with the motor off. Watching and waiting. He was sweating; everyone sweats in Florida. He wore blue jeans that hadn't seen a washing machine in over a month and a t-shirt with Ballard Jiffy Lube on the back. James noticed the Super 8's security cameras posted on each light pole and under the front canopy, not like he was going to shoot this guy in broad daylight anyway. He wanted to take him out in a back alley or shoot him from across a larger parking lot with the scope and rifle.

After thirty minutes of isolated wait time, a large bald guy on a black and white police Harley Davidson rode up and parked in front of the entryway. James watched as the big guy stayed straddled on his bike. He took out his phone and made a call. A few minutes later RJ came out of the front entrance. He stopped and talked to the bald guy. Then

RJ got on the back of the guy's bike, as a passenger. Two big guys riding together on a motorcycle, James didn't believe either man was gay but knew there was something odd about this. The two large men engulfed the motorcycle. They looked ridiculous.

James followed them in the Toyota as they rode out of the Super 8 parking lot. Cars were honking at them and people made snide remarks. James didn't think anyone felt they were a cute couple.

Twenty minutes later James passed them as they parked the bike in front of the county sheriff's office in Deland, Florida. James did a quick U-turn and paralleled parked across the street. He saw RJ get off the bike as the other big guy backed the Harley into the stall. Both men went inside the police station. Obviously not a good spot for a hit.

The two men came out after a few minutes, a short guy in a police uniform was with them. The sun was starting to set, not much daylight left. James contemplated his next move. Three men would be far more difficult. He decided he would continue to follow and play more of the wait-and-see game.

RJ got into the truck with the sheriff nd a dog while the other guy rode his Harley. James stayed with them through the streets of Deland then out of town on a rural county road. He hung back over a mile. The flat terrain and few trees or buildings made it easy to track and follow them.

James parked the Toyota and watched as the motorcycle went through the gate of an acreage posting a "We Found U Repo" sign. The Sheriff stayed parked on the bridge not wishing to enter. James watched as the sheriff got out of the truck, yelled something then saw RJ dash through the metal gate before it closed.

James watched as RJ walked across an acre of bare ground to join the guy on the bike. This was his chance. He grabbed the deer rifle from the passenger seat and got out of the truck. He heard a rustling noise in the long green grass and cat-tails in front of him. He watched as several alligators entered the black water, their two prominent eyes guiding them above the surface. James placed fi e shells into the magazine, fi e brass 243 shells. He rested his elbows on the hood of the pick-up, the rifle in shooting position. He found RJ through his scope, he took a deep breath, held it and pulled the trigger.

SALAS, RJ & GROFF

The sun was setting when RJ and Salas pulled the Harley in front of the County Sherriff's building. RJ riding on the back seat with Salas drew lots of stares, some snide comments, homophobic slurs and a request for a threesome from a lady in a faded green Pontiac Firebird.

RJ got off the Harley while Salas backed the bike into a parking stall. The sheriff's F150 was next to them.

Both men entered the station, Salas first. Groff was sitting in the receptionist's chair behind her desk. He was wearing the same coffee-stained short-sleeved shirt. He was drinking more of the same out of a stainless-steel travel coffee mug, the logo on the mug read "Gators" in bold blue letters.

"Well hello, boys. Didn't know if you had backed out or what. Was hoping you didn't go without me. Hate to arrest a fellow police officer Salas," Groff aid.

Bob came around the counter. He sniffed the shoes of both men. He growled at Salas.

Salas introduced RJ to the sheriff. And to Bob.

"We are with you, Groff. But I am telling you. This is not about stolen motorcycles. I just can't tell you what it is yet. Given Vincent's background, it has to be drugs. But why the bikes?" Salas had taken his Glock out from behind his pants and was looking it over. It was clean, oiled and loaded. He also made certain it was his gun.

"Salas this repo business, this Richard and Vincent drama and then you two, sum bitch. Hell, an out-of-town cop on vacation and a biker on probation. Yes, I looked you up RJ. You have a colorful resume. This whole shit makes my ass itch." Groff was using an oiled rag to clean off a classic Smith and Wesson .38. It was a six-shot revolver. His holster carried an additional 12 rounds of ammo.

"I understand. I'm just going to look around. I know they will be there and they know I will be there. It be best if you stayed here Sheriff Groff. The less you know, the better. If I find something, I will call you." Salas looked at Groff hen at RJ.

"Salas, I'm going with you. Only way you go is if I go. But I got good news. Got a local Judge to do some work today. I got a warrant to look at them bikes." Groff held up a piece of paper in his hand and waggled it at them.

"That is good news, Groff. See this will be a routine house call," Salas said.

"Yeah right. Routine. But you biker boy. I know this is your bike but you stay in the truck."

"They call me RJ," RJ said. "You can too."

"I don't care if they call you Martha Sweet Cakes Stewart. You stay in the fucking truck. Comprendo Amigo?" Groff sked.

RJ nodded.

Sheriff Groff grabbed two black vests from a standing metal coat hanger. "Wear this Salas." He tossed the vest to the detective. "Only way this is going down is you in the truck and you in that bulletproof vest." Groff pointed at RJ then at Salas. Groff grabbed another vest off the same rack, putting it on over his stained white shirt. The vest read "police" on the chest.

Taking off his leather jacket, Salas put on the vest. It went from his chin to his belly button. The vest smelled of sweat but not his. He put his riding jacket back on over the vest then placed his Glock in his pants.

The three men and Bob went outside. Groff carrying his travel mug filled with coffee, his gun in the shoulder holster. Groff got in the driver's seat, Bob sitting next to Groff. RJ got in the passenger side of the Ford. RJ's gun that Groff didn't know about was in the small of his low back. A felon with an illegal handgun. If shit hit the fan how would Salas and Groff xplain this?

RJ reached over and scratched Bob behind the ears. Bob crawled on RJ's lap and stuck his nose out the passenger side window causing Groff to say, "sum bitch, ain't never seen Bob do that before."

Salas rode out on his Harley, the Road King leading the way. He was retracing the same route from earlier in the day. Groff followed Salas a few car lengths back. None of them noticing the Toyota following them in the distance.

Salas crossed the metal bridge and stopped at the closed gate, his front tire nearly touching the metal chain link. The Ford was a few yards back of his rear fender, sitting on the bridge. They didn't wait more than five seconds when the gate suddenly rolled open, left to right. Salas immediately rode through.

Groff was reaching for the handheld microphone thinking he was going to have to request the gate be opened like he did before when the gate moved to the right. Groff jumped back, the coffee mug which was sitting between his legs tipped forward, the contents spilling on his lap.

"Sum bitch that's hot," Groff yelled while he got out of the truck and stood on the metal bridge, he was dabbing coffee off f his crotch.

Groff ooked up as the gate started to close.

RJ opened the passenger door and ran in front of the pick-up truck towards the gate; he crossed the entryway as the door was closing. A loud clunk signaled it locked. Bob followed RJ but stopped, not entering the compound.

"Damnit biker boy let me in," Groff yelled, he looked like he had just peed his britches.

RJ grabbed the gate, rattled it, forcefully pulling it back and forth. The gate was locked. "It ain't budging Groff."

"Sum bitch," Groff yelled. "RJ you two don't do shit in there. I mean it. First thing you do is find the button to open this damn door and let me in."

Bob was barking at both men.

Salas was sitting on his bike looking back at the two men, RJ on one side of the fence, Groff on the other. He shook his head. "You got to be shitting me."

RJ started walking across the flat acre of graveled and rocked road toward Salas, and Richard Lopez's home.

The Chevy Silverado was still parked facing the house with a tow truck beside it. Fluorescent yard lights lit up the compound. Salas could see Richard's house; the muscle head's modular, the mobile home, then the two metal buildings. The garage doors were open on both outbuildings, lights on but they could not see anyone around.

Salas parked his Harley by the Silverado, dropped the kickstand and dismounted. RJ was walking towards Salas, still several feet from Salas's bike. There was no wind, no breeze. Mosquitos were buzzing in their ears, moths flying around the bulbs of the yard lights. You could hear crickets and an occasional bullfrog.

A shot rang out, Salas looked left, and RJ was on the ground. Salas ducked down going near the truck. Another shot startled the still evening, the dirt beside RJ's head jumped in the air. RJ rolled away from Salas as more dirt kicked up by RJ's head and another shot echoed in the yard. Salas ran into the open and grabbed RJ under the arms and began pulling him towards the pickup and tow truck. Another shot, Salas felt it before he heard it. He fell forward on RJ, the impact knocking him over. Salas recovered quickly as RJ was helping, they both rolled behind the tire of the Chevy.

They looked at each other. "You ok?" Salas asked.

"Hit in the thigh. I think it's an in-and-out. But I'm good. You?" RJ was checking his leg. He had blood on his hand.

Salas was looking at his left shoulder, "Not bad, the leather jacket helped. I think it just grazed the delt. It burns a bit now but will likely hurt like a bitch tomorrow. Where the fuck those shots come from?"

Before RJ could answer, the two men jumped, both startled as Richard Lopez was kneeling beside them. Richard was crouched low, his head up.

More shots came. This time from the front left, an onslaught of automatic fire pummeled the tow truck. Salas could hear and feel the bullets passing over his head. Shooting then came from the front right, more shots, three in succession, then three more. They were virtually surrounded. RJ and Salas sat up in unison, pointed their guns forward, returning fire, shooting randomly into the night air.

"Cease fire. You are wasting ammo. You are not even aiming at anything," Richard said to RJ and Salas.

"I'm firing for effect. It makes me feel better," RJ said

"Give me your weapon soldier." Richard was looking at RJ. RJ followed the order and handed Richard his Glock. Richard was on one knee, Tim Tebow position. He quickly studied the weapon then aimed and fired, aimed and fired, aimed and fired, aimed and fired. Four shots and the four-yard lights were out. Darkness engulfed them. A sliver of moonlight reflected on the pond creating the same illusion as the moonlight off he metal roofs.

Salas said, "That was good fucking shooting Richard."

"Yeah, easier when they are not shooting back at you." He pivoted to his left looking across the pond and entry gate. "We have a threat at our rear perimeter. The threat is localized on him though." Richard was pointing at RJ.

"What do you mean him?" Salas asked.

"The shooter wants him." Richard was still pointing at RJ. "He wasn't trying to shoot you. You were in the open as much as he was. Four shots, all four at him. You were standing in the open; he was walking. You were an easy target, but he skipped you. Yes, he shot you but only because you were in the way trying to save his ass. The rear shooter wants him."

"Has to be a deer rifle," RJ added as he was applying pressure to the wound on his thigh. His blood dripping on the white and gray rocks of the driveway.

"It is a .243 or maybe a .270 but yes definitely a kind of rifle you would use to kill a deer. He is a way off, across the pond. He is neutralized without the yard lights. Unless he has a night vision scope." Richard was now facing forward left. "Our immediate threat is the semi-automatic weapon to the left."

Salas said, "Must be an AK-47." He too was bleeding, as a dark red sticky stream of blood was running off the tips of his fingers to the ground.

"AR-15 by the sound. And the shooter doesn't know how to use it. You could tell the strength and recoil of the weapon was driving his shots upward. If he hits anything, it will be pure luck. The shooter to our right. That is a 20-gauge shotgun. He was firing for effect." Richard looked at RJ.

They could hear shots coming from the area of the entrance to the compound. Three short bursts of two shots each.

The three men turned and looked at the front gate.

Salas looked for Groff. He saw the truck had sunk. The front end of the truck was under water, only the tailgate of the Ford above the water level. He knew they would have to call a tow truck to get Groff out of the lake. Irony at its finest as there were two tow trucks sitting in the parking lot of the compound. Neither tow truck could lift the truck from the front end up and out of the water, and neither truck could get on the other side to drag the back end out. "Are you shitting me?" is all Salas could think to say.

"That's Sheriff   roff," RJ said.

"That is a .38. But no return fire." Richard said. "Could be the sheriff is just shooting for effect, but I doubt it." Again, Richard looked straight at RJ.

GROFF

The gate closed with Groff on the wrong side, as if there were a right and wrong side…. Groff watched as Salas and RJ went into the main yard of "We Found You Repo." Groff could see the two men, Salas and RJ, under the yard lights. He heard the rifle shot, looked to his right. Too late for a muzzle flash. He turned to see RJ on the ground. Another shot. He rotated again this time able to spot the bright red and yellow burst of the third shot as it lit up the silence of the black background. The shooter was fifty to seventy-fi e yards north. Groff got into his pickup to call for back-up.

As Groff sat in the truck, trying to call his own 911, he heard a loud groaning noise. Suddenly the front of his Ford F150 was tilting forward. His truck was going engine first, head first into the pond. The bridge was folding away, diving into the water.

The truck was at a downward angle, Groff was being pressed against the steering wheel, his chest causing the horn to beep. He pushed back with both arms, like doing a push-up while sitting. Groff opened the driver's side door and got out, standing on the running board. Water was pouring into the cab, flooding the floor of the pick-up. The truck was sinking fast, the front end dropping while the rear end was rising. Bob was running in circles on the dry land barking at the truck, the shots, the alligators, the dark of the night, and to the sound of Groff honking the horn of the Ford.

Groff climbed into the back of the Ford. Water was past the doors, filling the back seat, creeping up the back window and now filling the truck bed of the pick-up. Groff considered standing at the front of the truck and singing "Distant Memories" or the song "Rose" from the

Titanic. Damn his wife for making him watch that stupid movie. The thought quickly left im and turned to saving his own ass.

Groff stepped back, slipping in the wet pickup bed. He stepped over the tailgate and stood on the rear bumper hitch. He was balancing on the hitch, his thighs against the tailgate of the Ford, the truck nearly under water. The sinking stopped. The truck settled in position. Groff thought the front end must be touching the bottom of the pond.

Something, someone hit the back of his calf, nearly knocking him off the precarious perch he was balancing on. His feet were under water, his hand on the tailgate. He looked down. It was an alligator. The beast was at least eight feet long.

"Sum Bitch," yelled Sheriff Groff. Panic could be heard in his sum bitch.

Two eyes were peering out of the water. They were large red eyes with white sclera's and puffy eyelids. The eyes liked the looks of Sheriff Groff.

Groff pulled his service revolver from the shoulder holster and fired two shots. Both rounds went between those eyes that were looking at him with so much love. He saw the gator go belly-up. The light of the moon shining on the white underside of the alligator. Another gator swam, crept, slithered, hell, came forward, and demanded another two shots by Groff. Double tap to the brain. No body shots. He had nowhere to go. Bob ran from the gate to the edge of the pond barking and doing circles. A gator sprang from the water going for Bob. Two shots by Groff killed the beast with blood spatter hitting the dog, causing Bob to bark even louder. Groff had to reload, dropping six empty shells into the dark water. The brass empties sank quickly. Groff watched them disappear as he put six more shells into his .38.

"Damnit Bob, stay by the fence!" Groff yelled. He then added, "Sum bitch."

VINCENT

S itting in the back office of the shop Vincent was watching the action unfold over two computer screens. The security cameras were set to watch the front gate, Richard's house, the shop, and garage.

Vincent laughed as he pushed the button to lock the gate, leaving the sheriff on the bridge. He wanted the other two men to die at the hands of his crew. He envisioned the police searching through the carnage while he was in the Freightliner well on his way to Canada with the motorcycles and the drugs.

When the shooting started from the far side of the pond, Vincent was confused yet delighted when a third party entered the fray. The more confusion, the better the chance of success for his escape. Let the guy fire away, if he killed the two bikers all the merrier. Vincent found himself cheering for the shooter while he watched the computer screen. He saw Salas and RJ by the tow truck; he thought they both had been shot. That is when he clicked on the icon to lower the bridge. He laughed out loud as the Sheriff climbed out of the cab of the truck and into the back. The truck sinking while Groff   as scrambling.

Vincent was shocked to see his brother join the two bikers. "Damnit," yelled Vincent. "What the fuck is Richard doing there?"

His anger rose again when Terry started firing and then, of course, more upset when Rod had to jump in emptying his gun too.

"Why are you firing let the other guy kill them!" Vincent yelled at the computer screens.

Vincent knew all the firepower would bring more police and encourage them to get there faster. One round, one gunshot at night, was normal in Florida like a random shot in the South-side of Chicago, it just happened, and you didn't report it. But this barrage of gunfire would bring more cops, a lot more cops. One-on-one, people can shoot themselves all week. Multiple shots at the same time in the same evening drew the major media. Were they winning or losing? No one knew. The truck was sinking, the troops were charging. He wanted chaos, and he got it. It was all going as planned. Chaos at its best. The look on Sherriff Groff's face was priceless. Now there was no way for the police to enter. Richard could drive out the rear entrance, through the swamp, and get away.

Leaving the computer screens up and running, Vincent thought it was time to leave. He stood, grabbed the .357 and speed-walked into the garage. The weapon dangling by his side weighed over two pounds. Vincent wanted to shoot it.

"Jake, get out of the truck," Vincent barked out the command.

Jake did as he was told. He opened the truck door and climbed down, hopping off he last step on to his good knee.

"What's up Vince, why all the shooting? Is the biker gang here?" Jake stuttered as he spoke. He was nervous and scared, really scared.

"Yes. They are here, and they brought more men than we thought. We need more firepower. Terry and Rod need your help. Now get out and take a position near the modular with Rod," Vincent said, pointing his gun towards the exit.

"No way man. I didn't sign up for this shit. I told you no guns and no killing from me," Jake told Vincent as he threw up his hands. He turned his back to Vincent and started walking away, towards the shop.

Vincent lifted his gun and shot Jake in the back, between the shoulders. The .357 magnum threw Jake's body forward. Two steps and he went from a truck driver to a dead man. Jake's body twitched for a few seconds then went quiet.

Vincent forgot the money and went back to his office to get the duffle bag. He told himself he didn't give a shit about Terry, Jake, or Rod. They were pawns and too stupid to know better. The next world, his world, was all about Vincent. He didn't need any of these people. Vincent had to make his exit while the men outside were shooting each other. Vincent's plan was to be gone while the two gangs battled for territory. Then when the dust, and the body count was completed, they were all dead, and he would be long gone.

RJ, SALAS, & RICHARD

"Salas, I need you to lay suppression fire towards the AR. He will respond by returning fire. I will then take him out." Richard stated the order to Salas.

"Richard, that is a fifty or sixty-yard shot and we can't even see the shooter in the dark, you shot out the lights remember?" Salas said.

"Listen. The shooter is smoking a cigarette; I saw a faint red glow the last time he fired." Richard was pointing. "After he shoots he will take a drag off the cigarette. That will make the glow even brighter. I will make the shot. Shoot Salas. Now."

Salas shot the Glock four times randomly into the expanse of darkness before them. Just as Richard had said, return fire was immediate. The spray of bullets from the AR-15 started in the dirt about fifteen feet in front of the tow truck with a quick upward trajectory. Bullets clipped and ricocheted off the metal hoist that was over fi e feet high in the back of the tow truck. More shots flew into the night skies above them. Salas thought, with any luck, that the AR-15 shooter would hit the guy shooting at them from behind of the pond.

Richard stood, pointed the gun towards the red ember, both arms extended outward, and pulled the trigger. The red glow vanished.

"You get him?" RJ asked.

"If the end of that cigarette was between his lips, I got him," Richard said, lowering his weapon.

They could hear more shooting by the bridge. Six shots in two round bursts. Again, no return fire.

"You, soldier." Richard was pointing to RJ again. "Go confiscate that weapon, the AR-15 and get to the bridge. Find the source of the shooting. Sheriff Gross must be in distress. Eliminate or neutralize." More shots came from the right, six shots from the shotgun. Richard again ordered, "Ignore those; they will not hurt you from here. Now go."

RJ ran with a limp, his thigh not functioning correctly after being hit. He had one hand pressing the thigh wound. He was soon lost in the darkness, but still no shooting from the guy with the deer rifle across the pond.

Richard and Salas leaned against the pickup. Both men were contemplating their next move. Richard started to laugh. Lightly at first, then a true belly laugh. With all the shooting, Richard was laughing. It made Salas smile.

"Am I missing something, Richard? What is so funny" Salas asked.

"My headaches. They are gone. I can't remember when the last time was I didn't have a headache. All I needed was to get back into the action man. I just needed to feel alive again. When this is over, I'm going back. Back to Iraq. I will work security. Free-lance. Something." Richard was grinning.

Salas looked over the tow truck. He could see the two muscle heads going into the shop.

"While you are enjoying yourself, and planning your future, I am going after the twins. You take shotgun boy then go into the garage and get your brother." Salas gave the order this time.

"Yes, sir," Richard said, still laughing, a bright smile on his face.

RJ

Crossing the empty driveway, the darkness was his friend. RJ's thigh tightened up as he ran, his face grimacing with every step. RJ found the dead shooter. The deceased man was flat on his back, having fallen off a shooting platform. RJ took out his cell phone, using the light of the screen to highlight the dead man's face. The deceased wore a crooked smile with missing teeth in the corner of the man's mouth. On the ground was a large pool of blood outlining the head and shoulders of the dead man

RJ found the AR-15, which was still on the stage where the man had been standing. Lying beside the rifle was a smoldering cigarette. He was surprised there was no blood on the gun. He popped off the clip. RJ counted ten rounds, with one in the chamber. RJ checked the shooting platform, the ground, and the body. No other magazine or clips. No other weapons.

Running caused the wound on his thigh to bleed more profusely. RJ continued to apply pressure to his thigh with his hand as he moved. The bullet went through the meaty portion of his outer leg. No major arteries ran through that part of his leg, and it didn't hit a bone, just two holes in his thigh. RJ thought maybe a couple of stitches would be needed, but Neosporin and a band-aid would suffice if he had them.

As he walked and jogged to the bridge, he heard two more shots. A third as he got to the gate. RJ could see the sheriff standing on the back bumper of his truck, most of the Ford was submerged in the water of the pond, the front end and engine were under still water, light bubbles outlining where it was. Groff's hand was on the tailgate holding himself steady. Water was nearly to his waist. RJ thought, "what happened to the bridge?"

As RJ approached, still in the cover of darkness he heard another voice from the other side of the pond; the voice was walking towards Sheriff   roff. RJ dropped to the grass laying on his belly.

"Sheriff, how are you this fine evening?" The man walking up asked Groff.

RJ looked towards the sound and the outline of the man. He could clearly see him, just not the color of clothes. He recognized that voice. RJ laid flat on the ground, the barrel of the AR resting on a chain-link of the fence. He held the AR steady aiming at the chest of the new arrival.

"I'm up to my nuts in swamp water here with gators on my ass. I've shot enough gators to supply Kanye and the Kardashians with clothes and suitcases for the fucking year." Groff imed and fired again.

"Seems to be an alligator infestation Sheriff," the stranger said, a slight drawl to his voice.

"Yeah hurricane Irma drove them inland, but it looks like these guys may have been breeding and feeding, the cocksuckers." Groff was looking left and right in the water. "And you sir. How you know I'm the sheriff? I don't think we have met."

"Saw your truck, before you sunk it. I saw you drive by my place a ways back." The southern drawl.

Bob had stopped barking and was sitting by the chain link fence near RJ.

"And you just happen to be out for a walk?" Groff sked.

"Why I am a concerned citizen Sheriff. I heard a great deal of shooting and was thinking I may have to call the police, but I see they are here and in control of the situation." The concerned citizen stepped closer. He was standing on the edge of the embankment, a sharp drop off o the water.

"Concerned citizen walking around with a deer rifle?"

"Gators my good man. As you are clearly experiencing." This time a little British accent. The new arrival put the rifle to his shoulder, aimed and shot into the water. A gator went belly up. "Hmmm, that my good man, was a crocodile. I had heard there were various species of the Nile Croc here in Florida. But I had never seen them before. Very interesting."

"Well kiss my interesting ass. A crocodile? Sum bitch and I thank you for that. I am down to my last three bullets." Groff aid.

"Why don't you just swim to the shore?"

"I can't swim!" Groff elled

"Swim hell, the gators will probably kill you." The man with the deer rifle swung his weapon towards Groff.

The AR-15 barked out. RJ shot the man holding the deer rifle in the chest. The man fell to his back and slid down into the water. A gator was there to greet him. The man and the rifle were pulled into the pond. The ripple created in the water slowly went flat. RJ and Groff staring at the now still pond.

Sheriff Groff looked at RJ. "I think that sum bitch was going to shoot me. Who was he?"

"An old acquaintance." RJ had the muzzle of the AR pointed at the locking mechanism of the gate. He fired. The lock sprung. He pushed the gate open. "How did you break the bridge?"

"I didn't break no bridge. It just went down; it is hydraulic. Someone triggered it from in there." Groff said pointing towards the compound. They could hear shots coming from the buildings.

RJ was standing in front of the bridge. He raised the rifle and shot a gator. "Are you going to swim over here?"

"Hell no. You heard me. I can't swim. And these gators and crocodiles, crocodilians, whatever the fuck they call 'em, are all over." Groff raised his pistol and shot three times into the dark waters of the pond.

"Sheriff, I have eight rounds left." RJ paused and fired three more shots into the water behind Groff's legs. "Make that fi e more rounds. What do you have?"

"I'm out. All I can do is talk sexy to the sum bitch and hope he likes me," Groff aid.

RJ shot again, twice. A gator exploded, twisting in the water, it's tail swinging wildly, narrowly missing Groff. RJ shot him a third time.

"I am counting another three gators just sitting right there." RJ pointed to the water's edge where he had just shot a man. He fired again. A gator's head burst open. He then shot the gator next to it. He was out of ammunition.

As Groff was turning to look where RJ had fired, another loud groan came from under the water. The bridge was starting to rise. The front of the pickup was being lifted out of the pond. Water running out the doors and out of the box of the pickup.

RJ stood back, Groff stepped over the tailgate and into the back of the truck. It took a few minutes, but the bridge locked back into its original position. The Ford was once again sitting level on the metal bridge as water drained out of the truck and back into the pond.

Groff swung his leg over the side panel of the pickup and stepped on to the metal surface of the bridge. He jumped up and down twice as if testing the integrity of the structure.

"Sum bitch you see that RJ? It was like Jesus parting the water of the Dead Sea. And now we have a way across the water." Groff spread his arms wide.

"It was Moses and the Red Sea, but I understand what you are saying," RJ replied.

Sheriff Groff opened the door of the Ford, stepping to the side as the water splashed on him, on the bridge and dropping back to where it came from. He had his revolver out expecting a gator.

"Why you pointing that pistol? Thought you are out of ammo Sheriff?" RJ asked.

"I know that, but that sum bitch gator don't," Groff replied as he was peering inside the cab of the truck.

Groff holstered his weapon and sat down in the driver's seat as water squeezed out the seams. The key was still in the ignition. He turned the key. The pickup barked, hiccupped, coughed and spat out water, he pumped the gas pedal and tried the key again. The pickup roared to life, water spraying out of the exhaust pipes as Groff laid on the accelerator.

"Sum bitch these Fords are kickass. A Chevy would've needed artificial mouth to mouth resuscitation." Groff drove the pickup off the bridge and onto the compound, he opened his door, and Bob crawled in, scooted under Groff's legs and sat on the passenger seat. RJ jumped on the back hitch where Groff had been standing. The shooting had stopped.

SALAS

Salas left Richard to deal with the man with the shotgun. He sprinted across the expansive driveway to the smaller garage. He ran unnoticed, covered in darkness as the moon was now hidden behind dark rain clouds.

The shop's garage doors were raised and fully opened. White light from long fluorescent bulbs was peeking out to the driveway. Salas walked into the shop with his gun in hand, his back against the metal side walls of the building. He squatted down, lowering his head and shoulders, looking right and left or the twins.

A car hoist was in the center of the building lying flat on the concrete floor. Automobile jacks, air compressors, barrels of oil, cleaning solvents and auto parts were strewn haphazardly across the width of the building. There were two work benches with various tools, mainly wrenches, screwdrivers, hammers, and sockets cluttering the flat surfaces. A socket set sat alone with most of the sockets missing.

Salas cut across the floor then stopped and stood in front of a workbench. He heard tennis shoes squeaking on the pavement and slowly turned. One of the muscleheads was standing there, twenty feet from Salas, the twin was grinning.

"Hey old man." The musclehead spoke. He raised his arm; a gun was in his hand. He pointed it at Salas. "Go ahead. Make my day," he yelled at Salas.

Salas raised his weapon before musclehead could react and squeezed the trigger. Nothing happened. He squeezed the trigger again. Nothing.

"You got to be shitting me," Salas said to himself.

"What's wrong, smart ass? You only bring one magazine?"

"Yeah, what can I say, I'm on vacation," Salas said, lowering his empty weapon.

Musclehead took his time. He aimed his gun at Salas and took a deep breath then pulled the trigger. His gun fired. Salas was hit and fell back, landing on the flat metal table.

Musclehead took his time, he took three more steps toward Salas and went into a shooter's stance. He placed the barrel of the weapon against his lips and kissed it. He slowly and deliberately aimed his gun at Salas, both hands on the weapon. Musclehead took a deep breath then pulled the trigger. His gun fired.

Salas was hit in the chest, the force of the impact throwing him to his back. He landed on the flat metal work table. He pulled frantically at the Kevlar vest that just saved his life; the pain was intense He was still on his back, on top of the table, his feet kicking in the air. Salas felt for the bullet; it was lodged into the vest directly over his heart. He was fi hting to breathe.

Musclehead walked to the table and stood over Salas as Salas struggled to breathe. Musclehead smiled. Salas brought his head up, extending his neck, trying to sit up, the wind was knocked out of his body. He was gasping for air while tearing at the Velcro straps of the vest. Salas saw the man up-close, the twin was bigger and uglier than he thought. A ragged scar stretched across the twin's forehead. His cheeks were pocked, marked from scores of old acne blemishes. Salas smelled sweat and body odor; he breathed in deep needing the air, but not the taste of the twin.

The man held his gun to Salas's head. "Damn, I was aiming for your face. I should just kill you now. But you know what? I want to see you in pain. He reached forward and grabbed Salas by the vest and pulled Salas to his feet.

As Salas rose, he grabbed a screwdriver off the workbench with his right hand. Musclehead lifted him up, Salas stood, now both hands on the tool and both feet planted on the floor. He drove the Phillips end of the screwdriver under the chin of muscle's head. Salas drove it up and through the back of the man's throat into his brain. The screwdriver stopped when it hit the back of the man's skull. Blood streamed down Salas hands and arms while he lifted the man off he ground.

He was looking into the eyes of a dying man. "Now I see why that little shit liked this so much that last night in Sturgis," Salas said to the twin as life left   is eyes.

Salas pushed up and away letting go of the screwdriver as the dead body fell to the concrete. Blood poured out of the neck of the muscle man turning the gray floor to crimson.

Salas took off the vest, pulled up his shirt and saw a deep purple bruise forming over his heart.

"Raphy, Raphael, my brother," the twin Marco screamed in the air. He ran forward, sat by his brother, taking his brother's head in his hands. He had tears in his eyes as he rocked the dead man back and forth. Salas watched as the brother cried.

Marco looked up at Salas. His face turned shallow, his eyes dark. There were no more tears.

"I am going to kill you." Marco stood. "I am going to kill you with my hands. I am going to tear you apart."

Salas had his wind back. He stood there looking at the twin. The twin stared back. No one spoke, no one moved.

"Well, you going to tell me a ninja turtle story about your dead brother and bore me to death or what?" Salas had his fists held tight.

Marco screamed and charged at Salas, head down, arms wide. Salas had been here before, several times. His instincts took over. Years of wrestling paying off. Salas stepped to the side, reached with his right arm across the body of the twin and arm-dragged him sideways. Salas used the twin's momentum to ram him into a barrel of oil. Marco hit head-first, a large dent was visible in the barrel. Blood covered Marco's forehead; the cut would need stitches.

The twin was on his knees. He shook his head as he spun towards Salas. Marco was met with Salas's left kneecap to the face. Marco dropped to the floor again.

"Stay down," Salas said.

Marco ignored the command and stood. He continued to shake the cobwebs out of his brain. Marco pulled brass knuckles from his pocket dramatically placing them on his fingers one at a time. Marco punched his fist into his other palm three then four times. He approached Salas in a boxer's stance. The brass knuckles in his right hand. He led with his left.

Salas and the twin circled each other, inching closer and closer. Salas's arm was stinging, a reminder he had a bullet hole in his shoulder muscle. Marco fainted a left jab, rearing back with his right arm. As his arm went back, Salas stepped straight ahead, following through with a right hand to the cheekbone of the twin. Salas could feel the zygomatic arch of Marco's face crunching under his fist.

The twin staggered, his instincts, conditioning and low IQ keeping him on his feet. Salas followed with a left hook to Marco's jaw; the twin didn't try to block the punch. There was more crunching noise. The man's head snapped to the right, back to the left, Marco was falling towards Salas who hit him again with a straight right then a left to the face. The left l nded on an unconscious Marco, who collapsed on the floor.

Salas checked Marco's pulse, with that last left Salas thought he might have killed him. Marco was unconscious but alive. Salas looked at his own hands, turning them over and back. Both fists were dark red. Salas had a cut over his right first knuckle; the finger was swelling. His shoulder hurt like hell.

Looking around the shop, Salas found a roll of silver tape. He put Marco's arms behind his back and taped them together. It wasn't as easy as it sounded. The man was so muscular in his chest, lats, and arms that Salas could not get the man's hands within six inches of each other. Salas then taped Marco's feet together at the ankles. Next, he wrapped tape around the twin's forehead and eyelashes so that when they ripped the tape off t would take the hair with it.

Salas found his empty Glock and returned it to the space in his lower back. He couldn't believe he hadn't counted the number of shots he had taken. Salas was rubbing his shoulder, the one the guy with the deer rifle had shot. Then rubbed his chest. He had been shot twice tonight, and he was on vacation. Blood was running down his arm from the bullet wound. It was mixing with Raphael's blood from the stabbing.

Salas saw two computer screens on a workbench. The monitors showed two dark fi ures at the entryway bridge. The lighting was poor, but he knew it was RJ and Sheriff Groff. Salas could barely make sense of it all in the darkness, but he knew it was Groff's pickup. The truck was under water, the tailgate in the air with the Sheriff balancing on the rear bumper. Groff   ith water up to his waist.

Standing over the keyboard connected to the monitors, Salas used the mouse to place the white arrow over the box in the upper corner of the screen and downsized it. Another window was open. On this screenshot was an icon that read, "Bridge." Salas put the mouse arrow on this icon. Within it yet another window and a square box that said, "enter." He double clicked that with the mouse. Salas looked at the screen as the Ford F150 was moving in the water. The hood of the pickup was rising, the truck leveling off. It took a few minutes, but the bridge was settling back into place. He could see Groff getting into the back of the truck then standing on the bridge. He could tell RJ was on the road across from the sheriff.

Salas heard the Freightliner's motor cranking over to start, he abandoned the computer and went towards the sound. He left the shop and entered the garage, keeping low, bending at the waist as he went. He heard several gunshot blasts, four or fi e in succession and dived behind a pallet of motor oil. He peered around the cases, all he could see was the trailer attached to the truck.

Salas started to move forward when the truck's engine was shut off. He heard the door of the truck slam shut. He could hear Richard talking then another blast from a gun. The noise vibrated off the metal walls and roof of the building. Salas ducked and hid as the rear garage door opened. He could see a black car entering. Salas stayed by the side wall and sprinted to the rear door of the structure. He was hiding behind a large portable tool cart on wheels. Salas had a gun, but no ammo, thus he had no weapon. He had to hide.

Salas couldn't see the two men talking nor could he hear their conversation. He saw two men with Uzi's, the 45-caliber kind. He watched as Vincent went back into the cab of the Freightliner. Vincent exited the truck carrying a blue nylon gym bag. The bag had an Adidas logo on the side.

He heard doors slam and the car start, Salas eased around the tool cart as the car drove out of the garage into the swamp. Salas knelt by the water's edge and felt around under the tracks of the black car; he found a metal road, like a flat bridge extending under the water and into the swamp.

RICHARD

Richard watched as Salas disappeared in the darkness. He had stopped laughing but was still smiling as he advanced across the green grass of his front yard, behind the modular, and was now behind the guy who was shooting the shotgun. Richard walked up and stood behind Rod. Rod didn't hear a thing; he was staring blindly into the darkness. Richard saw three empty Coke cans at Rod's feet as Rod was looking down the driveway. Rod had the shotgun leaning against the concrete pallet and a bag of Doritos in his hand.

Richard struck Rod on the back of his head with the butt of the handgun. The big guy didn't know what had hit him and he fell hard on the gravel of the driveway. Richard took the shotgun, emptied the shells and threw the gun into the rose bushes in front of the house. Richard hog-tied Rod with Rod's own belt, his hands behind his back belted to his ankles.

He could hear a truck starting then the roar of the diesel as it came to life. Richard jogged into the garage and into the well-lit interior of the building. Holding his handgun steady, Richard walked along the length of the Freightliner shooting out the tires until his weapon was empty. This truck was going nowhere.

Vincent was furious as he shut off the diesel's motor. He climbed out of the truck, hitting the ground with both feet then walked around the front cab where he met Richard coming towards him.

"Vincent," Richard yelled smiling. He had his arms open wide looking to embrace his brother. "You won't believe this Vincent. My headaches, my headaches are...."

Vincent raised his .357 magnum and pulled the trigger. The gun exploded, the projectile hitting Richard in the forehead from less than three feet away. The back of Richard's head splattered against the wall, as a pink mist hung in the air. Richard's body flew back through the mist and landed hard on the floor. A bloody cloud floating where Richard once stood.

"You stupid, stupid man. You have cost me my life. Why couldn't you stay in your fucking room?" Vincent was yelling at his dead brother.

The rear door of the garage opened. It startled Vincent, and he spun around pointing his handgun at the car. The driver demonstrated no indecision, no hesitation. He pulled forward, stopping the Audi A7 as the car's front bumper touched Vincent's knees. The driver pushed a button allowing his window to come down.

"Put the gun on the floor Vincent," the driver said. Then he repeated it again only louder. "Put the gun on the floor Vincent. Now. Do it now."

Vincent did as he was told. Vincent looked at his dead brother Richard, then back at the Audi. He put his head in his hands and began to weep.

"What have I done?" Vincent screamed.

The driver and passenger side doors opened. Two large men, dressed in black suits, white shirts, black ties and black shoes stepped out of the car. They each had Israeli machine pistols in their hands. Both weapons were pointed at Vincent. Neither looked around the shop for others, neither looked away from the sobbing man standing in front of them.

The driver of the Audi approached Vincent, placing his hand on Vincent's chest and pushing him backward. He then kicked the .357 magnum handgun underneath the car.

The back door of the Audi opened. German stepped out. He was wearing the Italian suit; he rolled his head to the right pushing his hair behind his ears. He slowly walked toward Vincent.

"Vincent quit your sobbing. Be a man." German yelled again, "Vincent!"

Vincent tried to stop. He took his hands from his face. Looking down, he saw that his chest was heaving. High pitched yelps came from his body when he took a breath.

German slapped Vincent with an open hand across the face. The impact echoed in the garage. Vincent's head snapped to the side. German then took his hand and lifted Vincent's chin until Vincent's eyes met his.

"Vincent. Listen. Listen, Vincent. My friend." There was a long pause before German spoke again. "Hear those sirens? Do you? Everyone is coming Vincent. County police. State police. The FBI Vincent, perhaps even the fucking coastguard." German yelled out "coastguard."

German looked from side to side. He could hear but not yet see the sirens.

"Where is my money, Vincent?" German asked.

Vincent pointed to the truck. "In there."

"Get it, Vincent, get it now."

Vincent rushed over to the truck, with two large steps he went from the ground to the side door, opened it reached in and brought out the duffle bag filled with cash. He handed the bag to German.

"Tie him up," German told the driver. "Bind him. Place him in the trunk. Vincent, where are my nephews? Where are Marco and Raphael?"

"I don't know German. I don't know anything." Vincent was crying again.

German stepped back as the driver placed plastic ties around Vincent's wrists. The driver zipped them tight. Vincent yelped again, this time in pain.

"You will die very slowly, Vincent. There are 100 pounds of product in those toys. We cannot take the truck now. The tires have been shot. The police are on their way. I am out millions of dollars, Vincent. My friend." He led Vincent to the back of the car.

"Vincent, I will mail you piece by piece to my other, shall we say, friends. To let them know to never fuck with me. Piece by piece until you are dead." The driver pushed Vincent's head down and stuffed him into the trunk of the Audi. German tossed hair behind his ear and slammed the lid shut.

The three men got back into their car. German in the rear seat with the bag of cash. The driver started the Audi, drove through the garage, turned around in the driveway then exited back the way they came. He drove into the water where a metal roadway was two or three inches under the stale surface and grass of the swamp. One-hundred yards later the car turned left n a remote road and was gone.

GROFF, RJ, AND SALAS

Sheriff Groff parked the Ford truck by Salas's bike; he told Bob to guard the pickup. Bob, as before, placed his two front paws on the steering wheel and barked in response. The two men, RJ and Groff, approached the garage. Groff still wet from the crotch down, had his .38 revolver drawn. RJ had tossed the AR15 into the pond and was walking with a noticeable limp. His pant leg and boot were stained with blood.

They walked slowly, glancing from right to left. The sound of sirens grew louder, the Calvary on its way

Both men stopped and stepped back behind the tow truck, ducking for cover as a black sedan came out of the garage. The car turned around sharply, went back into the garage and exited through the back door of the building.

Inside the garage, Groff yelled, "Detective Salas, Richard Lopez, Vincent, you guys in here? Are you ok? This is the County Sheriff. Anyone that hears this, come out with your hands raised."

While Groff secured the area, RJ opened the rear door of the trailer. He saw his Fatboy; it was the third bike in. RJ unhooked the lower latch of the trailer, pulling out a long ramp hidden under the bed of the unit. RJ climbed into the back of the trailer and snapped open the ratchet straps on the first Harley in line. He backed the bike out of the trailer and down the ramp. He repeated the same with the second bike. The third Harley was his. First RJ checked the saddle bag. Deuce was there. He sighed in relief, closed the bag and loosened the ratchet straps securing the bike. Removing those, he backed his own bike down the ramp of the trailer.

Groff was kneeling over, bent at the waist, examining Richard Lopez's body. He looked back as the sirens were getting louder. The police were approaching the turn nearing the bridge to go over the pond.

RJ swung his right leg over the saddle of his bike. His damaged left leg could barely hold his weight. He grunted in pain. He took the barrel key out of his pants pocket, turned the machine to on, then stuffed the key back into his jeans. His thumb found the start button, he stopped. The gas tank lid was on wrong, the threads not matching, the lid was at an angel. RJ removed the gas cap to reset it. Once off, the end of a black rubbery tube popped out of the hole of the tank. RJ grabbed the rubber ending and pulled it out. It was a long black flexible tube. He took out his pocket knife, set the blade and made a small slit into the rubber. A white-yellow powder spilled out. RJ put it to his nose; he smelled gasoline. He licked the end of his finger and touched the powder then tasted it. He knew it was heroin.

"Sheriff Groff, here is what they were up to. Check each bike for this." RJ handed Groff he black tube.

"Dope. I told you it was drugs." The voice belonged to Salas. He was holding his leather jacket; his shirt was bloodied, the left sleeve dark red from shoulder to fingertips. He was carrying the bullet-proof vest Groff had given him. He was walking in from the direction of the rear of the building. Neither, Sheriff   roff r RJ seemed surprised Salas was alive.

Groff repeated RJ's steps; smell, lick, touch, taste. "Sum bitch. Gotta be a pound or two."

RJ looked again inside his gas tank. "Got another one." He reached in with two fingers, removed the tube and handed it to the Sheriff. Gasoline dripped on to the floor of the garage and on the wound of his leg. It burned, causing to RJ once again flinch.

Salas looked at Richard, or what was left of Richard, and turned away. He lifted the gas caps from the other two bikes RJ had backed out of the trailer. "Yup, more tubes in here. Bet they all have them."

"Listen, guys. I should get the hell out of here. I am on probation, I have what I need and don't need the police on my ass." RJ said as he patted his saddlebag and fired up his Harley.

"What about the guy that was shooting at you?" Salas asked.

"I don't know nothing. And don't want to hear a damn thing." Groff said as police cars were screaming in the front yard of the compound.

"He's taken care of." RJ saluted a two-finger salute and road out the back exit. He could barely see the metal track. Water sprayed right and left when he hit the swamp. He kept his wheel straight, praying the architects of the makeshift driveway were smart enough to build the road in a straight line and that no gators were crossing the bridge. With his headlight off he blended into the darkness. Nothing but the noise of the Vance Hines exhaust. It wasn't until a brake light signaled that he was slowing that you could tell a man on a motorcycle was out there.

Salas asked Groff, "Where the hell is Vincent?" as a dozen police officers stormed into the garage, their guns drawn.

RONNIE

Ronnie woke to Doris kissing him; he groaned in pain as she pulled him forward into a bear hug. The nurse arrived to remove the IV, EKG leads, and to get Ronnie to the restroom. A successful urination, albeit with a slight reddish glow signaled Ronnie's plumbing was working. The doctor in the white lab coat entered the room. She told Ronnie he was good to go. Paperwork was completed, and Doris escorted Ronnie to the exit, arm in arm. She was busy planning his dinner in her head. The sun was setting as they got into their cars.

Following Doris in his Chevy, he was tail-gaiting, Ronnie re-visited the man with the dead brown eyes, his questions, and his actions. Making money off the Aztecs? Who was tipped? Who was his boss? As he pulled his car on to his driveway, Ronnie realized he gave the man Captain Green's name. Tom Green would be next.

He slammed his car into park with a jolt that made the car's tires squeal. Ronnie drove the gear shift into reverse and backed out of the driveway. He was calling Doris's cell as he drove away from her, he could see her yelling his name. Fifteen minutes later he pulled the police-issue sedan into the parking lot of the Fort Wayne Police Department. He pushed a button on the key ring locking the car as he ran towards the building. The few steps he ran sent spasms into his low back and abdomen. He stopped, then restarted with a fast walk, then a slower pace. He waited for the elevator, bypassing the three flights of steps. It was nearing seven in the evening as Ronnie stepped on the detective's floor. Green's door was shut, and his office lights off. He turned, again with pain, went back down the elevator to his parked car. Walking and heavy breathing increased his discomfort.

Ronnie drove to Captain Green's home, every bump in the road sent shivers of pain down his spine. He had been to Green's house once before, just a few months ago during the Christmas holidays. The gated community was still under construction, security at the entrance not yet active as Ronnie sped past the brick structure built to house the future guard. The Green's had been in the house less than six months; it was one of few in the new neighborhood. Ronnie practically grew up in Green's former split-level home located just four houses down from his parent's current place.

The driveway to Green's house was lined with hedges and planted; mature coniferous trees. The driveway formed a large circle extending from the wooden garage doors to the front glass doors. The concrete driveway running the length of the house. Ronnie parked his car behind Green's black four-door Mercedes sedan. He walked past large picture windows. Turning his head to the right, he could see inside the home to a huge formal room, void of light, that expanded to the back end of the house. Strategically placed flood lights lighted the front walk way under the eaves of the roof. Each light designed to enhance the landscaping, the manicured lawn, and the etching of the brick siding.

Ronnie approached the front entryway, two wooden doors forming an arch that was nine feet tall. The door was open four to fi e inches, Ronnie slipped through, leaving the door as he found it. His eyes adjusted to the light, his boots squeaked on the marble floor. He could see a light coming from his left; he remembered the kitchen was that direction. Ronnie unclipped the latch holding his service weapon in the holster; he had his right hand on the butt of the handgun.

"Please don't hurt him!" A voice came piercing through the darkness. It was his Aunt Ginger, the wife of Captain Tom Green.

Ronnie drew his gun, both hands on the grip, his right index finger on the trigger. It was the first time he had drawn his gun away from the shooting range. He flipped a small lever on the grip; the gun was now ready to fire. With both arms extended he slid his feet forward. Ronnie's entire body was shaking.

"We had a deal, Thomas. We were to have unencumbered traffic through this city. You broke our deal." Ronnie recognized the voice as the man with the salt and pepper goatee and dead eyes.

Hearing the words, Ronnie turned the voice recorder of his cell phone to on. He then placed the phone with the audio receiver facing outward on his belt cell phone holster. He continued to creep forward.

"You guys are the ones who screwed up. I told you I would have a bust this week. It was part of the plan. I bust a few low-lifers, and you get your drugs through town. Tell Estrada he is at fault. You were supposed to be hauling a few ounces, not a few pounds." The voice was Captain Green's.

"You are helping these men run drugs through Fort Wayne?" Ginger asked.

"Shut up you fool. How do you think we get all the shit you want." Green yelled at Ginger.

"I didn't want this house. I didn't want your Mercedes or your Rolex." Ginger snapped back.

"Quiet you love birds." The goateed man said softly. "You can quarrel later. Tom, we need reimbursed for our loss. One million dollars will cover you."

"Hell, take it. It is in my safe. I don't give a shit anymore. The combination is 33-23-15. Take it all and get the hell out of here. Tell Estrada I am done." Green yelled at the man.

"We have a million dollars in our safe?" Ginger gasped.

Ronnie turned the corner walking into the kitchen. He was in a shooter's stance; his weapon pointed at the man with the goatee. The kitchen area was larger than Ronnie's house. An island with a granite top lined by fi e high-back bar stools separated his relatives from the hooded oven, stove and double-doored refrigerator. Aunt Ginger was sitting in a kitchen dining room chair. She wore a white saffron dress with two-inch heels; the dressed was pushed up on her thighs. Her hair was pulled back, a widow's peak hairline. Her arms were secured to the armrests by silver tape. Uncle Tom was in the same position beside her, his arms also trapped to the armrest by tape, his ankles connected to the footrest of the bar stool. The man with dead eyes was standing beside Tom; he had a meat cleaver in his hand. All three looked at Ronnie. Ronnie aimed the gun at the man with dead eyes. The barrel of the weapon was shaking.

"Run Ronnie! Run," yelled Doris.

"Shoot this son of a bitch, Ronnie," barked Tom.

"Ronald. You are out of the hospital already. I must be losing my touch," the man said.

"Tom. Is it true? Are you running drugs?" Ronnie asked. He was trying to hold the gun steady. His hands were shaking; his knees were buckling. He couldn't hold his weapon up much longer. He could feel his back cramping, his abdomen was in spasm, the wave of nausea returning.

"Shut the fuck up and shoot Ronnie," Tom yelled.

"Yes Ronald, your boss is on our side. I apologize as I was told it was the guy on TV, the one taking all the credit. I assumed a young millennial could be bought. Not an old goat like this," the man said as he pointed at Tom. The man with dead eyes smiled at Ronnie as he raised the cleaver.

Ronnie pulled the trigger. The gun exploded. The force of the discharge threw Ronnie's hands upward. He accidentally pulled the trigger again with the second shot splattering drywall and paint from the ceiling. Ronnie fell to his back, hitting his head on the floor. He dropped his weapon as he scrambled back to his feet, his right side in spasms, the pain shooting into his abdomen. Ronnie winced grabbing his stomach with both hands. He looked at the man with brown skin, the goatee, and dead eyes. The man's mouth was opened wide in surprise. He had his hand to his chest. Blood was seeping through his fingers, dripping to the floor. He looked Ronnie in the eye, then dropped to his knees and fell to his shoulder. The man with dead brown eyes was dead.

"Get this tape off me, Ronnie. Now." Tom said as Ronnie was lost, staring at the dead man on the floor. "Now. Ronnie cut me free," Tom yelled again.

Ronnie came back to the present. "No, Tom. I'm calling the police. You are under arrest."

"Listen you little cocksucker; I will bury you. Cut me free now." Tom yelled struggling to be free from the silver tape.

Ronnie dialed 911. "This is Ronnie Higgenbotham, badge number 155. I am at the home of Captain Tom Green. There is a man down. We need medical services, more police. More police now. More detectives too. More of everything."

As he took the silver tape off his Aunt Ginger's arms, he read Captain Tom Green his rights then added "I have you recorded on my cell Tom. That, plus the million dollars in your safe. I think you are going to be going to jail for a while."

Within minutes the house was alive with police officers, medical personnel, fellow detectives and the assistant to District Attorney. Next to arrive were two Federal Marshalls and a local FBI agent. When police are told to go to the Captain's home with a man down, you get all the key players. Ronnie gave his first statement. Ginger was hauled away in the ambulance after she hyperventilated and passed out. Ronnie had to lie down. The medics gave him oxygen. Green was still taped to the chair asking for his lawyer.

RJ

R J rode his Harley, staying under the posted speed limit. Riding a motorcycle with blood covering your leg and a bullet wound was nothing you wanted to explain to the police because of a routine speeding ticket.

He had to stop twice, first because he needed fuel and a restroom to wash the blood from his hands. The next stop was for directions. It was after midnight. The streets were filled with bikers. RJ pulled into a liquor store parking lot/ While sitting on his Harley; he asked two kids in a Chrysler Minivan how to get to Daytona. The two boys gave directions then asked him to buy a six pack. He ignored the request and rode towards the ocean. The closer he got to Daytona, the larger the crowds, the greater the traffic and there were far more police were on the roads.

Riding down AIA, he passed his Super 8 Hotel and continued to Big John Ballard's Jiffy Lube. RJ rode past the building once, made a u-turn in the middle of the street to ride past the business again. He rode slowly, looking for people. He spotted the lookout, a kid, in the Son's colors, standing at the rear entrance of the store. The outdoor light gave RJ a full view of the young man. He could see Big John in the waiting room. John was sitting behind the desk looking at a computer.

RJ parked his Harley a block down the street on the same side of the highway as the store. He didn't have a weapon and wondered if he should wait until he was better prepared. He decided against it. By this time tomorrow, Big John would know his plan had failed and would be under heavy security.

Approaching the back-entrance RJ easily walked up on the kid who was supposed to be on guard. The young prospect had his face down, staring at the screen of his cell phone. RJ put his hand over the kid's mouth, pulling him in tight.

RJ whispered in the young recruit's ear: "Listen. I am going to let you go if you be quiet. You don't want to look at me. You don't want to know who I am. Understand?"

The kid nodded. His mouth and nose covered by RJ's hand.

"You are going to stay quiet and run the other way as fast as you can, and as far away as you can. You are not for any reason going to look back here or come back here. Ever. Do you understand?" RJ asked the kid. "Nod if you understand." The kid nodded as fast as his head could go up and down.

"Now listen again. You go back home to your parents. I want you to go to college. Never associate with pigs like John Ballard. Do you understand?" RJ asked.

There was no answer. RJ said, "Nodding would be advised."

The kid nodded faster than the last time. RJ let him go, and the boy took off running. RJ watched the kid run for two blocks. The young man did as he was told and didn't look back.

RJ walked through the front door of the store as if he was there to get his oil changed. Hearing the sound, Big John looked up, and his face went pale.

"RJ, how did you? Good to see you again RJ." John stood, the chair kicked back against the wall making a cracking noise. John was looking left to right and over RJ's shoulders. He was sweating, maybe he always sweated.

"The kid at the back door. He went home. It is just you and me John."

"Well, so it seems. What brings you here so late at night RJ?

"Question is Big John, why are you here so late? Are you waiting for someone?" RJ asked. John was still looking. Looking around frantically, trying to see anyone, hoping someone would walk into the store.

"I, I don't know what you are talking about RJ. I am finishing some bookwork on the stores. You know how it is. An owner's job is never done. I am just burning the midnight oil."

"Have you talked to your little brother John? You know, the one with the phony southern drawl. The one that talks too slow, thinks too slow, and is currently missing," RJ said.

"What? What are you talking about missing? Where is he? What did you do to him?" Big John was sweating even more. Droplets of moisture forming on his lip, water dripping from his chin.

"Let's just say he won't be coming back."

"You son of a bitch. What did you do to him?" Big John Ballard asked. You could sense he was scared, unsure of what to do next.

"He was shooting at me, John. He actually shot me. Once. He also shot a good friend of mine too." RJ showed John Ballard his leg.

"I don't know what the hell you are talking about RJ," John proclaimed.

"Why John? Why did you try and kill me? Just so you can run dope under our colors. You think you can peddle that crap up and down the coast? Cause you know it won't happen as long as I am alive and that's why you put out the hit isn't it? Ain't that right John?" RJ asked, his face was red. Blood still dripping from the gunshot wound in his thigh.

Big John reached into his desk; he pulled out a handgun, a .44 magnum. John raised his arm to point the weapon at RJ. RJ reached across the desk and grabbed John's wrist. He twisted it at a downward angle, John's arm folded at the elbow. John's body turned away from RJ to relieve the pressure. His elbow, hand and gun went behind John's back. John's hand cramping from the intense pressure of the wrist and arm lock. The cramping caused his finger to bend, the trigger finger. John's entire hand cramped, his fingers forming a fist, his index finger closed in and squeezed the trigger. He squeezed the trigger of his own gun. The .44 exploded within the confines of the small building. Big John Ballard had just shot himself in the lower back with a .44 magnum, the most powerful handgun in the world.

The bullet ripped through his spine exiting through the bottom of his enormous belly. John slowly fell to the floor as RJ released the wrist lock. Four-hundred pounds of dead weight molting on the ground. Blood was seeping out both bullet holes. Big John was paralyzed from the waist down. He couldn't move his toes. John had blown out his spine and was now going to bleed to death.

"It sucks to be you, John Ballard. Who would have thought you and your piece of shit brother would die on the same day? Your mother will be so proud," RJ said.

Big John wailed in pain. He was trying to touch his lower back, but his arms were not long enough to reach there. He then tried to stop the flow of blood stemming from the front exit wound. His aorta was hit, he would bleed out in minutes.

"Well, I'll be off John. When you get to hell, tell your brother hello for me. Oh, and you can keep the gun. You may even want to use it one more time," RJ added as he went to the front exit. He shut off the lights as he left he building.

RJ was walking towards his bike when he heard another explosion from the .44 magnum. He didn't look back; he didn't hesitate. RJ got on his Harley and rode south. He was ten blocks away from Big John's Jiffy Lube when he passed a young man in a leather vest running, sprinting as fast as he could in the opposite direction of Big John.

SALAS

The sun was an hour away from peeking over the horizon by the time Sheriff Groff and Salas finished giving the officers oral and written statements. The crime scene techs were still taking pictures. Salas had walked the FBI agents through the events of the evening, then repeated the same process with two Florida detectives. Groff played out the same scenario from his point of view, focusing more on the alligators and the crocodile.

The police officers found Rod tied up. He was crying like a baby and telling the detectives everything they wanted to hear. The agents had to tell Rod to slow down as he was talking so fast. He waived his rights and told them everything Vincent had them do over the past few months. Rod told them about the man named German, Marco and Raphael. He talked of shooting the shotgun at Richard and another guy. He said he saw guys loading drugs into the safe in the mobile home. He said he and Terry and Jake had been stealing motorcycles for nearly a year. He admitted he even fed three dead people to the gators. He said he didn't know who they were or who killed them, but Vincent was the one who gave him the bodies to dispose of.

Next, the police found Marco; the muscle man was alive but beat to shit. He was unconscious, thus wasn't as talkative as Rod. Of course, even if he was awake, he couldn't speak as his jaw appeared to be broken and his face was so swollen he could not see anything but the back of his eyelids. The police carried Marco away in a county ambulance. The silver tape still wrapped around his forehead.

The investigators found Terry, minus the back of his skull, and Raphael with a screwdriver lodged under his chin. Salas described how Richard took out Terry and the difficulty of the shot. Salas admitted to killing Raphael showing the detectives the bruise from the shot he took in the chest and the dent in the bulletproof vest. They covered Richard's body with a field blanket and bagged the .357 Smith and Wesson. Two men were still working on Raphael's body.

Groff said nothing about the deer rifle shooter taken under the water by the alligators. He was relieved to hear Vincent had fed dead bodies to the beasts. If they found body parts of the shooter, it could now be explained. Groff told the officers he found the AR 15, emptied the clip on the gators, then threw the weapon in disgust at an alligator in the pond.

Neither, Groff or Salas mentioned RJ or German. No one knew who the drugs belonged to, or where the drugs were going. They only said Vincent took off in a black car and showed them the rear garage door and hidden roadway through the swamp.

Salas was told he could leave, he got on his Harley and rode across the bridge leaving Groff alone with the other police officers. He rode without thinking about where to go and ended up on highway AIA along the coast, the beach and the waves. He rode his Harley to the water's edge. Salas had read about riding your motorcycle on the sands of Daytona Beach, and today he was doing it. He was the only bike on the beach. The sun was rising.

Today would be his third day in Daytona. Salas had been awake every day by six in the morning. He had yet to see the sun rise over the ocean. He had yet to visit a bar, a concert or a bike show. He had yet to have a beer. Three days in Daytona and beside the Loop, this was his first rally experience.

Salas stopped the bike on the sand. He turned off the motor and sat on his Harley. His left arm was covered in blood and ached. He felt nauseous. He needed a bath; he smelled a metallic smell, the smell of blood. Salas thought about jumping in the ocean while looking and listening to the water crash on the beach. He thought better of it as the salt water might not be a good idea on a bullet wound.

Salas studied a man by the water's edge. He was in a catcher's position, like in a baseball game. The guy stood and stretched his leg, he had a ponytail and a Son's vest. It was RJ; he held an urn in his hands. Salas could tell RJ was talking to the ceramic vase. RJ was talking to Deuce.

Salas watched as RJ slowly poured the black and gray ashes on the sand of Daytona Beach. The waves approached, and the ashes disappeared.

RJ faced the ocean and did a two-finger salute.

Deuce was laid to rest on Daytona Beach.

VINCENT

German's driver drove deeper into the confines of central and very rural Florida. Gone were the beaches, hotels, chain restaurants, and office complexes. The Audi turned down a deserted road; green weeds were growing through the cracks in the asphalt. The lane was edged by downed trees, a wooden fence outlining the property was collapsing under its own rotten weight. The driver slowed to a stop, allowing an alligator to cross the road; it wobbled along in no hurry to pass. The car pulled in front of a large building. A garage door was open; the Audi drove inside. The building, an abandoned feed mill, was long since vacated and left to decompose in the hot Florida sun and humidity. A yellow and green sign, bleached by years of exposure, read "Hoover Feeds." The painted sign covered the lower half of the concrete silo. The driver stopped the car inside a long vertical tube, once used to store grain. The ceiling of the storage bin was thirty or forty feet in the air. Moonlight broke through lost shingles. The walls of the mill were old and treated with oil to prevent moisture. The place smelled of grain, corn or wheat. You could see dust hanging in the air as it danced in the headlights from the car. The movement of the head lights sent small creatures running for safety. Mice, rats, squirrels, and a fox ran outside through the open door. You could smell the odor of a prior visit by a skunk.

Three passengers exited the Audi. The driver stood next to the automobile as he punched the key twice to pop open the rear hatch while the other man with the Uzi scanned the building more for animals than enemies. The driver reached into the trunk and yanked Vincent out by the plastic ties holding his wrists together. He was pulled out forcefully and fell to the concrete floor of the mill. Vincent cried out in pain. He sat up on his knees, head down as if he was going to pray.

"Good news Vincent. I've changed my mind, my friend. I have decided to make this quick. This will be easier for me, and for you, Vincent. I have better things to do than keep you alive," German said. He was standing over Vincent.

"German, please. You agreed it was a good plan." Vincent pleaded his case. "You agreed, just like me; you thought it would work. It was those fucking bikers German. It was that gang. The Son's or something like that. That was the name of them. It was those guys that killed your boys, Marco and Raphael." Vincent had tears running down his cheeks, and his nose was running snot from his nose to his mouth.

"You said you didn't know where the twins were. Are you lying now or were you lying then, Vincent?" German responded.

"I didn't lie. I was confused. I was in shock. For God's sake German, I had just shot and killed my brother. Someone had to pay. It was my brother Richard that betrayed me. So, I killed him. I killed him for you, German."

German put his hair behind his ears. "What else do you know Vincent? Is that it?"

"The bikers are with the Son's. Their leader, his name are initials like JR or JT or TJ, no wait, RJ. Yes, it was RJ. The guy that killed them is named RJ." Vincent wiped the tears from his cheeks. He was regaining his color. He felt hope. He looked up at German and smiled. "Yes German, it was RJ. We need to kill him and all his gang members. Kill them before they come for us."

"Very well Vincent. Thank you." German nodded to the driver. "Stand up Vincent. Be a man and maybe I will let you live."

Vincent stood.

The driver opened the button of his suit coat and pulled out a small caliber pistol from a concealed shoulder holster. It was a Walther .22 caliber. Without hesitation, the driver shot Vincent in the shin. Vincent fell back to his knees. He was screaming in pain.

The other man, dressed in black, grabbed Vincent under his arms, lifting and dragging him to a wooden support beam. The rounded beam, a pole near the entrance of the mill. He forced Vincent to stand. Vince grabbed the pole, hugging it as if it were his savior. German turned Vince to face him.

"Look at me. Look at me, Vincent," German said.

Vincent raised his head and met German's eyes, his back to the pole. The man in black tied Vince to the support beam by the elbows. His wrists still bound, the elbows flared out as if he was trying to fly. Vince screamed again. They tied a rope around Vincent's legs, securing both to the pole. This too elicited more screaming.

"You are so weak, Vincent. Your father would be ashamed of you," German said as he turned to his driver. "Diego. Shoot our friend in the belly."

A shot rang out. Another scream. Blood was pouring through his shirt and through the wound in his leg. A puddle of blood was accumulating on the floor.

"Vincent. My friend. I will let you live. No more shooting. No beatings. No cutting off our fingers or genitals."

"Thank you. Thank you, German. I owe you. You truly are my friend," Vincent yelled out, crying.

"We will leave you now. The blood, I love the smell of blood. I think our friends the rats, the mice, the alligators, perhaps a bobcat or a coyote may enjoy the smell and taste of blood too. What do you think Vincent?" German asked, again the hair flip.

"No. No German. No. They will eat me. Eat me alive," Vincent screamed.

"Hmmm. Perhaps you should sink down to your butt and let the rodents or the gators eat the rope off your arms first. Or perhaps they would rather eat your arm than plastic. Either way, you may escape. Let them decide. Yes, that would work. Or maybe they will eat one of your legs first. That would loosen the ropes and allow you to get the other leg free and kick at the coyotes. Oh, I wish I could stay and watch."

"You cannot do this German. German, have you no soul? German!" Vince screamed.

The three men got back into the car, German in the back seat. They drove away, again slowing for a gator to cross. They left Vincent tied to the pole, standing in a pool of blood. Vincent was alone. The dust settling on him. He was screaming. As the car traced its tracks down the lane, the driver slowed as an alligator crossed their path. The reptile heading into the building.

An hour and thirty minutes later the Audi passed a security guard standing beside a small brick structure the size of an outhouse which was wedged between two lanes of traffic. A water fountain sat behind the guard with four lines of water shooting up and lazily falling back to the surface. The guard recognized the car and waved it through. The Audi didn't slow down.

The car approached a large house, even in the darkness, you could feel the ocean. The depth of blackness behind the home extended past the curve of the earth. The driver pulled to the right as he approached the house. He pushed a button on the visor, a two-car garage door opened with the light turning on, filling the driveway. The Audi pulled into an expansive garage. The door closing behind them as the car parked. Beside the Audi sat a red Ferrari, beside it a 57 Chevy, beside it a Ford Shelby GT 500, beside it a Ford Aerostar van. The floor of the garage was painted as a black and white checkerboard. The five vehicles all faced a wall of cabinets. The Cabinets were decorated with glass doors. Inside the custom wood were rows of cleaning fluids, oils, glass cleaners, and leather cleaning supplies, degreasers, bug removers and lotions that made tires glisten.

German and the driver exited the car, then went through a double-wide door into the house. The third man stayed in the garage. He went to the cleaning supplies, removing what he needed, and went to work detailing the Audi.

Inside the home, standing in front of a wall of windows, German enjoyed the view of the Atlantic Ocean and the waves pounding the sand. The yard lights highlighted over fifty yards of private beach. "Ah, I love St. Augustine, Diego. Tell me. Do you feel we should hit these bikers? The Son's and this man RJ?"

"You are asking me, German? You know what you need to do," Diego said.

"Yes, I guess I do. How big is this club, we need to know. Could we be in a war, perhaps causing more problems than we solve?" German asked Diego.

"They are not the Hell's Angels. Some local club with weak men and weak minds. We send them a message, and they will break. Allow me to send the message."

"Call Sanchez and that Irish asshole McGinnis. Have them meet us here in an hour. Let's hit the bikers before they know why. Find their little clubhouse. Let's start there."

"What about me and Danny, we can do it. We do not need to outsource this," Diego countered.

"You saw Danny. He is weak. He threw-up. He cried for shit's sake. He is the broken one. Not tonight but next week. I want Danny taken care of. You understand Diego? There has been enough killing for today. Danny is next week's project. Be sure and feed him to those alligators he loves so much. A fitting end to his meaningless life," German said. "Use Sanchez and McGinnis. Point the blame at them. This way we are in the clear."

"Yes, German. As you wish."

"And you Diego. You enjoy killing too much. After Danny, I think you need a vacation. Maybe you go to Puerto Vallarta. There you will find the men you like."

It was two hours before Sanchez, McGinnis, Diego, and German sat down in German's den. The office was an east wall of windows with a view of the beach. The north wall was bookshelves, thirty rows high, sporting a ladder on rollers to get to the top. The wood was all a dark mahogany. The bookshelves, the ladder, and the desk were matching grains. The men sat in leather chairs with gold buttons. The south wall was a credenza supporting pictures of German with his children, German with his wife, German with several Jaguars football players and German with President Obama.

Diego had the address of the biker's club. "We go. We destroy them. We leave," Diego said.

"Kill them. Two for Marco and two for Raphael." German said as he looked at each man. He was drinking red wine as he spoke. German placed his nose inside the wine glass and took a deep breath, inhaling through his nostrils. "Aaaaaggghhhh. A pure Bordeaux. I love French wines."

"You drinking wine for breakfast? What the fuck?" Sanchez said.

Diego looked at Sanchez and said, "While you sleep, we work. Thus, why you are low-end scum to us. Do you wish to work today or die?"

"Sorry man, I didn't mean nothing by it," Sanchez responded

Ignoring the conversation, McGinnis asked, "Can we trust this address? Trust the source?" He was talking to Diego.

"Yes, we have intel within the police system. They are never wrong. They cannot afford to be incorrect," German said before Diego could speak. German was terse as he said it. He didn't like McGinnis, but he served a purpose.

The Irishman, Sanchez, and Diego exited the den, leaving German looking at the ocean and the early morning sun.

Once in the Ford van, the three-man hit team drove to Waldo, Florida, a two-hour drive from the beach. As Diego drove, the two passengers cleaned their weapons. The shooter's weapons of choice were Uzi's with 16- round magazines. They were fully automatic weapons, illegal in the United States but easy to obtain with the right amount of money. McGinnis also placed a 9 mm in the back of his pants; he never went anywhere without his 9 mm.

It was decided Sanchez and McGinnis would be the shooters. Diego was the driver and would wait in the van. German trusted them but wanted Diego to supervise.

The men arrived at the address in Waldo. Diego drove past the clubhouse then circled back. He was looking for cars, morning walkers, or joggers. The Son's building was a metal structure; metal frame with metal sidewalls and a metal roof. It was hurricane-proof but not hit-team proof. Diego pulled into the parking lot, made a short and tight U-turn parking in front of the building's entrance. His vehicle was parked facing the street, ready to move.

McGinnis and Sanchez got out of the van as if exiting a cab to go to an opera; they left he van's side panel door open.

Sanchez went to kick in the front door, hesitated then leaned forward and turned the doorknob. The door opened with ease and the two men entered.

Opening the doors allowed a bright glare of morning sunshine to enter, blinding the men inside. The men sitting on the sofa could see only the outlines of two men. They looked more like angels with the sun on their backs than killers.

Sanchez opened fire pointing his Uzi towards the three men on the couch. They were dead before they saw who walked in. Three soon to be dead men had bullets hitting their face, chests, and upper arms. Their screams were short bursts like the shots that rained down on them.

McGinnis fired to the right at two men sitting at a card table. They were playing cribbage, both shot multiple times and killed, dead before they hit the concrete floor. Neither of the card players had even bothered to look in the direction of the open doors. They too never saw who shot them.

The two shooters stood over their targets. Smoke still creeping out of the short barrels of the Uzis. The noise settled. It was eerily quiet; there was no crying or moaning. All were dead. You could hear the blood oozing on the floor; it made a slithering sound as if a snake was crossing in front of them.

Sanchez and McGinnis looked around, staying in the main room of the building. They kept their backs to each other. There was no movement, no sounds. Sanchez gave a signal, no speaking and the two men backed out of the building, facing the inside of the room. McGinnis was last out.

Diego had the car running, the door open and the air conditioning on high. Sanchez came out of the building first, his back to the auto. Once clear of the door, Sanchez turned lowered his head and entered the van, he scooted over to the window seat looking for McGinnis who came out next, same positioning as Sanchez. As McGinnis turned to enter the van, a man carrying a shotgun came around the side of the building and fired.

McGinnis was hit in the back. A 12-gauge fired from less than 10 feet. His intestines came out from the front exit wound; he was blown in two. Blood, body tissue and McGinnis's soul were thrust into the van. The man with the shotgun, his eyes were now locked on Sanchez. There was no emotion from Sanchez; he looked at the man that was going to shoot him. Diego was trying to get his gun from the holster, but the over-the-shoulder seat belt trapped his weapon.

"Go. Go," yelled Sanchez to Diego as the shotgun blasted again. Sanchez's face and the side window glass of the Aerostar showered the asphalt.

A third blast from the shotgun took the van's driver's side headrest and the back of Diego's head. Brain matter, blood, and pieces of the headrest sprayed the inside of the front windshield.

The van was parked, the motor was still running. The echo of the shotgun blasts had vibrated away. The man with the shotgun stood over McGinnis; he was breathing hard with sweat rolling into his eyes. Anthony Aaron Anderson dropped the shotgun on the concrete, blood splattering on his pants and boots. Anthony turned and ran inside the clubhouse. There on the floor, a cribbage board by his side, playing cards scattered over his chest, lay the body of Will Dosier. Dozer was dead. Tripp pulled his hair back behind his ears and took a cell phone out of his back pocket. Tripp dialed RJ.

RJ

Salas and RJ were sitting in a booth near the rear entrance of a Daytona Beach McDonald's, the seats made of Naugahyde, their rear ends stuck to the booth. The two men looked tired. After taking a shower at the beach, a cold shower at best, Salas had gotten most of his blood and the blood of Raphael off his arms. He drip-dried and re-dressed. Salas threw away the bloody 2015 Sturgis Rally shirt, switching it for a Daytona Bike Week long-sleeve T. He picked the shirt out off a rack of clothes that were sitting on hangers in front of a souvenir shop right off the beach. Two shirts for $25.00. He got Ronnie a medium.

RJ still had on the same jeans, one leg blue, the other a dark crimson, but no one seemed to notice. Both men had finished their egg McMuffin breakfast. They were talking about how good a bed would feel and getting some sleep after being awake for over thirty hours. Through the window of the McDonald's, they could see a group of men preparing for a bike show. Yellow cones marked off each section; a large banner was being hung between street lights. Two men with a Dodge Ram truck and a goose-neck enclosed trailer were unloading three motorcycles. Customized bikes with special paint jobs and all the chrome they could handle. RJ recognized a Bourget Dragon Softail and a V8 Chopper. The third bike was, used to be, a Harley, now dressed out in flames with extended front forks, eighteen-inch apes with the metal saddlebags skimming the street. More men in more pickups with more trailers were waiting in line to unload.

RJ's cell phone vibrated. He glanced at the screen as he said hello. He cupped the receiver and said to Salas, "It's Tripp" as he took a sip of coffee.

"Yeah, what's up?" RJ listened intently. Several minutes passed. RJ listened, his face was blank, no emotion, then he asked, "How many are dead?"

He had Salas's attention.

RJ stood, ear still to his phone. He took a twenty-dollar bill out of his leather wallet, laid it on the table and spoke again into the mouthpiece." Stay there I'm on my way. And no, don't call the police."

Salas grabbed the twenty; they had already paid at the counter when they got the fast food. RJ wasn't concerned about the money. They walked out the door. Salas said, "You going to tell me what is going on? Is Sami ok?"

"Yes. Sorry, I should have said that. She is fine. Not your worry brother. I have to get to Waldo." RJ reached in his front pocket getting the key to his Harley.

"Waldo? Where's Waldo?" Salas pursed his face together, his eyebrows up. "Are you shitting me?"

RJ was on his bike. "Mike, I've got five of my men dead, and the three men that did the hit are lying dead in the front of our building. I have to get there and straighten this out. See who did this."

"I'm in; I can help. And we aren't arguing about it." Salas started his bike, hit the kickstand up and followed RJ out of the fast food parking lot to find Waldo, Florida.

RJ did not have a GPS on his Harley but seemed to know the way. He kept the speed about five miles per hour over the limit. They stopped for gas at a Chevron. Neither man spoke. They were at the station less than eight minutes.

Finally, Salas saw a sign that read, "Waldo 20 miles".

They rode through residential housing, by a mobile home and RV park. The two men rode past retail businesses, auto repair shops, and restaurants. They then passed construction sites, cement plants, storage facilities and into the warehouse district, all void of people on a Saturday.

RJ took a right, his body leaning hard into the turn, the Harley's tailpipes just missed scratching the road. They went through an open gate into the parking lot facing a warehouse. A metal building sat in front of them. A blue Ford van sat parallel to the front doors.

They parked their bikes behind the van, the engines rattled and coughed as the motors relaxed. Salas and RJ stared at another dead body.

Tripp came out of the warehouse. RJ got off his bike, the two men embraced. RJ stood with his arm around the shoulder of the young man. Tripp then led RJ and Salas into the clubhouse, showing them more dead bodies. He showed them Dozier. RJ rubbed his eyes; he knew these men. They were his brothers, club members, his friends. Dozer was just a kid.

Salas listened as Tripp walked them through what happened.

"We left the girls, Mr. Salas. We needed clean clothes and cash, so we rode over this morning, I'm sure the girls are still sleeping." Tripp looked at Salas while he said this. "It is about a four-hour ride. I fi ured we would be back in time to watch them tonight."

Tripp continued. "When we got here, the guys were watching the news, having coffee. Will, Dozer, he asked Paulie to play a hand of cribbage. Dozer loves, loved, the game. So, I went to my room to throw some clothes in my backpack and then all hell broke loose. I heard guns firing, screaming. I grabbed my 12 gauge and went out the side door. I keep the gun loaded, I know I shouldn't, but it always has been since the day Deuce gave it to me. So, I see these two guys; they are carrying guns, looked like machine guns. I see them getting into the van. So, I shot them. I shot them RJ. I killed them, and I killed the driver too." Tripp spoke calmly. He had no remorse. He reacted as if he was trained that way, more of a Marine than a 23-year-old kid. "They killed Dozer, RJ. He was my friend. Why? Why did they do this?"

Salas said to the two men, "I got the license plate number of the van, let me check for IDs on the bodies. I will call it in, off the record. See who these assholes are." Salas was getting on his cell.

"And RJ, have you heard? Ballard, Big John was hit too. He is dead." Tripp added as Salas walked away.

Salas looked at RJ, RJ returned the stare. Salas knew there was going to be hell to pay. RJ was in a different zone. His face was stoic, his body alert, he had bloodlust in his eyes.

"Ballard wasn't part of this Tripp. I will take care of that myself. For now, call Junior, Junior Delos Santos. He will clean this up. The three shooters, we will dump them in a landfill or the swamp. As for our team, we will have a proper service for all of them."

RJ took the young man by the shoulder again. "Tripp, you did good. I am very proud of you. But son, I want you out of this. You have to go. You cannot be tied to this in any way. You have your whole life ahead of you. You are done with this life. This isn't for you. This is your last time here. Pack what you need, you are going to Chicago a few months early."

"But RJ, I want the guy that ordered this hit. I want the guy that killed Dozer," Tripp said.

"You got them, Tripp. You avenged his death. You did your part. Now let me do mine. This is at the next level. This is my job now." RJ still had his arm around Anthony.

SALAS

Salas dialed a familiar number. Ronnie answered as if he was expecting the call.

"Mike," Ronnie said, "You are not going to believe what happened."

"Yeah Ronnie I would like to hear, but I have a pressing issue right now."

"But Mike it is about Captain Green. I sho.." Ronnie was interrupted

"Ronnie, no time. Serious Ronnie. I got dead men here buddy. This is all out; shit has hit the fan right now. I need you to focus on this at this very minute. Green can wait. Got it?" Salas said.

"Yes sir, yes I understand. I can do that. What databases do you want me to explore?" Ronnie asked.

"I have a couple of dead guys, so someone else may be tracking this too or snooping around. Thing is, this is a "no one knows they are dead yet but us" scenario. Got it? We do not want the police to know. No FBI. No one else. The snooping may not happen for a few days. So, cover your tracks."

"Easy enough. Are you in trouble Salas? What have you gotten yourself into? You realize you are just on vacation. Can't you just vacate? How do you get into these situations, Mike?"

"I may have extended myself beyond the current limits of my professional code of ethics. You know I tend to make decisions based on how I feel at the time," Salas said.

"That you do, and you have a broader set of limits than most of us Salas, but it usually works out. What do you need me to find? How can I help?" Ronnie asked.

"Like I said, three dead guys only two IDs and a Florida license plate number. Again, there can be no trace of your searches." Salas said.

Salas fed Ronnie the info. With Ronnie repeating the numbers and names for accuracy.

"This won't take long. I already have the van's owner and address. Let me check backgrounds on everyone. Give me 15 minutes." Ronnie hung up the phone leaving Salas looking at a blank screen.

Salas walked through the crime scene again, this time alone. He was visualizing each move. Each angle of the shooter and each movement of the victims. He identified shell casings, blood spatter, bullet holes in the drywall and floor. He could tell where each man sat on the couch, where they were hit and how they ended on the floor or on each other. The men at the card table, one shot in the back, multiple times. Dozer took two rounds to the chest and one to the throat. None of the men had a weapon on them, not even a pocket knife.

Back outside, the sun climbing, the heat index rising, Salas traced the steps of Tripp and his exit out the side door. Tripp shot the first man in the back from close range with a shotgun. Salas guessed four-shot 12 gauge; it was an ugly wound. The back-entry point was less than two inches. In the front, the man's belly was blown wide open, intestines, blood, and the stomach contents still leaking out.

The second shot by Tripp hit the man in the van square in the face. The shot also took out the window of the Aerostar as gun pellets and body matter shattered the glass. The body was leaning back against the side door, still in the seat.

The driver was buckled up in the driver's seat of the van, his face was blown forward and hit the windshield. You could not see through the glass. The front window was intact, not a crack in it. The glass was covered with an inner layer of body tissue, blood, and stuffing from the headrest. The body was held upright by the safety belt, perfect posture. Blood was everywhere, it had been over two hours since the shooting, and the smell was getting worse. The flies had found the bodies quickly.

Salas pocket vibrated, he swiped his phone to the right and answered. "What you got?"

"Mike don't hang on me this time when I am done. Ok? I have got to tell you something," Ronnie yelled into the phone.

"Ok. I got it. Talk to me, Ronnie." Salas said

"Ok. The Ford Aerostar van is licensed to German, I think the G is like an H, but I will call him German. German Hernandez. Now you wouldn't think a hit team would use their own vehicle but in this case the owner of the car. Well, this guy is connected. Knows everyone, a high roller. Friends with the president of the Jacksonville Jaguars, former Governor Bush, and many others. But I do not see where he gets his money. And he has a lot of it. No tax records. German was born in Guatemala, moved to the States when he was a kid. I've never been to Guatemala. That reminds me, my parents took me to Costa Rica once it was a lovely place. Doris and I are considering…"

"Ronnie, German." Salas interrupted. "Is German dirty. Was the van stolen?"

"Yes, yes. Well. German is a US citizen, and he did it the old-fashioned way as his parents applied for citizenship and followed the legal process. Parents are deceased. German is married with three kids. Lives in a four-million-dollar house on the beach in St. Augustine. Very extravagant. Did you know you can see most of the homes on the County Treasurer's websites? And then, of course, I like google maps where you can zoom in on the home from the satellite."

"Please, Ronnie we are on a short time frame here buddy. And I thought you had something very important to tell me," Salas interrupted him.

"Yes, yes I do. I just get lost in the research. I will dig into more of his finances later but let it be said, that yes, he is dirty. He has a storied background of several affiliations with nefarious individuals. My initial search says he is related to a drug cartel. Rumor is that he is missing three fingers. As a kid, he saw the cartel kill a guy. The opposing drug lords took him in and questioned him. They tortured him by snipping off the end of his fingers to get him to talk. He held tight and didn't rat them out. When the people let him go, he left and came back with a gun and shot them all. The Cartel rewarded him with a position. He was 14 or 15 years old at the time. He hasn't gotten any friendlier over the years, just wealthier." Ronnie took a deep breath, "So. Have you been dealing with some drug type people on your vacation Salas?"

"Yeah. This is connected. It has to be the right guy."

Ronnie continued. "The driver's license you gave me was for Diego Murano. Diego is not a citizen of our great country. The Florida license says he is, but facial recognition software confirms his name is Ramone Diego. On the FBI's top 100 list. Wanted for murder in this country and others, extortion, drugs, and terrorism. Diego has been linked to at least a dozen murders. His name is in synch with the Rivera Cartel. He is their enforcer. I take it German may be the kingpin of this cartel. Salas, just who are you hanging out with in Daytona?"

"Let's say the FBI can cross Diego off their list. How about the other guy, McGinnis?"

"McGinnis is a local thug. Lives or lived in Jacksonville. Petty theft, armed robbery, assault with a deadly weapon. He has done two tours of the state penitentiary. His rehabilitation must not have been effective. You realize the penitentiary system has been studied closely over the years. The research on the effectiveness of incarceration and confinement as well as the combined effectiveness of confining multiple individuals with the same and varying degrees of sociological and psychological illnesses has been proven to be very ineffective. There is no formal retraining process. Just years in prison then released with a "good luck out there…""

"Ronnie. My battery is dying."

"Yes, of course. Salas, you said three dead. Can you send me a photo of the third dead body? A picture of his face. This facial recognition software is very sophisticated and very fun to play with."

"Sorry Ronnie, no can do. The third guy is missing a face right now. Text me the address of German in St. Augustine. You are the best Ronnie." Salas shut off he call not able to hear Ronnie yelling at him.

The phone vibrated stating a text had arrived. Ronnie had sent the address in St. Augustine with a note in capital letters "I HAVE TO TALK TO YOU."

Salas ignored the caps, he punched the screen, dialed another number. The phone rang twice and was answered.

"What," was the greeting.

"Sheriff Groff, Salas here. Tell me; you know anything about those two muscle-heads?"

"Well good day to you too Salas. About those two dip sticks. I know one sum bitch is dead and the other is beat to shit. Remind me to never piss you off alas," Groff eplied

"If you don't shoot at me you probably won't piss me off. You got their names? Last names? No way were they working for Richard. Must be an outside source. Most likely they were there to safeguard the drugs."

"Makes sense. Let me check the system, hold on." Groff put the phone on mute; all the background noise was gone. Then a click and the sound of phones ringing and people talking backed up Groff's voice. "Yeah, the boys' last name is Przybyszewski."

"Prybzski? What? Are you are shitting me?"

"Yeah, I'm shitting you. The last name is Hernandez. Did those two-sum bitches look Polish to you? What are you working on Salas? You are supposed to be on vacation at a motorcycle rally." Groff reminded Salas of the purpose of his two-day ride to Florida.

"Can we talk off he record?"

"Yes. But I don't know if I want to hear this. Did it happen in my county?" Groff sked.

"No. Not yours. RJ's team got hit. Five dead. Well, eight dead. Five of RJ's team. I am sure it has to do with the twins Marco and Raphael. Especially if their last name is Hernandez."

"Yeah, I am sure it is Hernandez. Sum bitch. Let it go, Salas. Tell RJ the same. Let it go. Let the police do their job," Groff aid.

"That ain't gonna happen Groff. I can see it in his eyes. Those twins and that Vincent started this by stealing RJ's bike. They had the chance to give it back to us. Then they shot at us first, you know that."

"Yeah, Salas I know that Rambo first blood shit. Last night I had more fun than a dog licking his balls, but you two went there looking for a fi ht," Groff aid.

"Yeah, a fi ht, not a shoot-out. Not drugs, not AKs and not killing Richard. Now they did a direct hit on guys that had nothing to do with any of this. Groff, you got to keep this to yourself. But we are going after Hernandez," Salas said.

"I don't want to hear it. You know I will keep this off the record. But you are running solo on this Salas. I wish I could help," Groff said as Salas terminated the call.

RJ

R J was relieved when Tripp finally had his gear packed, got on his Harley and rode off. He didn't want this young man to be involved in the club, much less with what he thought would happen next. His heart broke for the boy. He had no parents, the man that raised him was dead, and now he lost a good friend. RJ watched Tripp ride until he could not see him anymore then stood listening until the roar of the Harley died away.

The man named Junior had arrived and was cleaning the room where the shooting took place. He wore long yellow gloves that went to his elbows and a white body suit. He had a blue mask over his mouth and blue slippers over his boots. By the end of the day, Junior would have the drywall repaired and painted, new carpet, new furniture even a new deck of playing cards and a cribbage board.

Two men in Junior's crew took the dead bodies of RJ's friends to a local morgue the club had connections with. All the bodies would be cremated, today. Cause of death would be a heart attack, accidental slip and fall, a suicide and two died in a single-car accident where it would say the driver fell asleep at the wheel. There would be no mention of gunshot wounds.

RJ made more calls. Other club members would arrange a group funeral for the fi e men and their families. RJ knew the service would be attended by hundreds of bikers, club members and rivals giving their respect. Deuce usually spoke at such events, and he was good at it. RJ would assign the speaking duties to another person.

A fourth member of Junior's team loaded the three hitman bodies from the Aerostar into the back of a white Chevy panel van. Three bodies in three separate plastic wraps. Human burritos stuffed into a delivery van. The Chevy had no identifiable markings. Where the bodies would end up, was the diver's decision. Not even Junior would know.

One last soldier on Junior's team was cleaning the Aerostar. He was dressed like Junior. The blue mask, white suit and yellow gloves. The smell wasn't as bad in the van as inside the clubhouse. The morning breeze swept through the broken window and opened doors. The man was more ripping the van apart than cleaning it. The gray carpet and cloth seats were removed and going to be burned. The ceiling fabric was ripped out and the dashboard removed, to go into the same burn pile as the carpet. The instrument panel was left intact, sprayed with Clorox and deep cleaned as blood had entered every crevice and crack. The young man was scrubbing the interior and exterior side walls as blood had slid down the side panel of the van. RJ wanted to dispose of the automobile, but Junior thought he could salvage it, change the VIN, the vehicle identification number and use it for disposal work.

Salas watched it all in disbelief of what he was seeing and that he was still an officer of the law. Was he crossing a line or justifying it? Right now, he didn't care; he was helping RJ.

RJ came forward, breaking the trance Salas had fallen into "Mike, you should ride back to Daytona then leave the state. Get the hell out of here. I will fi ure this out. You got no dog in this fi ht."

"Yeah, you are right RJ. I have no dog. But I'm in, and I have a plan." Salas said.

This was now a two-man fi ht. RJ didn't want any of his guys involved, and Salas volunteered because he was, well, he was Salas and known for his decision-making skills.

RJ showed Salas the ammo closet located near the front exit of the clubhouse, Salas grabbed a box of 9 mm shells and an extra magazine for his Glock. He wasn't going to be short of firepower this time. Salas also found a six-shot .38 and an ankle holster. He buckled it to his calf and ankle. It felt secure.

Putting on a pair of black leather gloves he found in the closet, RJ also chose a double-barrel shotgun. He placed two 12-gauge four-shot shells in the chambers and placed two extra shells in his front pants pocket. RJ wiped blood off of the 9mm Glock taken from the dead

Irishman, not like McGinnis was going to be using it any time soon. RJ pulled back the slide of the weapon, popping a shell out of the chamber of the handgun. The bullet rolled under the sink. He didn't bother to look for it.

"Salas, toss me one nine mil. I need it to top off his clip," RJ said.

Salas grabbed a shell from the box and tossed it to RJ.

Salas planned to remove the seats from the now confiscated and cleaned Ford van and load his Harley into the back. Both men would be driving the van to German's house, using the electronic garage door opener found on the visor of the Ford as their means to gain entry. Once in the garage, the plan took a turn for the random. Whatever happens next, shoot it. Find German, eliminate German. If the wife and children are there, take German and shoot the "sum bitch" in the garage. Unload the Road King from the van and Salas and RJ ride out.

RJ agreed and thought it best if he rode in the back with his shotgun ready to fire out either window. They had Junior's van guy take out the passenger side glass. They also had the van guy replace the blown up and torn out bloody driver's seat with the passenger side cloth seat. It took the mechanic less than fifteen minutes to make the change.

Salas removed the license plate from his bike and placed the plate, the two screws and a screwdriver in the side pocket of his leather jacket. Plus, as Salas thought of Raphael Hernandez, there are plenty of uses for a screwdriver.

Before they got in the van to leave, Salas followed RJ's lead and put on his leather biking gloves. He didn't want his prints on anything.

The drive crisscrossed the state of Florida from Waldo to St. Augustine. RJ tried to sleep, maybe dozed off for a few minutes. Salas got coffee and *Redbull* when they got fuel. He was wired. It was early evening when the two men arrived. Driving into the neighborhood, they were unprepared for the security guard and the gated community. Salas's source, Ronnie, talked of the beautiful home but not of any security detail. Salas slowed the van as they approached, the guard standing in the middle of the street.

"Are you shitting me? What should I do now?" Salas asked, looking at RJ in his review mirror.

"Shit, stop. And tell him we are delivering this Harley to German Hernandez." RJ was laying the shotgun flat against the side panel.

Both men sighed in relief as the security guard waved the van through into the high-end residential neighborhood. The guard mouthed hello at the van. He stepped to the passenger side, not the driver's as the car passed. He wouldn't be able to see Salas's face through the passenger window and RJ laid down out of sight.

Salas said, "Great security guard."

RJ responded, "Just hope he lets us get out when we come back on the bike."

The Hernandez home was lit up, floodlights on each corner, and every ten feet under the eaves. Motion lights popped on when they got within fifty yards of the home. The long flowing green grass looked like a soccer field with a fountain of bubbling water over rocks as the goal. The dull red cement-tiled roof gave the home a hacienda look.

Salas had RJ stay low. He kept the driver's side window up with his elbow on the window sill, hand on his head. He was trying to hide his face from the multiple security cameras they passed.

Seeing the home, it was a tall single-story building, most likely a walk-out to the beach. The front door was at least twenty feet tall with a window over it. They had the option to turn left and park in front of the house on a large U-turn driveway or turn right and head towards the garage. Salas took a right and hit the button on the remote control clipped to the visor. The middle garage door responded and opened, the door sliding up and back.

Salas switched a knob in the van and turned the headlights to high-beam as he entered the garage, anyone looking at the car would be blinded by the bright lights. He could see a man dressed in a black suit rubbing a cloth on the hood of what looked like a Shelby GT.

"Sweet car," Salas said then he told RJ. "Guy on the right, take him out when I stop the van. Through the window. One shot fuck the noise."

The van stopped, RJ rose to his knees as the barrel of the shotgun came through the window. He used both triggers of the Remington. The blast shook the garage, the guy cleaning the GT flew backward flat on his back where the Ford Aerostar van used to be parked. Blood splattered the floor, the wall, and the Shelby.

Both men opened the van doors and rushed into the garage. Sweeping the building left to right, Salas saw a large panel against the wall. The panel read "A-1 Security." He pointed out the box to RJ who loaded another shell into the shotgun and blasted it. Salas hoped that shot would turn off he cameras.

They ran past the Audi with Salas slamming a shoulder into the metal door going into the house. Salas led the charge then did a side roll to his right, the Glock extended with both arms. He settled on his knees, his back straight behind a leather couch. RJ did the same but a roll to the left. RJ was now behind a granite counter-topped island in the center of the kitchen. He sat up with his handgun, the 9 mm pointing straight ahead.

German Hernandez stood in front of the window facing the beach. He slowly turned towards the two men. German was wearing his signature glossy blue suit coat with matching pants. The pants were the straight-legged kind. He wore black penny loafers and a white shirt with the top three buttons open. His hair was pulled behind his ears and tied in a ponytail. He was short and muscular. Even with an expensive tailored suit, German looked awkward. Salas knew the feeling and the look. German was sipping on red wine, holding onto the stem of the glass.

"Well gentlemen, as you can see, you are not whom I expected," German said as calmly as if he was talking to his mother. "I am sorry I do not have anything prepared for you."

RJ focused his aim and shot him in the forehead. German fell back. He landed flat, his arms extended out like he was trying to make a snow angel on the carpet. The wine left the glass, splashing against the window and running down the wall.

Salas stood then went to the rooms connected to the kitchen looking for a wife, children, or other men.

RJ stood over the dead man. He yelled out loud as he pointed his finger at him. "You got what you asked for. I never wanted any of this."

Salas was looking out the bay window, onto the grounds of the estate. He was looking for movement, knowing others were bound to be out there, more security to come.

Salas said "Most people in the movies make their speech before they shoot someone. You know like… "Forgiveness is between you and God; it is my job to arrange the meeting." Or as Tony Montana said, "say hello to my little friend.""

RJ looked at Salas. "I always liked Outlaw Josey Wales, "Dying ain't much of a living, boy." RJ tossed the Glock on the floor and watched it slide under the leather couch.

"Let's get the bike unloaded; we got to go. You know he has back up somewhere, they have to be on the way."

Inside the garage, RJ opened the rear door of the gutted-out Ford van. Salas went to the other side to help unload. As he passed the Audi, he glanced inside. The rear window was down. Salas saw the Adidas duffle bag from the garage at "We Found U Repo." Salas reached inside the Audi, through the open window and grabbed the bag.

At the back of the Ford RJ had unhooked the nylon straps. The two men lifted the one thousand plus pound bike out of the van and onto the checkerboard floor of the garage. Salas stuffed the duffle in his side saddle bag. RJ didn't say anything.

Both men were on the Harley, Salas in front. RJ had the shotgun, the barrel tucked into his boot, the stock against his shoulder as he rode high in the passenger seat. No helmets, no glasses, the windshield protecting Salas. RJ was squinting from the wind in his eyes. Mosquitos were hitting his face as they raced out of the garage and down the driveway.

They went by the security guard going over 70 miles per hour. The gate was up, the security guard in his brown outfit and yellow shoulder stripes was sitting on a lawn chair in the other lane. He was on his cell phone and smoking a cigarette as the bike passed in a blur.

Ten miles out from German's house, Salas pulled the Harley into the back corner of a Burger King parking lot. Salas put the license plate back on the bike, returning the screwdriver inside his leather jacket. You never know when a screwdriver will come in handy.

RJ opened the double barrel as if to load a shell into it; then he snapped the weapon into two pieces. He threw both sections of the destroyed gun into a large dumpster behind the fast-food restaurant. It blended into the left-over fries, burgers, garbage and paper towels.

They arrived in Waldo at 10:00 at night riding back to the clubhouse so RJ could get his bike. The door to the club was open. It was deserted, the interior immaculate, Junior did great work. There was no sign of the death that was present just a few hours earlier in the day. Even the blood stain on the concrete in front of the building was gone. The place was clean, yet a sense of gloom hung in the air.

They rode out of the club's lot to the first hotel they could find. The vacancy sign was lit. They parked their Harleys under the canopy covering the entryway. Both remembering to lock the handlebars. They each got a room.

In the hotel lounge, they shared buffalo wings, shots of Jameson, three pitchers of Miller Lite, then another shot of Jameson. Talking was limited. They left the bar at the same time and went to their rooms. Both men exhausted. Both asleep by midnight.

GROFF

Sheriff Groff arrived at the county office at six in the morning. He parked the Ford, the interior still damp from the bath in the pond at "We Found U Repo." He exited the truck, twisting his back to see the butt of his brown pants turned dark. His ass was wet. A lingering effect from the pond.

"Sum bitch," Groff aid.

Walking up the steps to the office, he saw a manila envelope taped to the front door of the building. He studied the package as he approached. In bold black letters, was printed "County Sheriff nly."

Groff ripped the tape and envelope off the door and went inside the county office. He made coffee and turned up the air conditioning then sat down at his desk. He took a drink of hot coffee, looked again at the yellow/brown envelope then tore the top section open. Inside was a hand-written letter and a clear plastic ziplock bag. Inside the ziplock was one spent/empty brass shell casing. Groff thought it looked like a 9 mm.

Groff took a sip of his coffee, leaned back in the chair and examined the letter. The paper was a plain white sheet, most likely copy or printer paper. The writing was partial printing, some cursive. One large paragraph. The lines started straight then swooped upward. Most of the words were misspelled, there were no commas and only a few periods. Groff read the words. "Sheriff, sorry I don't know your name. I saw you, and a big bald guy at "We Found U Repo" the other day. You had just driven into the lot when I came behind you and parked on the bridge. That's why I am writing. That day I dumped a body of German Hernandez's wife into the pond. Her name was Michelle. I liked Michelle she treated me good. But I didn't kill Michelle Hernandez; her husband choked her to death. I have been dumping bodies to them gators for near a year, but I didn't kill any of them. It was my job to get rid of them bodies. I did as I was told. Anyway, I saw the two of you and your pickup so I knew where to come. I saw the bald guy at German's house last night. I was patrolling the beach at German's place. That is my job too. I walked to the house and saw a muzzle flash, so I hid in the bushes. The big bald guy then stood by the window. When they left I went inside and found the dead body of German Hernandez and his body guard Raul. Raul always hit me on the side of the head and called me names. I was glad he was dead. I also found this empty shell and fi ured when the cops came they would run finger prints and find out it was the bald guy." Groff rank more coffee and went on reading.

"I want to help. German was going to kill me this week. I heard him tell Diego to kill me. Diego likes to kill so I knew I was done for this world. So, the bald guy, by killing German well he saved my life. German was a killer Sheriff. I didn't see him kill anyone, but I know he ordered it. Diego, who I was told is dead too, was the guy that did the killing. I feel safe now with both dead." Groff looked at the plastic bag, held it in his opposite hand and continued to read.

"I am free now. The two that want me dead are gone. They killed DayVonte Robinson in the Atlantic. It wasn't a boating accident like they said on ESPN. I was there I saw the whole thing. Diego cut DayVonte's friend throat and fed him to the barracudas. Then they blew the boat up after torturing DayVonte. And they killed Michelle. They killed Javier Rosalis, I dumped his body, Garcone Diaz, Chuck Kennedy, Pete Jenkins. Those are the names of the people I gave to the gators. They were all bad men. Michelle and DayVonte were good people. They loved each other, and German killed them. And DayVonte's friend, I am sure he was a good guy too." Signed Danny.

Groff ead the note again. Drank another cup of coffee.

Sheriff Groff took the casing out of the bag. He held it in his hand. The bottom read 9 mm. He squeezed it, pinching in the sides. He threw the casing and the bag in the trash. He then took a Bic lighter from his desk drawer and burned the letter from Danny. He dialed a number on his cell phone.

"Yeah," Salas answered his phone. It was his first word of the day. His voiced creaked and scratched from a need for water. He was lying flat in the Holiday Inn's king-sized bed.

"Sum bitch. I wake up your ornery ass Salas?" Asked Sheriff   roff.

"No, I just jogged a couple of miles on the treadmill. Getting my breath back. What time is it?" Salas asked.

"Pert near eight in the morning sunshine. You still in Daytona?"

"No, In Waldo Florida."

"Waldo? Hell, people in Waldo don't want to be in Waldo. What, three days in Daytona too much for you?"

"Yeah too much. Like I got to see any of Daytona. What you hearing on the police chatter?" Salas asked. He was standing over the stool peeing while talking to Groff.

"Let's see Detective. First. Big John Ballard is dead. He is or was a friend of our friend RJ. Seems John committed suicide by shooting himself." Groff aid.

"It happens, Sheriff. The best of us go through those down times in life when the world just shits on ya."

"You don't commit suicide by shooting yourself with a .44 magnum. Twice. Once in the low part of your back and then in the head, Salas."

"Maybe he was scratching an itch and got carried away." Salas countered.

"Yeah, you can call an alligator a lizard until it bites you in the ass."

"I don't know what that means Sheriff   roff."

"It means, I don't know what the fuck it means," Groff elled back.

"Anything else Sheriff. Hell, I was with you most of the time, so was RJ."

"You two are not on the radar. Ballard was under an early watch list for running meth. So, no one cares. He has no wife, no kids. He has a brother named James that is worse than John. Seems James hasn't showed up for work or at his momma's house. And thing is, no one gives a shit." Groff aid.

"Don't you waste your time on James Ballard. I think he took a dive with the gators at the repo place."

"So that's who that was?" Groff sked. "That sum bitch."

"Per RJ, he was going to shoot you." Salas was now brushing his teeth while talking to Groff.

"Well yes I think he was, but I had my eyes on those sum bitch alligators and crocodiles. Crocogators or allicrocs."

"So, is everything's over?" Salas mumbled then spit into the sink.

"Well. There is a bit more. German Hernandez is dead. He is big shit from Saint Augustine. They say he was executed. You recall Marco and Raphael Hernandez Salas?"

"Yes, I do. How is Marco doing? I hope he is feeling better."

"He is awake. He can't talk. His jaw is wired shut. Face needs reconfi ured. Hell, he will end up looking like the elephant man. But you were right; German is, well was Marco and Raphael's uncle."

"Really? Are you shitting me? The twins are related to German? And German? Who killed him?" Salas tried to sound surprised.

"Fingerprints on a gun, a 9 mil Glock they found at the scene say Joey McGinnis. Total loser. Major search is out on him."

"Good luck with that search. Bet he lays low for a spell," Salas said.

"Yeah, I imagine he is six feet laid low. Or burnt to shit or maybe gator bait."

"Imagine you are right Sheriff Groff. You are very perceptive, ever thought of being a detective?"

"Right Salas. Why take a downward pay grade? Funny thing about a van they found in the German's garage though. It was torn inside out. No prints yet. Checking for blood. Looks like someone Clorox'd the hell out of it."

"So, there's nothing huh?" Salas asked.

Groff was quiet for more than a few seconds. "Nope. Not a damn thing. No spent shell casings were found. The hit team must have picked up the spent shell. Thought they could get a print off the casing but can't find her." Groff as quiet.

Salas was quiet.

"Well, would make sense the shells belonged to McGinnis if the gun did," Salas said, his mind tracing their steps.

"Yeah, I suppose. They said the security system was shot to hell. The cameras show a van coming in with a white dude driving but nothing after that. Nothing they can identify. There are pictures of a man in the backyard. They fi ure an on-premise security guy. But we can't find him. I am sure he is in hiding too. Not like German kept records or had a human resources department for his employees."

"Man, in the backyard huh? He didn't get in the way? Didn't try and protect his boss?" Salas asked.

"Nope turns out he hated his boss. Says he knows German killed his wife and fed her to the gators at We Found U Repo."

"Thought you said you couldn't find him?"

"Sum bitch Salas. What? You playing twenty fucking questions? Can't a guy just speculate? It is called hypothesizing detective. And that Security guard at the entrance of the subdivision, he don't know shit," Groff said.

Salas didn't know whether to feel better or worry. He didn't see anyone in the backyard. And how did Groff know about German, the wife, and gators?

"Anything new from here in Waldo?" Salas asked.

"No why? What you two do there for shit's sake?"

"Nothing Groff. We sat here and had some beers. Killing nothing but time."

"Yeah, everybody goes to Waldo to kill time. I will make sure I keep Waldo on my list too," Groff aid.

"What is next Sheriff?"

"I will let you know when I know Salas. Take care. Whatever I can do here I will. Ride safe and put on that sum bitch helmet." The phone call was over. The Sheriff ropped the call.

SAMI

Sami and Anthony spent the night on the sand of Panama City Beach. Several college-age kids created a bonfire fueled by scrap wood from an abandoned work site, old wooden pallets, and driftwood found randomly on the beach. They were a mile downwind, on private property. Supposedly the owner was there. The ten to twelve people sitting around the fire were coupled together; each caught in a private moment. It was the last night at PCB for most of them. The group preferring a quiet night with friends over the wild party and street scene. Each staring at and lost in the flames which were dancing a few feet in the air.

"What's wrong Anthony? Is something bothering you?" Sami asked

Anthony said, "Sorry. A lot happened today. Sami, I decided I'm going to Chicago early. I called my grandparents, and I can stay with them until I can find an apartment near campus. So, if you don't mind, we can spend more time together."

Sami was thrilled, excited to hear the news.

A cool spring breeze brought slight chill; it bit at their shoulders. The couple had a blanket courtesy of the hotel Sam was staying at, the smooth velour wrapped around their shoulders. Anthony told Sami about his parents, how they were killed in an auto accident. Since his father was an attorney, he had a will set up that placed Anthony with his mom's brother Harold. They called him Deuce. His grandparents on his dad's side were deceased, the ones on his mother's side were, as his mom called them, "out there." They disagreed on religion, politics and how to raise children. Deuce was the answer. A trust fund financed by life insurance, investments and an inheritance from his dad's parents left   nthony a college fund and living expenses.

"I was thinking you could ride with me tomorrow."

"Tomorrow?"

"Yeah, I can pick you up. We can follow your friends in their car. I have an extra helmet, and I got you a leather jacket."

"We are riding a motorcycle?" Sam asked.

"Yeah, that is all I have. I know Chicago gets cold, so I will probably get a car once I get there."

"What about your furniture, your books, you know knick-knacks and stuff? Your pictures, your clothes?" Sami asked.

"I lived pretty cheap Sami. I don't have much. I was young when my parents died. My grandparents, well, we weren't close then. But we are now. That is why I chose Chicago for law school. That, and well my dad, he went to Pritzker at Northwestern too. Everything I own, well just about everything fits on my bike."

The couple settled into a conversation about their futures. The rigors of law school, the cold Chicago weather, Notre Dame and a motorcycle ride. The conversation slowed. Anthony drifted back into a dark mood; tears trickled down his cheeks.

"What is it? What's wrong?" Sami asked as she took a tear from his face.

Anthony told Sami about Dozer, that he was shot and killed in a random drive-by that morning in Waldo Florida. He didn't tell her about him shooting the three men, about her father and RJ or even that others were killed in addition to Dozer. He said he just couldn't stay in Waldo. He wanted to be back here, in PCB with Sami, that she was the first person he thought of when he found Dozer.

Sami didn't know the two men had even left PCB. She thought they were asleep for most of the day. She was shocked and sat in silence, hugging Anthony. For the first time he could remember, Anthony cried. He cried in Sami's arms. Sami cried too. She pictured Will's red cheeks, how he blushed when he smiled. How he grinned when he saw Steph running on the beach.

At some point during the night, they fell asleep on the sand. The bonfire and blanket keeping them warm, Sami was nestled in Anthony's arm. Anthony woke when the sun rose. As the morning light was peaking over the water, Anthony nudged Sami; she sat up too. They watched their second sunrise together.

SALAS

Salas was up early. He felt feverish. The deltoid where he was shot was red and inflamed. Salas brushed it off and made another call to Indiana. The voice on the other end of the phone said, "Yes?" It was Doris. Multiple-night sleepover. Good for Ronnie.

"May I speak to Ronnie, please?" Salas asked.

"Same guy sweetie." Came across the phone.

"Salas? You again?" Ronnie groaned and said, "ouch" into the phone. "Can't you call a little later in the day?" Ronnie asked.

"You ok? What have you hurt lying in bed with your lady?"

"Funny guy. If you would listen to me, you would know. I have been trying to tell you. You just call and want things. Maybe I need you too, Salas." Ronnie was stern with Salas, something he had never been.

"Well, I do need one more thing. And of course, quickly," Salas said, as humbling as he could.

"Salas I am not doing anything for you until you listen."

"I'm all yours Ronnie."

Ronnie started with the man with dead eyes, meeting him in downtown Fort Wayne, the kidney punch, what the man said, and the trip to the emergency room. Ronnie told Salas about the drive to Green's house, the pain in his lower back, the open front door, what he heard, and how he recorded it on his cell phone. He told Salas about the million dollars in cash found in Green's personal safe. He told Salas how he shot the man with dead brown eyes and killed him. He talked about the arrest, how he read Green his rights and how Ginger passed out.

"Salas, I killed a man," was how Ronnie ended his talk.

Salas was quiet a few seconds then said, "You have got to be shitting me."

"No. Salas, it is all true. Green is in prison, no bail. Ginger had a nervous breakdown; she is with my mom. The FBI has taken the case due to the money, crossing state lines, tax evasion, all sorts of charges."

"Listen, Ronnie. I am so proud of you. I will be in the office in a few days. We will talk this through step-by-step. Please do one thing for me after you do this other one thing for me."

"Sure, what's that?" Ronnie asked.

"You shot and killed a man. Always remember Ronnie that man needed to be shot and killed. You did the right thing. You made the right decision. That was great work Ronnie, but let me tell you from experience. Right or wrong, it will still eat into your head. Dreams, nightmares, night sweats, feelings of anxiety, apprehension, angst. Have you felt any of that?"

"Yes. The dreams have started. I keep seeing his face after I shot him."

"That is normal Ronnie. Go to the shooting range today. Shoot a box of shells. And, call the officer crisis support line. Talk to someone there. I have called them several times. It helps," Salas said.

"You called for help?" Ronnie asked, surprised.

"Absolutely Ronnie. You should too. Call them. Agreed?"

"I will."

The line went quiet. Ronnie was thinking. Salas was listening.

"Now what can I do for you, Mike?" Ronnie asked.

"Please text me the address of Corinne Lopez in South Carolina. I don't know the city. She lives with her parents, and I don't know their names. Her husband is, was, Richard Lopez. You have his information. Text it to me as soon as you can. I need it within the hour. And Ronnie? Again, I am very proud of you." Salas swiped the cell to off.

After the free breakfast at the Holiday Inn Salas went to his room. Waiting on the call from Ronnie. There was a knock on the door. Salas opened. RJ asked him if he wanted to get breakfast. RJ went by himself.

A text came in with an address.

Salas texted back: "This address has to be correct. Sending a VIP package. You 100% positive this is right?" Salas texted back.

"Yes, ONE hundred percent," was Ronnie's reply text.

Salas went back down to the lobby; the smell of coffee was still lingering in the air. RJ had a stack of cinnamon rolls with white frosting stacked on a plastic plate in front of him. He had his arms around the meal, guarding it.

At the front desk, Salas asked for a box, "a container the size of a shoe box would be perfect." The manager on duty according to her front lapel pin went into the back room. Minutes later she returned with a box and handed it to Salas. Next, he asked for packing tape; she had that sitting on the shelf in front of her. Salas thanked her and went back to his hotel room.

In the room, Salas emptied the contents of the duffle bag onto the sheets of the bed. Packets of one-hundred-dollar bills spilled on to the linen. He then stacked them neatly into the shoe box. He counted over 200,000 dollars. Using the notepad and green-capped pen compliments of the Waldo Holiday Inn, Salas wrote out: "Corinne, Richard wanted you and the kids to have this. Please use it for their college education. One of the greatest gifts you can ever receive is the love of another. You were loved." He left o name, no return address.

Salas went back to the front desk returning the packaging tape to the manager. He had the box taped shut, the forwarding and return addresses the same. Salas asked if she had any stamps. She said yes and pulled out a fresh roll of one hundred stamps.

"Can I buy them from you?" Salas asked.

"Sure, how many do you need?" The manager asked back.

"All of them. I got to be sure this gets to South Carolina. It is a little boy's birthday present," Salas said.

"Oh sir, my husband is a mail carrier here in Waldo. Let me take the package and mail it for you tomorrow. I will be sure it gets there. And I can text you the tracking number."

Salas gave her a fifty-dollar bill and his phone number. She called his phone while he stood there. It worked, they were now connected. The manager tried to give him back twenty dollars, but he insisted she keep it. He just trusted two-hundred thousand dollars to a random person at a Holiday Inn and the United State Postal Service.

RJ and Salas reloaded their gear on the bikes. The saddled the Harley's to ride the four hours to Panama City Beach. Salas wanted to see his daughter get in her car and ride safely back to Indiana. He was thinking about following her all the way to her apartment in South Bend.

The two riders took highway 27 through Bradford and Mayo. Salas was surprised how a state can differ so much geographically and demographically. From the beach to the swamp to wasteland, to farm ground then back to the beach. From designer clothes to J-Z and Che t-shirts to bib overalls and back to beachwear. The only thing common to all of Florida was baseball and football jerseys with the name "Tebow" on the back.

At Perry, Florida, where highway 27 turned into highway 98 they stopped for fuel. Back on the highway, the road went through more wetlands, a wildlife management area, then crossed over St. Marks River. Now on highway 267 which later would magically turn into highway 20, the pair rode with Salas in the lead. RJ was just riding, relaxing, enjoying the ride, the road, the weather and the wind. He let Salas do the navigating.

Cutting through the north-east edge of the Apalachicola Wildlife Management Area, they stopped in Hosford. RJ's leg was cramping up, the quadricep pierced by the bullet was red and inflamed RJ, had a different pair of jeans on, throwing the bloody ones away at the hotel. He went inside the men's room, dropped his pants, pulled off the blood-soaked band-aids on the entry and exit wounds. He dabbed on Neosporin; then he covered both bullet holes with more band-aids.

In the parking lot, RJ handed Salas the Neosporin.

"Nah, I'm good. Mine was nothing like yours. It is a little stiff is all. Jacket looks good with a bullet hole in, don't it?" Salas smiled, showing RJ the shoulder of his leathers.

Hosford to PCB was 90 minutes. Once again, they were riding on Front Beach Road, stopping under the canopy of the Beach Tower Hotel.

It was one o'clock in the afternoon. Salas had texted Sami without a response. He fi ured she was still asleep.

RJ texted Tripp, whose returned text stated he would be there in ten minutes.

The time past, still no word from Sami. Salas was walking into the hotel lobby to ring her room when RJ waved as he watched Tripp ride up to join them on his Harley. Salas recognized the bike as a Dyna Wide

Glide. Tripp had a passenger sitting behind him. They could tell it was a girl's fi ure with a full face mask helmet. Tripp pulled beside RJ's bike, planted both his feet on the ground as he shut down the bike. Tripp's hair was pulled back in a pony-tail, he wore a long sleeve FSU Seminole Football t-shirt. His passenger unstrapped her black helmet, pulling it back over her head as she shook her hair free. It was Sami Salas.

"Sam?" Salas asked loudly.

"Hi, Daddy," Sami said with a smile.

"Don't 'hi daddy' me. What the hell is this?" Salas looked at RJ, who smiled, shrugged his shoulders and looked at Tripp.

"Mr. Salas. I can explain," Tripp spoke up.

"I'm not talking to you, junior. I will deal with you in a minute. Samantha, what the?" Salas turned to Tripp "How did you? You. You were just supposed to keep an eye out on her." Salas got off his bike and was facing Sami and pointing at Tripp.

"Don't be mad at her Mr. Salas. I am the one that introduced myself to her," Tripp said.

"I'm not mad. Hell, I don't know what I am." Salas said.

"You only call Sami Samantha when you are mad or upset with her," Tripp countered.

"How much have you told this kid Sam?" Salas asked Sami.

"As much as I have had time to. Daddy, it just happened. We met and are hitting it off. I think I love him, Dad." Sami put her hand on Tripp's pony-tail, pulling it slightly. She was still sitting on the back of the Dyna, Tripp straddling the gas tank, both feet on the ground.

"Love? I have only been gone for three days in Daytona, and you fell in love? That is impossible Sam," Salas said.

"Daddy, you told me the moment you met Mom you knew she was the one. You knew you loved her." Sami was calmly talking to her father.

"Yeah, and look how that turned out." Salas wasn't as calm as his daughter.

"She still loves you dad. She just can't take you being a police officer." Sami said it.

"She said that?" Salas went quiet. No one spoke for a few seconds as Salas absorbed what his daughter just told him.

"I'm riding with Anthony to South Bend Dad. He is moving to Chicago, then starts law school at Northwestern in the fall," Sami said.

Anthony nodded.

"Anthony?" Salas looked at RJ and Tripp.

"Yes, sir. That is my given name. Tripp is just a nickname," Anthony said.

"We are following my friends in their car. We were just heading out when you text. We wanted to surprise you." Sami said

"Well, you did. I am surprised," Salas responded.

"Well," RJ interrupted. "We have to ride or have a drink, but we can't drink and ride. So what is it?" RJ asked.

Salas saddled his Harley. Three bikes were switched on; three bikes revved their engines. Three bikes left the Beachfront Hotel. They were soon following a Chevy Impala with Indiana license plates. Steph waved at Sam and Tripp. Tamara was driving.

The caravan followed Highway 81 to I65 to Montgomery Alabama. At Birmingham, they stopped for fuel. RJ and Tripp had a discussion away from the girls and Salas. Salas hugged his Sami.

RJ came back to the bikes and said to Salas, "I will be turning at Interstate 22 to Memphis, got to get back to Denver. My emails are blowing up with business issues, and then we have a funeral for the team in Waldo. I will be flying back out for that."

"What do you think RJ, should we ride to Laughlin?" Salas asked

"Let's plan on it. I need a vacation." RJ said.

"Thanks, man. Keep in touch," Salas said. The two men hugged as men don't often do. RJ smacked Salas on the shoulder. Salas winced.

"You should get that wound looked at." RJ got on his Harley, started it and gave Salas a two-fingered salute.

Salas and Tripp watched him ride off.

"Ready kids?" Salsas asked the new couple on the Dyna and the three rather hung-over girls in the Chevy. All six looked like they could use some rest.

"Let's ride," Sami yelled out.

RJ

Riding on Interstate 22 through Memphis, Tennessee, RJ crossed into Arkansas on Interstate 40. RJ stopped for the night in Little Rock. He had ridden nearly 400 miles since leaving Tripp and Salas. His body ached from the gunshot wound to his leg, ached from the riding, and ached from the lack of sleep. After a shower he checked his emails as he waited for a pizza to be delivered by Papa John's or Dominos, he couldn't remember which, just that it tasted like cardboard with red sauce. He ignored a text and email from Sheila fi uring he hadn't responded all week and a few more days wouldn't matter. He hoped she got the hint. With no Deuce to look after, RJ was asleep early.

The sun rose in the east, lighting up his hotel room. He showered quickly, re-bandaged his wounds and applied more Neosporin. The edges of the wound were clear, the damage healing. He felt he probably needed stitches but at this point, the healing was happening, so he would be just be left with a larger scar. He dressed and was riding by eight in the morning. The next leg of the trip was easy; I40 through Tulsa, I35 to Wichita, Kansas. The further north he rode, the more the temperature dropped, and the more layers of clothes to put on. Good news; in March there were no bugs, better news there was no rain and best news, no snow.

Seven hours later he decided to spend the night in Salina, Kansas, at a truck stop motel. He had a room on the first floor of what used to be a Super 8 or Motel 6. The business long ago losing its franchise as well as the credentials to qualify for a chain hotel. He paid $35.00 for the room by sliding the cash under a bulletproof glass window. His room smelled of cologne, smoke, and sweat. He didn't want to lay on the bedspread, pulling it off and throwing it on the floor. He spread it over the carpet.

The sheets were clean with the faint odor of Clorox emanating from the pillowcases. His bike was parked in front of the door to his room, he didn't trust the neighbors, and didn't sleep well rising with each noise to check on his bike. Around midnight he stood outside his doorway letting the cold March air produce goosebumps all over his body. He watched as two local hookers worked the trucks going cab to cab offering their services. They were dressed in short, short skirts, high heels, and what had to be wigs. One of the girls got lucky and crawled into the cab of the truck. The other girl saw RJ and started walking his way. He waved her off nd went back inside.

He fell asleep and for the first time in years, slept past eight in the morning.

The last 435 miles was Kansas boring. Straight interstate, no trees, no lakes, no mountains no scenery. Welcome back to Kansas.

RJ crossed the Colorado state line with the distant view of the snow-capped Rocky Mountains as his destination. Eastern Colorado wasn't much better than Kansas, you just knew the scenery was going to get better, so you stayed optimistic. He rode through Denver to Boulder without incident, turning at the Pearl Street exit to Deuce's house, his house. The home was located near the Foot of the Mountains Motel, had easy access to recreation; fly fishing but no actual fish in a city park, and rock climbing on boulders, thus the name.

He rode up the same incline he recently and quietly coasted down, in second gear. RJ downshifted to first as he turned into the driveway. Shelia's Subaru was still there, the same place as when he left. A Chevy Tahoe sat next to it. Both vehicles sported Colorado plates.

Again, he rode the bike on his grass, parking his Harley in front of a two stall garage. He knew that the inside the garage there was no room for a car. The parking stalls were filled with boxes, an old and tattered coach with matching recliner, and the summer patio furniture. There was just enough space for his Fatboy. He turned the bike at a sharp 180-degree turn, ready to back the bike into the space reserved for his Harley.

RJ lowered the kickstand and dismounted. There was no one there to greet him, no noise coming from the house.

He climbed the four steps to the back door which led to the kitchen. He tested the doorknob, the door was unlocked. RJ never left a door unlocked. He entered his home. RJ could hear muffled voices, whispering, a slight high-pitched squeal. RJ pulled the 9 mm Glock from the space between his lower back and belt line. He switched the safety to off. He was ready to fire. RJ was in shooting position; his arms extended, both hands on the pistol as he inched towards the living room. His mind was racing, could it be one of Ballard's crew, German's men, the Mongols, Angels, maybe the Bandidos or the Pagans, he only had run-ins with all of them.

RJ was at the end of the hall; the whispering was over, the muffled sounds now eerily quiet. He stood, waiting, hoping for something; a voice, a yell, a scream for help or of any signs of what to prepare for or do next. Nothing.

He heard footfalls, stocking feet on a wooden floor. RJ was still, his breathing stable, his pulse rate the same. He was ready for what was next. RJ pointed his weapon straight ahead.

"RJ! Honey is that you?" Sheila yelled out. It was her stocking feet. She turned the corner seeing RJ with a gun in his hands. "What? RJ just what do you think you are doing? Put that silly thing away," She said loudly.

RJ lowered his gun, he put the safety back on and placed the weapon behind his back. "Sheila. What are you doing here? Whose Tahoe is that?"

Sheila stepped forward and gave RJ a hug. She got nothing in return. She kissed him on the cheek. No response from RJ.

"RJ. Are you ok? So happy you are home. We missed you," Sheila said over her shoulder. "Honey I have a surprise for you."

"Surprise? What kind of surprise? I don't like surprises," RJ said back.

"Bobby, Becky. Mom. Come meet RJ," Sheila said.

RJ went pale. "You got to be shitting me," He said to Sheila.

"Honey. You never called or texted me while you were gone. I sent you an email. I told you I had a surprise for you when you got home," Sheila said, as her two kids and mother entered the kitchen.

"Hi RJ," the two kids said in unison.

"Ugghh Hi," replied RJ.

"You didn't tell him did you, Sheila," the mom stated and didn't ask.

"Honey, I thought we could live here. It is such a nice neighborhood. Much better than mine. The same school district for the kids. Closer to work for mom and for me," Sheila said to RJ.

"Live here?" RJ asked.

"The kids can have the two rooms next to us. Mom, the basement. This home is just lovely," Sheila said. "The lease at my place is up this month. Perfect timing." She was all smiles.

RJ turned and went back outside, down the steps to the garage. He walked to his Harley. He swung his leg over the saddle and pushed the ignition starting the bike.

Sheila followed him, her mother beside her. They stood on the back porch, her hands on the railing. "RJ, what are you doing?" she asked.

"You didn't tell him did you, Sheila," Mother stated again.

"I forgot something," RJ said over the roar of his Harley. He put the bike in first gear, rode on the grass back to Pearl Street.

"Where are you going?" Sheila yelled again.

"Daytona," RJ yelled. He turned left and rode off. He rode the other way.

"Sum bitch." He said to himself, leaving Sheila with her mom and two kids at his house.

SALAS

"Let's get as far as Bowling Green tonight ladies," Salas yelled over the roar of his and Tripp's/Anthony's motorcycles; he was talking to the three girls in the Chevy. "I know you girls could drive all night, but the bikes have to rest."

Stephanie looked curious; her painted eyebrows arched upward. "Rest? Why? Do they get tired?"

"The guys don't like to ride their bikes at night Steph," Sami said. "The guys are tired."

"I'll get the hotel rooms. One for you girls and one for us guys," Salas said, easing any and all questions about habitation for the evening.

The girls nodded and drove away, a cloud of purple smoke puffed out of the Impala. They were followed by Salas on his Road King with Anthony and Sami on the Dyna.

In Bowling Green, they found a hotel with a green neon sign announcing a vacancy. Salas got the two rooms as promised. He ate a room service hamburger in his room, by himself. The four girls and Anthony had pizza delivered to the lobby. Salas knew he was running a fever; he had body aches, his shoulder was red, it felt warm and was inflamed. He chewed on some Advil and went to bed early. He was hurting from being shot in the shoulder, shot in his chest and from being awake for 38 plus hours in Daytona. Salas woke briefly when Anthony came into the room. The clock read 10:35 but Salas was asleep before Anthony got into the twin bed next to his.

Morning came, the six of them struggled to wake up, all were in need of more rest. They needed a vacation from their vacation. Sami rallied the girls as Salas and Tripp took turns in the bathroom and shower. They didn't talk much other than bikes and the weather. Salas was flushed, his face red, he felt warm. He noticed red streaks running from the bullet wound to his neck. He dried off, redressed in the same jeans and Daytona shirt and went outside to his bike. The hotel offered no breakfast just coffee. Salas had three cups before the kids came outside.

The car and two bikes left Bowling Green at 9:00. Sami still riding with Anthony, Salas following the couple who were following the girls in the Chevy. They stayed on Interstate 65 through Louisville, then a straight-line ride to Indianapolis. Traffic was light, the weather was good. A great day to ride.

Salas admitted to himself but not to his daughter that he was seriously sick. He rode, his body shaking from a fever. He knew when he got to Fort Wayne the first place he was headed was the emergency room.

Going north from Indy they were on Highway 31. They stopped at the Plymouth, Indiana exit and Highway 30. It was Salas's turn to depart the caravan, his exit to Fort Wayne. Salas knew he didn't have it in him to ride to South Bend, see Sami to her apartment and still be able to get back to his city. His shoulder, the infection was getting worse by the second. He was sweating from a fever, and red streaks were now running down his arm, he felt nauseous.

Salas gave Sam a kiss, then shook hands with Tripp telling him to take care of his girl. He said goodbye to the kids and watched them ride and drive away. The girls and Tripp were less than an hour from South Bend, Salas had an hour and twenty minutes to his place in Fort Wayne. He was unstable and felt light-headed, maybe even dizzy. Not the best physical condition to be riding a motorcycle.

In Plymouth, Salas set his Harley's GPS for the DuPont Hospital in Fort Wayne. He wasn't a fan of the DuPont family ever since that psycho John DuPont shot Olympic Champion Dave Schultz, but he knew this hospital was owned by a bunch of doctors, not the family. Just a bad choice for a name.

Less than an hour and twenty minutes later Salas parked his Harley in front of the DuPont emergency room entrance doors and walked unsteadily into the three-story brick building. First thing, as with any institution was personal information, full name, address, phone numbers, medical history and of course insurance. He completed the necessary paperwork, gave them copies of his ID and insurance card then sat and waited.

His thoughts turned to Deb and what Sami had said, that her mother loved him, but she couldn't handle him being a police officer. He had always thought they just grew apart, when maybe if he had quit the force he would still have her. With all the excitement and RJ, he had forgotten about Candy and her friend at the Fairfield Inn. He had forgotten about Deb. Maybe that is how and why he lost her. When he worked, he forgot about everyone.

Salas sat thinking. He had graduated from the University of Nebraska with a degree in criminology; his lifelong dream was to be a detective like his father. Fort Wayne was his only offer. He viewed Fort Wayne as a stepping stone to Chicago, Indianapolis maybe Saint Louis. He met Deb during his first month on the job in the new city. As an Assistant County Attorney, Deb was assigned cases each week by the judge, usually those citizens guilty of a crime with no source of money to pay outside counsel. Deb was the attorney, Salas, the arresting officer. They met over a deposition with a stenographer, two other lawyers and the victim witnessing Salas overt flirtation with the attractive young female lawyer.

After the deposition they met for drinks, then a date, then Salas never again wanted to leave Fort Wayne. They were married in less than a year.

Salas took out his cell. He texted Deb. "Hey. Sami is good. She should be back in South Bend."

He got a response almost immediately. "Yup, on the phone with her now. You like Anthony? He is all she can talk about. She is so excited."

Salas texted back, "Yeah, he is a nice kid. Smart." Salas did like the boy, though he didn't like how shooting three men didn't have much of an effect on the young man. But then Salas thought about it, shooting people never bothered him either. Maybe that's why he liked him. He was mentally tough, responsible, independent, loyal, and self-sufficient. He did what needed to be done. He was like Salas.

Deb didn't return his text. Five minutes passed. Salas was keeping track. He hated texting etiquette. Salas texted her again after two more minutes. "What you up to? How you been?"

The return text came within the minute reading "John and I are going to play Bridge. I just love the game."

Salas shook his head. And said, "You got to be shitting me."

"Salas, Mike Salas." The nurse said his name and looked into the empty waiting room. Only Salas, Mike Salas was there. "This way please." A heavy-set nurse with broad shoulders, a square jaw and dressed in dark blue scrubs gave him directions. She was holding the door open to back offices. She had a clipboard in her hand, a stethoscope around her neck and a cell phone in the front pocket of her scrubs.

First stop was height and weight. He hated this. Ex-wrestlers, current wrestlers have a distaste for scales.

She weighed him and said loudly as if announcing to the media before a prize fi ht: "Height of six feet. Weight of two-hundred and fifty-eight pounds."

Salas rolled his eyes. He was now not only heavier but shorter than in his college days. What happened to six-feet one-inch and two-hundred -and fifteen pounds?

Salas said, "Shit, these boots and jacket must weigh a ton."

"Yeah, I bet that is it." The nurse said directing Salas to sit in a chair. She tried to take his blood pressure. The cuff was too small. She left and came back with a larger unit and took his blood pressure manually.

"One-forty-eight over one-hundred." Again, the announcement to a crowd that wasn't present. "Running a little high, Mr. Salas. Do you usually have high blood pressure?"

"No, and I don't take any medications. I'm usually right at one-twenty over eighty. But I have been riding a motorcycle all day. And I'm feeling sick, thus why I am here."

"Yeah, I bet that is it." The nurse said again, not believing Salas. She proceeded to take his temperature by placing a white cone attached to a device that looked like a remote control for his TV inside his ear.

Salas said, "Man I'm glad that isn't a rectal thermometer."

This time it was the nurse that rolled her eyes, "One-O-three. Your temperature is too high as well."

Salas decided she must talk loud for effect or is used to men not listening to her. So, she yells at them. "Come with me," she said as she took off   alking.

Salas followed the nurse past several three-walled rooms, each with a curtain as the front wall and entrance. Salas had been here before but never as a patient, always as a cop bringing someone else in for care. She directed him to room number 33. She opened the curtain and gave Salas a gown. Yes, the ones like a dress that is open in the back. The color was pale blue with white strips and three green tie-downs in the back.

"Put this on. The doctor will be right in," The nurse said as she placed the clipboard with his information in a slot by the front curtain on the left.

Doing as he was told, Salas took off his clothes. He had trouble taking the t-shirt over his head. The shoulder was swollen with his range of motion limited. He adorned the gown. He couldn't reach back to tie it together so left it open. Salas sat down on the exam table, the white paper crinkling under his butt.

He saw a hand reach up and grab the curtain pulling it to the right. She entered. An attractive she.

"Mr. Salas. I am Dr. Harper, welcome to our ER. It seems you have a fever and a rather high temp. Let's take a look at you, love."

Salas was looking her over first. Brunette hair pulled back, high cheekbones, a nice neck. She had light blue eyes that smiled when she smiled. Her white doctor's coat went to her knees, but you could see she had a nice fi ure. She looked like a runner, a lean face, long legs. Yes, he was checking her out, but he was a detective, it was his job to notice things. He also noticed she looked nothing like Deb. Still the comparisons.

"Have you had any recent cuts, exposed to anything?" She asked as she was reviewing the notes on the clipboard. "Says here scratch on left shoulder. Let me take a look, love."

"Yup, I got a deep cut here," Salas said as he let the gown drop to his waist.

"Well love, from your ears, your chest and your arms you are either a former wrestler or MMA fi hter and were very bad at protecting your ears," Dr. Harper said. She put on pink latex gloves then pulled and pinched on his shoulder muscle. Salas winced.

"And that's a nasty bruise on your chest," She said, eying the black and blue circle over the heart. She pressed on the ribs above and below where Raphael had shot him. Salas winced again.

"Mr. Salas this on your shoulder. It isn't a scratch. You have been shot. It is severely infected. And this bruise. You may have a broken rib."

"Nah. It's just a scratch. Don't worry about the ribs, not like you can put a cast on it."

"Both of these are gunshot wounds, sir. I would say a Kevlar vest saved your life, Mr. Salas. Do we need to get the police and security in here?"

"No, I feel safe with you. And besides, I am a cop. My badge is in the pants pocket." Salas said pointing at his jeans laying on the chair.

"Great. You are my second cop this week. Tough profession. I can see though, that you are going to fully cooperate."

"Who was the other cop?" Salas asked. "I probably know him."

"Doctor and patient confidentiality Mike. If I told you, I would have to kill you. First, let's get some blood work love." The doctor said.

"Did you just call me lover?" Salas asked.

"No, sorry I have a habit of calling people love."

"You said, lover."

"No. It was love."

"Lover, Doc."

"I know what I said, Mr. Salas."

"I know what I heard. Love." Salas was smiling. The doctor was smiling back, reaffirming the smile that matched her eyes.

"Blood work for now. It will take a few minutes. I'll be back." The doctor closed the curtain as she left.

Salas said, "My doctor quotes *Top Gun* and *The Terminator*. Gotta love that." He said it loud enough; he knew she heard him.

The blood was drawn, the nurse taking three vials from his vein, each one a dark red almost purple color. The nurse had Salas sit back on the exam table. She put a blood pressure cuff on his arm, the same problem with the fit. Next were the EKG leads, she placed four on his chest. A small off gray colored cap, like a thimble, went over the end of his index finger that was connected to a computer. The monitor was beeping. She said his pulse rate was good and his blood pressure had dropped to one thirty-two over eight-nine. Next, she put an IV in a vein at the crease of his elbow. The nurse telling Salas they were putting fluids and an antibiotic into his system. She taped the plastic tubes to his forearm.

Doctor Harper entered the exam room twenty minutes later. "Yes, you have a nasty infection, Mr. Salas."

"My lovers call me Mike."

"Not going to let that go, are you?" Dr. Harper asked.

"If it keeps you in the room, I'll keep going with it," Salas said.

The doctor placed a hand on Salas's shoulder, the good one and said, "In addition to the antibiotic we gave you in the IV, we will be giving you a shot of dicloxacillin. It's a stiff antibiotic as well. You will feel a little better pretty soon. We got this before it went septic. You came in just in time. Also going to give you a prescription to get filled on your way home. You will take the pills two times a day, twelve hours apart. The antibiotic is called Ciprofloxacin or Cipro. Take all the pills. You will feel better before you are out of the medication but be sure and take them all. Finish the entire two weeks of pills ok?"

"Got it. Take the pills two times a day, 'til all the pills are gone." Salas said.

"Now we are going to clean this wound up a bit. You may need a stitch or two."

"I'm in your hands Doc."

"Tell me Mike, how long you been with the force?"

"Over twenty years."

"Are you married? Or a significant other?" She asked as she was looking at the chart again.

"Does this have anything to do with my infection doc?"

"Maybe. I fi ured it could be a good wife that shot you."

"Let me be the detective. Love. But you are right, a majority of the time it is the spouse. But no, I am no longer married or significantly with an….. other."

The Doctor put *Betadine* on a large Q-tip. She dug the device into the wound. Again, Salas winced. She took a scalpel removing some dead tissue on the boundary of the injury. She removed small black pieces of the leather coat embedded in the wound.

"Damn Doc. That hurts," Salas said.

"And getting shot didn't?"

"Not like this it didn't."

"So, you did get shot?"

"No. Just seeing if you were paying attention."

Dr. Harper used a small syringe to inject the area around the wound with an anesthetic then opened a sterile package containing what looked like a fish hook with line attached. She pierced the skin then hooked it through the opposite side of the cut, brought it back through and repeated the process three times. Three stitches were tied off. She then went to the other end of the so-called scratch. With similar technique, she completed four more stitches on that end. There was a two-inch open wound between her sewing techniques.

"I could ask for a skin graft Mike, but I don't think you are the skin grafting kind of guy. This will leave a nasty scar I am afraid." The Doctor said. She then covered the wound with white gauze, taping each end to Salas's skin.

"Shane Falco said chicks dig scars," Salas responded looking at his new stitches. "What do you think?"

"Shane Falco? Who is that?" The doctor asked as she completed cleaning the wound.

"You know the Replacements. The movie. Keanu Reeves and Gene Hackman."

"Never heard of it. I must have missed that one during medical school, residency, work or just living a life."

"Well, maybe we could watch it sometime on Netflix. You heard of that yet?" Salas said with a smirk.

"Perhaps. I have Hulu'd." Dr. Harper smiled as she reviewed her handy work. "Ok, Mike, my love. You should be good. The nurse will be in soon to give you the shot of the antibiotic. Here is the script for Cipro," Doctor Jennifer Harper said as she handed Salas a slip of paper. "Remember two per day till gone," she said as she left he room.

It was another ten minutes before the nurse returned armed with another syringe. She instructed Salas to roll on to his right hip. She let the gown fall to the sides and injected a large needle of clear fluid in his left butt cheek. The heavy-set nurse smiled when Salas flinched. She patted him on the ass when she withdrew the needle. The nurse then placed a white cotton ball under a clear strip of tape and covered the injection site.

When the fluid in the IV bag was empty, the nurse said he was free to leave. It was approaching six in the evening, and Salas was wrestling with the idea of riding to the Harley Davidson dealership.

Salas redressed, it was easier to put the shirt on than taking it off. He laced up his boots, signed off the paperwork and left the three-walled cubicle. The same nurse escorted him to the exit doors. They didn't speak as they walked. He looked for Doctor Harper on his way out. No such luck.

Back on his Harley, Salas rode to his favorite Walgreens, filled his script then rode home. He went past his house, turned at the corner and rode past it again. The motorcycle, as if thinking on its own, took him to the Fort Wayne Harley Davidson Store. Was it lust? Was it love? He rode into the parking lot of the dealership, stopping parallel to the front double doors and large picture windows.

Salas looked to his right and saw Candy. She had her back to him; she was standing inside the front window, dressing a mannequin. The headless mannequin had breasts with nipples standing at attention. Candy placed a short-sleeved, V-neck t-shirt on the dummy, leaned back and examined how it fit. Salas thought Candy's butt looked amazing; he could remember how it felt, the shape, how firm her bottom was. He smiled at the thought. Candy bent over, the crack of her famous rear-end smiled back at him. Tattoos were going up her back and hiding inside her pants. Deb would never get a tattoo. He promised himself to quit comparing. He wondered if Doctor Harper had any tattoos.

The pocket of Salas's leather jacket vibrated. He took out the cellular phone and looked at the screen. He didn't recognize the number. It was a text message.

"Hey, Mike. How are you feeling?" The text read.

Salas responded. "Who is this?"

The response, "Jenny."

Salas sent back, "Jenny who?"

"Jennifer Harper, the doctor that just stitched you up and didn't report you to the proper authorities."

"Oh, hi." He texted. "I feel better. Thanks. Is this a new service of DuPont ER?" Salas asked via the text.

"Yes, we aim to please. Would you like to meet at *Delfrescos* for dinner?" Jennifer asked.

Salas looked from his cell phone to the front window. Candy was looking at him now. She was smiling. A beautiful smile. Candy looked happy to see him. Salas thought maybe she had gotten her hair cut; it highlighted her face. She was really beautiful.

"Figured you as a vegan," Salas texted to Jenny.

"I'm a steak and eggs kind of doctor. There aren't many of us left," Jenny texted back.

"Does this violate some kind of patient-doctor code or a HIPPA law?"

"Yes, it could. What are you going to do? Call the police?"

Salas looked from his phone back to Candy. Standing in the front window with his arm around her shoulder was her husband, Warren. He was smiling, wearing the same bibs. Candy looked displeased; Warren looked like he had put on some weight.

Salas went back to his cell and text, "Yeah, I would enjoy *Delfrescos.* Perhaps dinner and a *Netflix?* See you at 7:30."

Putting the cell phone back in his jacket, Salas looked one last time at the woman he thought he might love. He remembered advice someone once told him: "Ride the other way."

Salas gave Candy a two-fingered salute and rode out of the parking lot.

THE END

ACKNOWLEDGMENTS

Thank you to my loving wife and children for their enduring love, loyalty, encouragement and unwavering support.

Riding along the beach and experiencing the sun rise along at Daytona, and watching the sun set over the Gulf on my way home are memories I'll never forget.

Daytona Bike Week and Biketoberfest® draw me back to the area, while providing the perfect backdrop for "Three Days in Daytona".

A special thank you to my crew, they know who they are, and especially to my best friend and son who has made every ride and rally a special memory and an adventure to remember and share.

ABOUT THE AUTHOR

JJ Spain

JJ Spain is a 25-year veteran of Bike Rallies, including Daytona, the Sturgis Rally, and Laughlin. His captivating crime are set at his favorite venues, bringing the Daytona ride and experience to your fingertips. Take the ride. Enjoy the rally.

ALL BOOKS IN THE MIKE SALAS SERIES

IF YOU ENJOYED THIS BOOK OR FOUND IT USEFUL I'D BE VERY GRATEFUL IF YOU'D POST A SHORT REVIEW ON AMAZON. YOUR SUPPORT REALLY DOES MAKE A DIFFERENCE AND I READ ALL THE REVIEWS PERSONALLY, SO I CAN GET YOUR FEEDBACK.

THANKS AGAIN FOR YOUR SUPPORT!

ONE MORE THING

Please take a minute and sign up at my website. I won't spam you but will alert you when new books are released and when I am offering specials.

Visit MikeSalasNovels.com for the latest updates and a chance to win autographed books.

You can also follow me on Instagram JJ Spain

And Facebook

I look forward to seeing you there.

Thank you for buying my book, I hope you enjoy the ride!